Second Harvest

Dennis Rogers

To Gener,
Hope you like it —
Best Wishes

Dennis Rogers

The News and Observer

Raleigh, N.C.

Also by Dennis Rogers:
Home Grown

Cover photograph by Gene Furr

Artwork and cover design by Jackie Pittman

This one is for my daughters, Melanie Dale Rogers and Claudia Denise Rogers. They are my joy and we love each other.

Contents

The Part Nobody Reads

This is the part of the book most people don't read.

This is where I get to say how wonderful it is to have a book and how indebted I am to a lot of people.

Friends will read this part to see if their names are here.

A few others will read it because they're like that, the kinds of people who sit through the credits at the end of the movie and never remove tags under penalty of law. It is there so they read it.

Everyone else is just being nice; they're the kinds of people who enjoy browsing through your high school yearbook and love your vacation pictures.

This is my second collection of columns from The News and Observer. The first collection, called *Home Grown,* came out in 1979 and you seemed to like it. I hope you will welcome this effort as warmly.

We call it *Second Harvest* and that seems to fit. We've tried to save the best and throw away the rest. The people and places of Eastern North Carolina are here, leavened by the fads, funnies and foibles that have found their way into my column.

Writing may be a solitary craft but it takes an awful lot of people. My thanks go to all of those who have opened their homes and their lives to me. I have tried to be true to the stories they told.

Owen Davis put it all together. He is a good friend and a good editor. It is difficult to do both well.

News and Observer publisher Frank Daniels Jr. made it all

happen and took all the chances. I like his style.

David Martin, Jack Andrews and Macon Harris and his composing room crew made it into a flesh-and-blood book.

Any writer's work is an extension of his life and my life is infinitely richer for the people who share it. They know who they are: the good friends from Boylan Heights, the kickers and the cowboys from Raleigh to the coast, and all who were there with warm words on a cold night.

Look What They've Gone and Done Now

Lady Diana Spencer is probably the best thing to happen to the English royal family since Shakespeare stopped writing those blood-curdling stories about them.

I know she is the prettiest thing to happen to that lot.

Maybe it is because of my professional standing as an arbiter of ugly, what with my being the Wake County president of the North Carolina Ugly League, but the royal family always has struck me as being a tad on the homely side.

Now I, of all people, know there is nothing wrong with being ugly, and I certainly mean no disrespect to the crown (I know a good deal when I see it), but you would have thought that somewhere along the line a cutey would have popped up somewhere, wouldn't you?

But not in that family. About the best thing you can say about them, concerning their looks, is that they all seem to have excellent posture.

But then along comes Diana. "Shy Di" the British press dubbed her, 19 years old and as cute as a button. You'd have thought the royal family would have welcomed her with open arms, happy to have some gorgeous genes in the family for a change.

But no, they sent her to be inspected.

It seems she had to prove her "purity," as the news stories so delicately put it, as well as her ability to bear children.

And then, to make things worse, her uncle announced the results to the press.

Now I'm not one to criticize kings and queens, but isn't that a little tacky? Is that the sort of thing one calls a press conference to announce?

I don't know how things are in jolly old England, but if you told some Wilson County farmer that his little girl had to be inspected like a prize sow before she could get married and that the results of the test would be announced to the press, you'd wake up one morning to find a combine in your bed.

That could be why it has taken Prince Charles 32 years to find a wife. I don't know too many women who would go through that just for the honor of waking up each morning and looking at Charlie before he brushed his teeth.

But what's done is done. It is time to turn to the real issue before us:

Wedding presents.

I'll bet you a Pepsi and a pack of square Nabs that Charlie and Diana don't get a single toaster or a blender or a set of six matching straw place mats or even a hot dog cooker on the big day.

They'll probably get useless things like ivory footstools or sterling silver shoe buckles or a matched set of kangaroo luggage.

And, because no one thought to be practical, they'll rattle around their 35-room honeymoon cottage starving to death.

I'm sorry, but there is no way to make a late-night bowl of popcorn without a proper popper, one of those jobs with the plastic top that gets so greasy it takes two washings to get it clean.

Will anyone give them a can opener? Don't count on it. If you're such a big cheese that you get one of the 2,500 wedding invitations, you're going to be so impressed that you'll spend a bundle on some tasteful gift, like a picture frame made from parakeet beaks, when what they would really like to have is a handy salad spinner, something in royal purple plastic.

What a shame. Charlie and Diana are not going to get one thing they can exchange for what they really wanted — a nice clock radio.

Does That Mean It's Hot?

Do you give a hoot what the temperature is in Celsius degrees?

I didn't think so.

Then why, since we agree that the only temperature that is meaningful is the Fahrenheit one, do those time-and-temperature signs outside banks insist on giving the temperature twice — once in Fahrenheit and once in Celsius?

Would the republic fall if they left that Celsius part out for one day? People walk into parking meters waiting for the Fahrenheit to come around again.

I know what you're talking about if you tell me it is 97 degrees outside. Don't bother to tell me it is 36 degrees.

Ninety-seven degrees is hot. Thirty-six degrees is cold. Any pea brain knows that.

Why do television weather people insist on giving us the Celsius temperature? Do they really think people are sitting out there in TV-land waiting for that nonsense?

It's part of that metric business, and I don't care for it at all.

Take those two-liter soft-drink bottles, for instance. They got rid of two-quart bottles and went to two-liter bottles. That way, you have to buy more each time and the stuff goes flat before you can drink it up. Plus the accursed bottles do not fit in my refrigerator. They wouldn't fit in the last refrigerator I had, either.

Some people think two-liter bottles are a good idea. I don't know why.

Have you bought gasoline at a station with a metric pump? I know it's only paranoia, but I fear I'm being cheated. All I want to know is how much the stupid gasoline costs, and they're giving me an international arithmetic lesson. Metric gas always looks cheaper until the pump starts, and then watch those numbers fly by.

I hope by this time there is a metric lover out there saying, "Doesn't this dimwitted fool know that the metric system is simpler, that it is more rational and logical than the system we use now?''

OK, hotshot, then you define a meter — the basic unit of measurement in the metric system — for us all. Where did the rational, logical meter come from?

I'll tell you. The wonderful French dreamed up this baby. They decided that a meter would be a 10-millionth of the distance between the North Pole and the equator.

Then the wonderful French realized that the Earth's surface moved around, and that wouldn't do at all.

So they came up with another simple, rational, logical definition of a meter. A meter, the wonderful French decided, is "1,650,763.73 wavelengths of the orange-red light of excited krypton of mass number 86."

How's that for rationale, logic and simplicity? Is that something you need to know every day? Is that so sensible that we should change an entire nation's system of measurement?

The traditional measurements, while not based on wonderful French scientific gobbledygook, seem simple enough: An inch is from the tip of your finger to the first knuckle; a foot is based on a man's foot; a yard is based on a man's stride; a cup is about how much water you can hold in cupped hands; an ounce is one average swallow.

I can see how that might have caused some problems in the beginning, but we seem to have things standardized and worked out all right. I know how much two cups of water are, don't you?

You can approximate with the traditional system, but you can't do that with the metric system. If you try to step off your back yard in meters, you'll look foolish and get a hernia.

The metric system is arbitrary, cold and lifeless. It is based on nothing but some number plucked out of the air by a wonderful Frenchman 200 years ago.

If the French insist we go metric, the least they can do is buy us all new refrigerators.

3546-54B-16/79473 O

Something has to give.

We are being numbered to death.

I have been a nice guy about this number business, but things seem to be getting out of hand.

I was doing all right until news stories reminded me that the post office planned to increase our ZIP codes from five digits to nine.

I had heard it before, but I assumed that, like this metric madness, it would go away. Well, it won't.

A fourth of the members of the U.S. House of Representatives sent a letter to the Postal Service telling it what it could do with its nine numbers.

Did the Postal Service quake? Not on your number, big boy. The Postal Service wrote back and told the congressmen what they could do with their letters.

It seems that the Postal Service is above the Congress in this matter. It does not need the approval of our elected officials to lengthen our ZIP codes.

And we have no choice but to go along.

So get ready. The new ZIP code for The News and Observer could very well be 176029784 or something equally forgettable.

They are everywhere, those ubiquitous numbers that rule our lives.

The first number I ever had to learn was my Army service number. I had to learn it so well that even standing in a gas chamber, choking on tear gas, I could spit it out. I did, all two letters and eight digits.

Then they changed it to correspond to my Social Security number. That one has nine digits, but I had to learn it.

Telephone numbers in my hometown went from four digits to five digits to seven digits.

My driver's license has a number, one I am required to put on checks. I know the number, but no sales clerks believe I do, so when I write it on checks they still demand to see my license.

I have three check-cashing cards that permit me to give my money to someone else. Two of them have 14 digits; the other has 18.

The card identifying me as an employee of The News and Observer has a number; so does my health insurance card, my library card and my Veterans Administration card.

I have a card in my wallet from a large department store. In big letters it says it is not a credit card, but it still has a 13-digit number.

I carry 10 credit cards, from oil companies, department stores, banks and other sources.

All together, they have 113 digits — not counting expiration dates and ZIP codes.

I have a checking account and a savings account (I don't know why I have the latter.). My checks have 32 digits on them, not counting the ZIP code.

I have a card from a motel chain that does absolutely nothing but keep me from having to fill out my name and address when I check in. Six digits.

The big winner in my wallet is a card that says I give blood away. To let me give blood, the American Red Cross gave me a card with 38 digits on it.

When I travel and make official-business long-distance telephone calls, I have to reel off 24 numbers — in order. If I get one wrong, I have to start all over. Try that while shivering in an outdoor phone booth as the trucks roar by.

Add 'em up.

Just in my wallet, on my front door, on my home telephone and license plate I have 407 digits, all of which I use with some regularity.

So as not to overstate the case, I have not mentioned insurance policy numbers, automobile title numbers, engine identification numbers, receipt numbers, prescription numbers, telephone numbers of all my friends and business contacts, shoe sizes and birthdays.

And now the Postal Service wants to add four more.

Did you ever hear the one about the straw and the camel's back?

They Must Be Kidding

Everyone thinks bureaucrats are dull, colorless gnomes who cringe in their rabbit-hutch offices, shuffling papers from In baskets to Out baskets with nary a bright spot to lighten their weary days.

What people don't realize is that bureaucrats have a great capacity for rib-tickling humor.

The problem is, they don't know when they're being funny.

Take the case of Kenneth Franklin.

Franklin moved to North Carolina a few months back, and, like most newcomers, he had to get a new driver's license.

So he got a copy of the Driver's Handbook for North Carolina and studied like a good resident, all ready to ace the test.

He then proceeded to the Blue Ridge Road examining office in Raleigh to take his driver's test.

Things went splendidly. He took the written test and passed it, and then took the road test and passed that.

That's when things started getting funny.

Franklin has a nerve disorder that does not allow him full use of his legs. His car is equipped with hand brakes, and he uses a motorized wheelchair to zip around his house.

So Franklin paid close attention to page 105 of the handbook, where it says that operators of motorized wheelchairs have to get a special driver's license.

It makes no difference if he only goes from the bedroom to the kitchen to get a glass of milk, he needs an official North Carolina driver's license to do it. So says the law.

The scene is the examining room. It is raining outside, so the kindly examiner says Franklin can take his wheelchair road test inside.

So Franklin drives his wheelchair, with a top speed of 4 mph, from one end of the large room to the other. He executes a three-point turn and comes back.

And even though he thought the test was silly, he passed.

That's when they told him about the license plate.

Yes, friends, Franklin not only must have a driver's license to go get his glass of milk, but he also must have a license plate affixed to the back of his wheelchair.

So off he went to the Department of Motor Vehicles, where he was told that, yes, he must get a license plate. And to do that, the law says, he must show the title to his wheelchair.

A title? To a wheelchair? Yes, indeed, a title.

Of course, he didn't have a title. They don't give titles to wheelchairs.

How about a bill of sale, the bureaucrat wanted to know. That would do.

But the wheelchair was donated. There was no bill of sale.

Reluctantly, the state issued a permanent license plate for the wheelchair, but warned Franklin that he'd better come up with proof of ownership soon.

You can't have people running around in a hot wheelchair, now can you?

And to make the point, DMV sent a letter a few weeks later reminding Franklin that he'd better come up with that proof of ownership.

Zeb V. Hocutt is in charge of driver's licenses for the state. And as you might imagine, he just loved hearing from me about this one.

"It is preposterous as hell," Hocutt said.

Sure is, I said, and what are you going to do about it?

He said he'd have his boss call me.

His boss is Elbert L. Peters Jr., the fellow who signs your driver's license, The Commissioner of Motor Vehicles.

Peters also loved hearing from me.

"Oh, no!" is what he said.

"I can only hope it was a new examiner," he said. "The idea is that anyone who is in traffic with a wheelchair should be licensed so they'll know the safety rules.

"It should not have applied to Mr. Franklin."

But that's not what the book says, I pointed out. The book says you must have a license and a tag, regardless.

"We're going to change that," he said. "And we're going to refund Mr. Franklin's money, too."

That's good. Because if Franklin's driver's license ever were revoked for any reason, he'd also lose his wheelchair license, which bears the same number. And he'd have no legal way to go for that glass of milk.

May I Spit in Your Coffee?

Being of somewhat rebellious stock, I have a soft spot in my heart for creative anarchists.

The slogan "First in Freedom" that graces some of the state's license plates is more than some ad man's creation. It aptly describes much of our history and temperament, witnessed by the young man who challenged the law by taping over the slogan and then winning the case.

The nation was all hot to ratify the Constitution until Tar

Heels dug in for a fight. The result was the Bill of Rights.

We have an honored tradition of telling the world to take a hike, and for those reasons, I find the anti-smoking tactics amusing.

But be advised I take no stand in the fight — funny is funny, of whatever stripe.

Take the case of the young handicapped man in the Midwest. He had gone to the governor's office to thank the governor for his support of rights for the handicapped.

While waiting in the outer office to see the Big Cheese, the young man rolled his wheelchair off to the side and lit a cigarette.

There was also a woman waiting to see the governor. She was there to lobby for anti-smoking laws. She saw the young man light his cigarette and walked over and demanded that he extinguish it.

The young man, not wanting to cause a fight, agreed, and as he turned toward the ashtray he put the cigarette to his lips for one last drag, as smokers are prone to do.

With that, the woman picked up a pitcher of lemonade and dumped it over his head, drenching the young man, cigarette and wheelchair.

A scientist in New England has come up with what he calls his "H-Bomb," a vial of chemicals that, when opened, emits an odor the scientist describes as "a cross between athlete's feet and Limburger cheese." That is easily my choice for Descriptive Phrase of the Year.

And I love the Englishman who is credited with perhaps the funniest counter-slogan of the campaign. When told by smokers that a few puffs calm their nerves, he responded by saying, "May I spit in your coffee? It steadies my nerves."

A New York woman has hit on what she calls the "restaurant solution." Her trick is to call up restaurants and make reservations for 10. Once she has the owner foaming at the mouth in anticipation of a hefty check, she slyly asks that the table be in the no-smoking section. When the poor manager tells her there ain't no such place, she huffs and cancels the reservation. Since she knew in advance there was no such area and never intended to eat there in the first place, it smacks of misrepresentation and fraud, but it is clever.

Then there is her checkout-line gimmick. The non-smoker goes into a grocery store, loads her cart to the gunwales and then

marches to the checkout line. If someone carelessly decides to
have a smoke while waiting to spend his money, she demands that
the manager throw the bum out. When the manager naturally
refuses, she stalks out, leaving an innocent stock clerk with the
job of putting her groceries back on the shelf.

The same woman has a friend who goes to movie theaters
armed with a flashlight. She blasts smokers with a full, five-cell
beam in the eyes if they dare light up in her presence.

How about the newspaperman who created SHAME, which
stands for the Society to Humiliate, Aggravate, Mortify and Em-
barrass Smokers? His trick is to stand up in a theater and yell at a
smoker. In restaurants he throws wadded napkins at smokers and
has been known to blow out their matches with an air gun.

He also sticks his fingers in smokers' water glasses, operat-
ing under the theory that if they can pollute his air, he can pollute
their water.

While what these people do is funny, it also can be dangerous.
You tend to get punched in the face a lot, I would suspect.

In light of all the anti groups, with cute names like ASH, DOC,
CAPS, TAPS, SENSE and GASP, I propose yet another organization.

Our group takes no stand on smoking; in fact, we take no
stand on any issue.

We call it GUPPY, or "Give Us Peace and Privacy, Y'all."

We are opposed to any group that is opposed to anything. We
are also opposed to any group that is for anything.

Our slogan is "Fanatics Are Fun," and we plan to laugh at all
of you.

I Would, but My Adidas Died

I need not waste my time telling you not to do it, for when the
shaping-up bug strikes, it strikes deeply.

We of a proudly self-indulgent inclination frankly don't care.
You won't shame us; long ago we turned a deaf ear to those sinis-
ter "Shape Up, America" commercials. We know that if God had
meant man to be in shape, he would not have invented 100mm
cigarettes and Little Debbie Cakes.

But if you insist on making an utter fool of yourself with your
sweaty panting, at least do it with knowledge aforethought.

Most likely you will begin with senseless jogging. But remember this, you cannot merely trot out of the house in your high-top black tennis shoes, a ragged sweat shirt and shorts of indeterminate origin.

What I suggest is that you observe experienced joggers so you can become the jogger that is the real you. Since jogger identification is a mystical science, here is help in the form of my Guide to the Native American Jogger, Southern Edition:

The Loping Lothario: The most easily identifiable of that loathsome lot, Lope wears a thin gold chain, a gift from a mysterious lady he will never identify. Although it may be cold and raining, Lope is well-tanned, has blond hair on his well-proportioned chest, wears green satin shorts and shoes with funny names. He has worn out more blow dryers than you have hammers, knows no words of more than three syllables, drives angry-looking cars, dates "chicks" who dot their i's with little circles and has more varieties of cologne than you do. He is not overburdened with intelligence.

Bouncing Bambi: The female equivalent of Lope, she runs with arms cocked high, cooks everything in a wok, drinks booze in pink drinks, sweats only on her upper lip, has never heard of Bruce Springsteen and wants a kitten named Muffin. She changes singles bars the way others change their socks, has hair ribbons matching her jogging shorts and will break every bone in your body if you so much as wink at her. She loves to date Jaycees.

Strident Strider: Here is a real threat. He jogged before it was fashionable, knows all about stretching exercises and diet, has met Frank Shorter, is convinced that he will live forever and gets high when he runs. His face is gaunt with pain. The only thing he watches on television is "60 Minutes." He eats oatmeal with no sugar, tinkers a lot and bores his wife to tears.

The Dynamic Duo: They come in pairs, his and hers. They gave each other matching jogging suits for Christmas, have 1.4 children, drive earnest little cars, serve on worthwhile committees, have never had a nickname in their lives nor care for people who do. They drink only white wine, prefer white bread sandwiches and white sheets and haven't really looked at each other in months. They help clean up after other people's parties.

Stumbling Stumbleweed: Every time he runs out of his driveway, he almost falls over a wheelbarrow he borrowed from his neighbor four years ago. He drinks beer to replace body fluids, wears black socks while running, claims he played a little football in school when it was really two weeks in seventh-grade physical education and he made a C-minus, never shaves on weekends, wants to nuke Iran and bemoans the passing of polyester leisure suits.

Determined Dasher: He approaches the whole thing scientifically, gets a physical that cost him $150 and reads three books on running before moving the first muscle. He plans his route carefully, swears he feels better after the very first run, plans to stop smoking, drinking beer and cursing all at the same time, keeps hoping to get all the family photos in one album one day, gives the whole thing up after six weeks and spends the rest of his life poking fun at joggers.

He writes a newspaper column for a living.

Hi Yo, Mercedes

Waylon Jennings sings a song that goes, "Mamas, don't let your babies grow up to be cowboys."

And there is another line that goes, "Cowboys pick guitars and drive them old trucks, make 'em be doctors and lawyers and such."

Good advice. Cowboys do have it rough, herding them little dogies, riding them fences and, of course, there is the weekly ruckus at the Last Chance Saloon after everybody gets a snootful of Red Eye on Saturday night.

Well, don't look now, Mama, but your doctors and lawyers and such have grown up to be cowboys.

Hi yo, Mercedes, cowboy flash has come to town.

Everybody wants to be a cowboy. Cowboy hats are hot sellers at every store in town. The price of a good pair of pointy-toed boots is heading for $100. A simple feathered hatband — if feathers from exotic birds can be called simple — sells for $25.

Goodbye disco, time to saddle up the import car and mosey on down to the cowboy bar. Hide those gold chains and get yourself a bandana.

Willie Nelson started it all. It was the Grammy Awards show in 1975. Suddenly, in homes all across America, there was old Shotgun himself, pigtails and all, singing "Blue Eyes Crying in the Rain."

Within six months, the landmark cowboy-outlaw album

called "The Outlaws" was out and the stampede was on.

Rock 'n' roll radio played "Luchenbach." Old boots came out of closets. Discount stores started stocking hats.

Yippie, pardner, it was time to play cowboys again.

There is a popular myth that goes something like this:

The reason for the resurgence of the cowboy in society is that the stoic cowboy represents what all of us want to be.

And if you don't think cowboys are popular, try watching television and counting all the commercials with cowboys in them, everything from hair dryers to makeup to soft drinks.

The cowboy is a return to basic American values, so the sociologists say, a reflection of the conservative mood of the country.

He is the great American hero, riding alone, fighting and, most important, always winning. The cowboy is the good guy.

Balderdash, I say.

The reason the cowboy culture has taken over is simple:

Men get to dress up in fancy clothing.

This great revelation came to me in a shopping center the other day. I was standing in front of a famous men's clothing store. There, stretched down 40 feet of wall, were men's suits.

They came in two colors, drab and drabber, all blue or gray, all very proper and dull, dull, dull. Business was terrible.

Then I wandered into a department store that stocks cowboy duds. There was a line at the counter.

The jeans I selected were, of course, blue, but those boys fit like a glove.

The shirt was white, with blue and green roses embroidered on the front.

The hat, ah, yes, the hat, was a white number with a woven brown band and a goodly part of a beautiful bird tacked on one side in a graceful spray of flashy colors.

And what I had was conservative.

Don't look for the deep meaning in the cowboy cult, Mr. Scientist. Man has always been the dandy of the sexes, forced into dull suits, but now he is rebelling — at least on Saturday nights.

Gaudy is in. You simply cannot overdress. The male bird of plumage is flying high again, soaring to his rightful place as the fancy dresser he has wanted to be since they took away our plumes and capes 200 years ago.

From quitting time Friday night to go-to-work time Monday morning, in cowboy bars everywhere, he can be free.

Don't Read This on Monday Morning

Psychologists call it "burnout."

Simply put, it means you've reached the point in your job where you don't think you can cut it anymore, and even if you can, you don't care to.

Burnout does strange things to people. Doctors become carpenters. Carpenters become short-order cooks. Computer scientists chuck their diodes for a garden rake. Journalists become drunks.

Recently I came across a self-help quiz on burnout.

"Has your work become boring and routine?" it wanted to know. Of course, work is boring and routine. That's why they pay you to do it. If it were a lot of laughs, it would be your hobby instead of your job.

You get the picture: all-purpose questions for individual problems.

So I've come up with my own self-help quiz on burnout.

My quiz is different from the others. If one of these questions applies to you, you'll know whether it's time to change jobs.

For instance, when the alarm clock goes off in the morning, do you pull the covers up over your head and whimper softly for 30 minutes?

Do you get lost driving to work more than twice a week?

When the telephone rings at work and you answer, and it's for you, do you say: "I'm sorry, I'm not here now. Could I take a message?"

When you go to see the boss, do you have to introduce yourself and tell him what you do?

Do you always know who you are and what you do?

Did you ever have a sneaking suspicion that you could do your job blindfolded with one arm tied behind your back, and then tried it and found out you could?

When you goof off all morning, do you make excuses by saying, "I'm an afternoon person" — and then, after lunch, goof off by saying, "I'm a morning person"?

Do you hide under your desk for more than 20 minutes each day?

Do you know, to the day and hour, how long you've been working at your job?

When the phone rings at home, do you answer by giving your company name?

Have you set fire to your desk within the last two weeks?

Do you say "Yes sir" when your wife or husband speaks to you at home?

Have you begun looking lovingly at submachine guns lately?

At work, do you spend more than 30 minutes a day in the bathroom?

When you daydream about being the boss, do you think your first act would be to fire you?

When people ask you where you work, do you begin by saying, "Right now I work at ..."

Are you reading this at work?

Snow White Gets a Divorce

Hollywood sequels are big business these days.

Let a real money-maker hit the big screen, and you can bet your popcorn a sequel will follow.

There was "Planet of the Apes," "Jaws," "The French Connection," "The Godfather," "The Exorcist," "The Omen," "Love Story," all of which spawned sequels. But the biggest of all probably will be "The Empire Strikes Back," the follow-up to "Star Wars."

Here are some you can look for in the coming years:

"Snow White and the Seven Dwarfs II," starring Bette Midler as Snow White and McLean Stevenson as all of the dwarfs. Snow and the boys have gotten back together after Snow's bitter divorce from Charming and have formed a rock group. Watch the hilarious high jinks as they all share a swinging singles apartment next door to "Three's Company." Music by Paul Williams.

"The African Queen, Again." The Queen has been resurrected as a cruise ship on Lake Erie. Don Knotts is the skipper and Farrah Fawcett plays the social director. Watch the fun begin as

Knotts and crew get stuck in the Love Canal and begin to glow in the dark. Music by Paul Williams.

"Exodus, Two." The Jews have gotten to Israel and they don't like it at all. They have chosen the one Middle Eastern country with no oil, and since Lawrence of Arabia is on the other team, the Jews decide to leave for Connecticut. Watch the perilous journey across the Triborough Bridge, watch the fight to the finish in a New Rochelle 7-Eleven store. Music by Paul Williams.

"Revenge of the Grapes." This gripping remake of "Grapes of Wrath" stars Gary Coleman and Marie Osmond as a pair of hate-filled midget winemakers who leave California and find a lair in Duplin County. The dark secret is that they use permanent dye to color the wine and everyone who drinks it has a purple tongue for life. Music by Paul Williams.

"Casablanca: Play it Again, Sam." Rick, played by John Travolta, leaves Casablanca and moves to Pickens, S.C., where he opens a disco in the Holiday Inn. Kid (as in, "Here's looking at you, kid") is played by Loni Anderson. Sam the piano man is now a disco jockey and is played by Paul Williams. There is no plot.

"The 11th Commandment." Moses, played by David Brenner, leads the children out of Hollywood after it is discovered that Charlton Heston missed one commandment: Thou shalt make no other sequels. It means the end of the industry. Hymns by Paul Williams.

Dean Smith Is a 10

So Bo Derek is a 10, huh?

Good for her, we need more 10s; there are a gracious plenty of threes and fours around.

By being ranked a 10, Mrs. Derek has reached that plateau upon which mortal feet shall not tread, or so the ratings game goes. Ten is tops, reserved for the few, the best of the rest, the ultimate, The Perfect Ten.

I don't intend to debate Mrs. Derek's ten-hood, but I must admit that I am usually (but not always) more interested in what is between a woman's ears, but then I have often been considered a mite strange.

But the point is, there are a lot of 10s around if only we'd take the time to think about it.

There lives in Creswell a woman named Donnie Smith who fries shrimp that are 10s. By comparison, frozen fish sticks are a weak one.

A simple wire coat hanger is a 10 because it works perfectly at what it is supposed to do. The paper strip across the toilet seat in a motel is a zero. It does nothing.

Janis Joplin is a 10. The Captain and Tennille add up to a three.

Flying a 40-foot dragon kite in a snapping wind on a Sunday afternoon is a 10. Letting the dog in out of the rain is a two.

Take a one-inch-thick slab of toasted Sara Lee pound cake, top it with two scoops of Breyer's vanilla bean ice cream, dribble heated Hershey's chocolate syrup over the top and you have a 10. A stale Twinkie from a reluctant vending machine is a one.

Dean Smith is a 10. Lefty Driesell is a six.

Watching the World Series at the 42nd Street Tavern in Raleigh is a 10. Watching "Wide World of Sports" bring you the arm wrestling championship live from Petaluma, Calif., is a two, maybe a three if some yahoo breaks his arm.

Richard Petty is a 10. Drag racing is a four.

Katharine Hepburn is a 10; Suzanne Somers is a five, and Charlie's Angels, added together, are a three.

Sunset any summer night at Ocracoke is a 10. Saturday night on the circle at Atlantic Beach is a two.

Sitting on the patio on a sunny Sunday morning in April while reading the paper and drinking a cup of brewed (not instant) coffee is a 10. Lying on the beach anytime in August is a zero.

George Burns is a 10. Shecky Greene and any television show on which he appears is a three.

The bell tower at UNC is a 10, but digital watches are a quarter past seven.

The movie "From Here to Eternity" is a 10; the TV series of the same name is a one.

Clam chowder, especially Banks style, is a 10. Chitlins are a two, and then only once a year.

A brand new, sharpened, No. 2 lead pencil is a 10. A stubby No. 3 is a four.

Baggy, tattered, comfortable corduroy jackets are a 10. All tuxedos are threes as long as they are black. Pastel tuxedos are ones.

Backgammon is a 10; bridge is a seven, and jogging a four.

Doug Sauls in Nashville makes barbecue that is a 10, but any hamburger that has a name is a two.

Weaving is a 10; decoupage is a five; ships made from nails and wire are a zero.

Heineken beer is a 10, Lone Star a strong seven, Coors a weak five and Red, White and Blue is a one split three ways.

Walter Cronkite is a 10; Barbara Walters is a seven and whatever happened to Geraldo Rivera?

"M*A*S*H" reruns are a 10; "Brady Bunch" reruns are twos.

Old N.C. 86 between Carrboro and Hillsborough is a 10; U.S. 70 anywhere near Raleigh is a deadly one.

Travis McGee is a 10, but Nick Carter is a zero.

Warren Zevon is a 10. Any singer with the last name of Gibb is a four.

And I'm still waiting for a politician 10.

I Still Miss Janis Joplin

Everyone in the media has had, or will have, his shot at the '70s, and most of the reflections will be devoted to all the terrible things that happened. You will be reminded of Watergate and the collapse of Vietnam and the rise and fall of Idi Amin, the brief presidency of Gerald R. Ford (quick, who was Ford's vice president?) and whatever happened to Spiro Agnew?

Actually, I think the '70s were pretty good. Admittedly, they didn't have the excitement of the 1960s, but who needs that again?

Think back for a moment. How could you dislike a decade that featured as one of its stars a man who called himself Bebe Rebozo? I love the name. Rebozo, a verb meaning to bozo again.

Remember the biggest cosmic joke of the 1970s? For the first half of the '70s we spoke of little but the impending Bicentennial. Billions were spent, and the folks from Walt Disney Productions had enough fireworks in New York Harbor to launch the Statue of Liberty to Venus. And what happened? It rained cats and dogs. I loved it.

It was a decade that featured a girl from Texas who went from obscurity to Farrah Fawcett to just Farrah to Farrah Fawcett-Majors and back to Farrah Fawcett and then home again to obscurity, leaving nothing more than a hairstyle to mark her passing.

It was a decade of learning for all of us. Now we know all about skateboards, hot tubs, biofeedback, est, designer jeans, OPEC, the China syndrome.

We jogged, played tennis, an ancient Middle Eastern game called backgammon became bigger than checkers, discotheques came, went away and came back again as disco. And everyone spoke the word boogie far too many times.

It was a decade in North Carolina that began and ended with Bob Scott in the news, a decade that featured a witch trial in Morganton, the century's only Republican governor (so far) in the state and a sheriff or two sent to jail.

Anybody seen Mark Spitz lately?

We talked about test-tube babies; we cried when a pope named John Paul I died and sold T-shirts when his successor came to call.

We went from burning the American flag during the rage of Kent State to burning the Iranian flag during the rage of Khomeini.

We lost John Wayne and Groucho Marx; someone stole Charlie Chaplin's body, and Miss North Carolina kicked her crown.

The best rock 'n' roll song of the decade came early, with Dobie Gray's "Drift Away" ("Gimme the beat, boys, and free my soul, I wanna get lost in your rock 'n' roll and drift away.") He never had another hit.

Women discovered the Annie Hall look, and men wore three-piece suits with no ties like John Travolta. Hollywood, after all these years, can still do that to us.

For all our sophistication we remain impressionable innocents.

And I still miss Janis Joplin.

A Place Just Down the Road

Snow Hill

Is is 10:30 a.m. on the last Wednesday in August.

The sign at East Federal Savings says it is 71 degrees.

A blue sky is half full of mountain-sized white clouds, pushed along by a breeze from the northeast. The same breeze flutters the sales tags on the front porch rockers outside Potter's furniture store. It is the only movement on Greene Street, the main street.

It is quiet. For long minutes you don't see a soul on the street. A pickup coming to the drive-in window at the bank is cause for notice.

In the distance a dog barks, drowning out the sound of insects humming in the morning air.

Harry's Restaurant is quiet now, the morning coffee drinkers have gone back to work, and it is too early for the lunch crowd that will jam every seat at the eight tables and six booths.

The four women who work there are sitting at the front table, catching up on the latest news.

"She wants to get married?" one says.

"Who does she want to marry?" her friend asks.

"Anybody," the first one says. "She just wants to get married. All she wants is red-checked curtains. She is the countriest thing I've ever seen."

The courthouse, half a block from Harry's, is equally quiet. A man patiently trims the lawn out front, a lawn that would be the envy of any golf course. No one is in the halls. The sound of a typewriter comes from an office somewhere. The typing is slow, the cadence regular.

Two men sit in Ye Olde Fat Frog pool hall, playing cards and ignoring the black-and-white television set turned down low. Next door is the auto parts store that's also the license plate agency and the Western Union office.

It seems that no one is home at the big mansions on Greene Street in the first block up from the middle of town. All of them have been lovingly restored to their former elegance. All but one, that is, and it would make the perfect haunted house for any little town.

Snow Hill is an old town. A sign at the bridge over Contentnea Creek says the first settlers arrived about 1710. It took a century for the town to be formed and another half a century for it to be incorporated as the county seat of Greene County.

The settlers called it Snow Hill because it is more hilly than most towns in the East and because the white sandy soil reminded someone of snow.

That is about it for local history. A marker on the courthouse lawn records that, in 1713, a group of settlers fought the Tuscarora Indians five miles away in a bloody battle over land. The Indians lost and moved to New York.

The rest of Snow Hill's history rests beneath the fragrant magnolia tree in the yard of St. Barnabas Episcopal Church, an old church rarely used these days that sits on the highest hill in town.

The town, surrounded by major highways but undisturbed by them, seems an island of tranquility this Wednesday morning. It is prosperous and clean, the kind of place where young lovers still scrawl their initials in fresh sidewalk cement, recording for all time that "W.J. loves M.V.," and "D.W. loves C.G."

Harry's comes alive at 11:30 when the lunch crowd comes in

for pork chops or barbecued beef ribs at $3 a plate, tax and drink included. The fried okra is crisp, the potatoes boiled in ketchup tangy, the tea sweet.

But by 1 p.m., it is quiet again, the pace slowed.

A visitor sits on the steps of St. Barnabas, beneath the magnolia, a soft breeze washing over him, and tries to figure out the lure and charm of the little town.

Just before he dozes off, sung to sleep by the birds and the drone of a distant push lawn mower, he understands.

Snow Hill is the little hometown you always imagined little hometowns were like on a summer morning in August, calm and safe.

Miss Mary Keeps the Faith

Hadnot Creek

It never was a heavily populated neighborhood here in western Carteret County.

There were vast tracts of land but only a few people, so the Hadnot Creek Primitive Baptist Church never was a busy place on Sunday mornings when the circuit-riding preacher would come.

Over the years, as has happened to many churches of that faith, the old people have died and the young haven't joined, choosing instead to forsake the church of their forefathers for the uptown faith of modern religion.

At Hadnot Creek, in the unpainted church founded in 1791, in the church built when each member was assessed a certain number of board feet of timber to be cut from his own farm, here in this elegantly poignant memory of how it used to be, there is now but one member.

Her name is Mary Taylor. She is Hadnot Creek Primitive Baptist Church.

"I'd say there were probably never more than 20 or 25 members," she said of her beloved church. "We'd have more people than that, since people from other churches would come here and we'd have some outsiders, but it never was a big church."

There have been times when there wasn't preaching at Hadnot Creek, even on those second Sundays of each month when it was their turn. Primitive Baptist preachers are hard to find sometimes, and for three years the old church sat quietly beneath the Spanish moss. But now it is alive again. On a recent Sunday, 12 people were there.

"We've had some problems with vandals," Mrs. Taylor said. "Now we've got everything out here a big town has. They're not from our community, but they're a-comin' and a-goin' through here all the time. We had to get a lock for the door. Why, we didn't used to have to lock it. Isn't that a shame?

"They took a table from in front of the pulpit that was as old as the church. Man doesn't know how to make tables like that anymore."

There is no electricity in the church, but there are handmade fragile benches crafted when the church was new. There is no running water, but you can still see the fingerprints of the men who built the church, the sweat of their hands blending with the oil of the pine to leave lasting evidence of their love and strength. There are no carpets, but there are the old slave balconies where the young sat with the slaves so they'd be quiet.

There are no parking places, but there is the old wagon road still visible through the woods, the ruts cut deep in the sandy soil.

There is no heated baptismal pool, but they still dress the graves of their dead with whelk shells, the old way.

The church is all of wood, hand-hewn from these stubborn swamps. It glows on the inside in the way that only ancient pine polished by generations of preaching, pride and family can do.

There have been those who said fix it up, wouldn't a coat of paint look nice?

"So many wanted it painted," Mrs. Taylor admitted, even now aghast at such a silly notion. "But it would take all the beauty out of it.

"Some of those historical societies have wanted to restore it, as they called it, but they'd want it to be a museum. I still want it for a church.

"We got us a new tin roof a few years ago and it could probably use some other things, but we're Primitive Baptists, we don't go a-beggin'.

"If this church stays here, it will be according to what God calls."

There may be but one member left at Hadnot Creek Primitive Baptist, but when that one member is Mary Taylor, that's all it takes to make a church.

A Hot Dog, With Relish

Rocky Point

"My ambition was to sell 1,000 hot dogs a week," Beverly Paul said. "Now we do that in a day and it isn't a big deal."

It is hard to explain the magic of Paul's Famous Hot Dogs; it is hard to explain why this roadside hot dog stand sells close to 400,000 hot dogs a year when other restaurants come and go like sunburns; it's especially hard to explain why they've been able to do it for so long — considering every customer has to drive to the place because no one lives within walking distance.

One part of it is easy to understand. The hot dogs are good, very good. Don't even bother ordering just one.

Paul thinks he has the secret: "You don't have to be perfect, you just have to always be better than the competition."

But what makes it even more remarkable is that Paul's Famous Hot Dogs violates that most sacred of hot dog lovers' rules of life. The one true way to eat hot dogs is all the way — mustard, onions and chili.

But you don't get chili on your hot dogs here; you get Beverly Paul's own concoction, a pickle relish.

"We used to have chili," Paul said. "But during World War II meat was rationed so I had to come up with something else.

"And when the war was over we started to go back to chili, but people said they preferred the relish, so we stuck with it."

It has been 52 years since Addie A. Paul first opened his general store and filling station at the intersection of U.S. 117 and N.C. 133 in Pender County. Beverly decided he wanted a business of his own so he opened a hot dog stand nearby.

"I figured if I sold 1,000 a week for 5 cents each, I'd take in $50 a week and clear $25; that was good money in the Depression," he said. "That's what nurses and teachers made."

As World War II brought hundreds of thousands of people to this area to work at military bases and shipyards, they all started lining up to buy Paul's hot dogs.

There was no chili and even onions were in short supply, so Paul whipped up the relish from local produce.

That relish is now sold in grocery stores all over Eastern North Carolina, bought by people who have stopped by this country crossroads for "two all the way."

It is not a place that changes much. The present building was built after a fire in 1932 and Paul is proud to say it was remodeled — in 1951.

You can buy hot dogs, drinks or ham sandwiches. That's it, and you get the feeling nobody much cares about the ham sandwiches; they're for hot dog haters dragged in by hot dog lovers.

"Everything else here is scenery," Paul said. "If you beat us over the head, we may let you put catsup on a hot dog but that's about it.

The place is open seven days a week, 17 hours a day. People usually are in line when the doors open, ready to have a hot dog for breakfast.

Train crews have been known to stop on the nearby tracks and run over for a sackful. Pilots have landed planes in nearby fields at lunchtime. Judges and construction workers jostle for counter space. Cadillacs and pickups sit door to door. All are equal in a good hot dog joint, and therein lies part of the charm of these places.

"Think about it," Paul said. "When you eat a hot dog, it's because you're hungry and a hot dog is exactly what you want. And when you're hungry and get just what you want, you'll love it. That's the secret of hot dogs."

First there was Addie, then Beverly, now Dave is at the cooker, and young Jonathan, the fourth generation of hot doggers, is toddling around behind the counter. The tradition lives on.

"You've got to get new customers every day," Paul said, "because customers die every day. That's what we try to do."

It Can't Happen, but It Does

Johns

It is an old road. You can tell by the giant trees that stand in neat rows on either side.

It is officially called State Road 1613. It slides through Scotland County farmland, past Gray Pond Baptist Church, the old houses and the new mobile homes.

It runs downhill for the last half-mile or so, all the way to where it meets in a T-intersection with State Road 1619, right in front of the path that goes up to Rudolph Locklear's house.

It is there, at that very ordinary rural intersection, that a most curious thing happens.

When you stop at the stop sign at the intersection, you realize that you cannot see what is coming either way on 1619. High weeds block your view to the right, a sharp hill and curve block your view to the left.

So you cheat, roll a few feet past the stop sign, maybe a car length or so, to get a better view.

And then, with the front of your car nosing out into the other road, you put the transmission into neutral.

Now take your foot off the brake for a moment.

You will not roll forward into 1619, although you are apparently going downhill and that is what should happen.

You will roll backward several feet, back to safety behind the stop sign.

You will roll, you will be convinced, uphill.

Cars do not roll uphill. Everyone knows that. Sir Isaac Newton figured out the laws of gravity and those laws say that nothing rolls uphill.

Try to remember those laws when you're sitting there, feeling and seeing your car roll uphill.

Because that is what happens, or seems to, anyway.

The only logical answer is that it is an optical illusion. You come down a long hill and right at the end it levels out some, but from every angle it still looks like you are going downhill.

As you might imagine, there are legends aplenty having to do with this intersection.

The oldest one goes back to the Civil War. That legend has it that two soldiers were crossing the intersection when a runaway horse and buggy came around the curve and killed them both.

They say that many years back a young woman drove down 1613 and pulled too far into the intersection, trying to see around the curves on both sides.

Her car stalled, the legend goes, and she got out to open the hood and see what had happened.

It was then that a car came around one of the curves and killed her.

Ghosts have been there ever since, gently nudging the careless driver back to safety, or so the legends go.

But what happens if you choose not to believe in ghosts? What if you don't believe the theory that a magnetic deposit is beneath the intersection that somehow pulls metal cars back a few feet?

And don't misunderstand, cars don't roll backward just a few inches. A full car length would be more like it. And they move with some speed.

The farther you pull into the intersection, the farther you move back up the hill. And the farther you are past the sign, the faster you roll, always ending up in exactly the same spot, in my case with the stop sign beside my front window.

People have been coming to this spot for years to feel the strange sensation for themselves.

I sat near the intersection for most of an hour. Of the 15 cars that stopped, six of them played the game. And all six of them rolled up that hill, or appeared to, at least.

"Yeah, I've heard of the place all my life," said an elderly man in nearby Johns. "But I ain't never been there. Wanted to some, but I never did. I don't believe in the mess."

I offered to give him a lift, let him check it out for himself.

"That's all right," he said, "I don't like to stick my nose in a mess like that. Some things you just never know about. Best not to mess with it is what I say."

But if you want to try it, drive on U.S. 501 South from Laurinburg to Johns, about five miles. Take a left on State Road 1619 in Johns and go about two miles. State Road 1613 is on your left.

But be careful. It is a dangerous intersection. There are curves blocking drivers' views and who knows, you could become a ghost story yourself.

White Christmas and Steamed Oysters

Rodanthe

The surf began building a half-mile or more offshore, rising rapidly from the churning slate-gray sea in a race to see which wave would next slap the battered beach with a watery fist.

Out on the horizon, where the sea usually looks as flat as a pool table, 30-foot waves made mountains.

The wind was blowing a steady 40 knots and gusting to 50, a full-born January gale screaming ashore on these tiny islands.

The temperature hovered in the low 30s. That means that a combination of wind and temperature made it feel like zero.

And in case the wind and the cold weren't enough, it was snowing.

The snow didn't come down in big fat flakes to rest easy on the live oaks and sea oats. It came hard and icy, parallel to the ground, a solid wall of stinging white, bringing the sparse traffic on N.C. 12 to a cautious crawl.

It occurred to me that night, driving south from Whalebone Junction, sliding on the icy Herbert C. Bonner Bridge, that maybe this year they would cancel the traditional Old Christmas celebration at Rodanthe. I mean, who wants to stand outside in that kind of awesomely rotten weather and eat oysters?

Most everyone, it seemed.

The crowd may have been smaller at the old schoolhouse that now serves as the Rodanthe community building, but you couldn't tell it. If there had been more people, they would have stacked one atop the other.

It has been going on for longer than anyone knows, this annual blowout on Jan. 5, the traditional date of Christmas. It has, all will agree, no religious significance. It is a party, pure and simple, and Bankers party hardily.

They were all there, the old families — the Midgetts, the Paynes, the Herberts, the O'Neals — families with roots deep in the sand and sea that is their home.

There were children and fishermen and matrons and hippies, three-piece suits and rubber boots, drinks poured in monogrammed glasses and bottles grasped by weathered hands.

And there was Old Buck.

Legend has it that Old Buck was a magnificent bull who swam ashore from a shipwreck — but then, legend has it that practically everything out here came ashore from a shipwreck — and was first spotted standing proudly on the beach.

Local residents, impressed with the size and beauty of the bull, went home and turned all their cows loose so they could breed with him. Old Buck, they say, fathered many calves during his life. Children rode Old Buck's back. He led the procession on Old Christmas. He was part of the people's lives.

Being of a wandering nature, Old Buck met his end when he walked down to the Trent woods and was shot by a hunter.

To honor Old Buck, the locals made a replica of his head and for years carried it high on a pole during the Old Christmas celebrations, celebrations that were far different from the bourbon-and-boogie party that survives today.

Each celebration began with shooting apples off people's heads, William Tell style, and ended with a procession through the village by people dressed in disguises.

Now Old Christmas is a raucous party, covered by two television networks and, at $3 a head, a money-maker for the community.

But when the gales howl and the seas crash, and the Banker fishermen crowd into the little building to dance, eat and drink, time stills.

And nothing tastes better than a steaming oyster slurped from the shell, while around you snow falls on Eastern North Carolina's only white Christmas.

The Black Water of Waccamaw

Lake Waccamaw

A day on the lake:

At noon the lake is still. The glassy reflection of the towering cypress trees lining the shore wavers gently in the spring sunshine. The far shore is lost in the haze.

A family of ducks slides by in perfect formation, seemingly oblivious to the danger that threatens just across the road.

There, in the ominous swamp surrounding this huge lake, alligators live. Still a protected species, the gators are out this warm day.

Two of them, a hundred yards apart, move like silent death; one heads west, one heads east, on patrol.

They show nothing but snouts, eyes and the occasional guiding flick of a powerful tail.

The water is black; the gators blacker. If they only knew the ducks were there, just a fast flip away.

But they don't. The ducks will live this spring day.

"You used not to hardly ever see gators," a lake old-timer

said. "Now you see them all the time. You want to see chaos? Let a gator be spotted in the lake. Them people walk on water to get out of there.

"People find them in their yards all the time now. And the fools feed them chicken necks. Wait until they open the door one night to let the dog out and one of them gators is hungry for a chicken neck."

● ● ●

It is an old place, this lake called Waccamaw. Legend has it that Osceola, the great Seminole chieftain, was born here of a white father and an Indian mother.

Later the chief would lead his swamp-living people against the might of the U.S. Army in the Florida lowlands. And he would win, something few Indian tribes could claim.

They don't know whether the lake was born when a great fire began in the peat swamp and burned off all the vegetation or if it were one of the bay lakes, born when a shower of giant meteors crashed into Southeastern North Carolina in the days when the Earth was young.

● ● ●

"Lake Waccamaw is a secret, and frankly, we'd like to keep it that way," Betty Timberlake said.

That may not be difficult. There was a time, back around the turn of the century and for many years after, when Lake Waccamaw was one of the plushest resorts on the East Coast. The wealthy Cannons of Cannon Mills came every summer to bask in the mysterious breeze that comes every afternoon and blows all night, calming every morning, as regularly as the sun comes up.

There were hotels along the lake; excursion trains brought people by the thousands. There were cottages to rent, an active social life. In fact, the social life was so active at one time that many staunch people cast a wary eye at this lake where the orchestras played, and there were miles of moss-laden lanes where a young couple could find a few moments alone.

"But it has changed," Mrs. Timberlake said, standing in the Lake Waccamaw Museum. "It has changed from a summer resort to more year-round residents. I'd guess that 60 percent of the homes here are year-round now.

"I guess I'm typical. I used to come here for the summer in the late '20s and every year, just after Labor Day, I'd start dreaming about coming back next summer. We moved here permanently in 1974. I love this place."

• • •

Nature always has been the draw here. The lake is good for fishing; the water is made for sailing in the afternoon breeze; the cypress trees are huge.

It was those cypress trees and the shingles made from them that first brought commercial interests here.

North Carolina Lumber Co. had more than 400 men in its work crew on the swampy south side of the lake, cutting shingles from the mighty cypress trees.

They hauled the shingles by boat across the lake and up the small railroad that ran to the main Wilmington-Manchester line, said to be one of the longest straight stretches of railroad track in the world.

There are people still living from the cypress. At Crusoe Island, tucked back in the Great Swamp, hardy men make dugout canoes the Indian way.

Lake Waccamaw is a place of beauty, remarkably protected, lovingly visited.

If you come, drop by the museum in the old depot.

"We want people to appreciate what a unique place this really is," Mrs. Timberlake said.

All They Do Is Eat Barbecue

Whitakers

The club rules are strict.

No liquor is allowed, no gambling, no women except on ladies' night, and — best of all — no speeches.

"It is the only club I know of with no purpose but to promote the enjoyment of Eastern North Carolina's principal delicacy — barbecue," said Judge Ben Neville.

"All we do is eat barbecue."

The 55 members of the Whitakers Barbecue Club meet each Thursday from May through August on the banks of Fishing Creek, where, at 12:15 p.m. sharp, Lee Ward reaches into a big pot and starts dishing out barbecue, slaw, mashed-up boiled potatoes and corn bread. You bring your own drink.

They have been doing it since 1919 — 62 years of eating pig at the same place.

Membership in the club is restricted. Someone has to die or quit to create an opening, and there is a waiting list to join the select 55. And you even have to live in the right place.

"We select 55 because that's how many people you feed on one 85- to 100-pound pig," the judge said. "The rules are that 33 come from Nash and Edgecombe counties and 22 can come from up around Enfield. It started just for Whitakers, and they didn't want Enfield people taking over."

The club, made up mostly of farmers, but with a sprinkling of small-businessmen, bankers and others who can choose their own lunch hour, began at a spot on the creek that years ago was a favorite swimming hole.

Time was, the judge said, when upward of a hundred people would gather to swim, and on one such occasion a group of local farmers got together and cooked some pig.

It went over well, and since 1919 — five years before the first commercial barbecue restaurant opened in nearby Rocky Mount — they've been doing it the same way.

"Used to be, one member was in charge of each meal," the judge said. "He'd have to go buy the pig and pick up the cook and come down here and build the fire so they could get the pig on about 2 or 3 in the morning.

"We cooked for years in an open pit, and then we built a cookhouse with a grate at waist level to cook it."

The cook since the early 1950s has been Lee Ward, a 70-year-old man with 50 years' experience cooking barbecue, and one of the legends you hear about anytime you mention good pig.

"I didn't like staying down here all night by myself," Ward said. "I know it's foolish, but I don't like snakes. Actually, the only snakes I'm afraid of are the little ones and the big ones."

Being a professional barbecue man, Ward developed his own gas cooker and now cooks the weekly pig at his business in Whitakers.

"But I still have to get up at 3 in the morning to do it," he said.

Dues for the club are $20 a year and $2 a meal. You can eat all you want, and after everyone is finished you can take the leftovers home with you.

"The ribs are the first things to go," Ward said. "I've been looking for a pig for 20 years that is all ribs, but I haven't found it yet."

Ward's pig is cooked to his own exacting standards. His sauce, sprinkled on the pig only after it is chopped up, is nothing but a mixture of vinegar, salt and pepper. He believes you ought to taste the pork.

"I don't get as much barbecue from a pig as some others because I don't think everything in a pig is edible, and I drain it to get the grease out," he said. "I may not be the best barbecue cook around, but I ain't scared of none of the rest of them."

The club likes to brag that when Bob Melton opened his first barbecue joint in Rocky Mount in 1924, his cook was a fellow who learned while cooking pigs for the Whitakers Barbecue Club.

"Ward's barbecue is good, but it doesn't seem to be as good as it used to be," Judge Neville reflected, his cigar in one hand and a fork in the other. "We used to buy our pigs from a man that fed them on peanuts, and the aroma of that pig cooking in the open air added something to it."

By 1 p.m. the diners were mostly all gone, the open-sided shelter and benches swept clean, only the gurgle of Fishing Creek, the rustle of drying corn and the songs of the birds to accompany Judge Neville, at 69 the oldest member of the club, as he walked to his car.

"I've had many a good feed down here," he said.

Death Chair at a Country Store

Bear Grass

It is known to some as "The Death Chair."

To others, it's just that ratty old chair in the back of Mottie Belle's drinks-and-crackers store in the southern Martin County town of Bear Grass.

"Lord a-mercy, the story's done gone to Raleigh," Mottie Belle said when I mentioned it to her. "Now ain't that something."

What we're dealing with here is your basic Media Event. Fame has come to Mottie Belle and her old chair — fame she didn't expect, nor especially want, but she's doing very well under the strain. Might even sell a few more drinks and crackers.

Mottie Belle runs a little place right at the intersection in downtown Bear Grass. It is an old place, "about to rot away" as she says, and it is a favorite with Bear Grassers looking for an excuse to come in out of the sun.

There's a bench outside where folks sit to pass the time in the cool of the day and see who rides through town. Folks like Swamp Rabbit, the fellow who fell off his motorized bike just once and parked it for life, sit outside on the bench.

But the real action is inside, back around the stove where you can sit on the bench by the wall. Or if you're a regular, or just an uppity newspaper fellow from Raleigh, you can sit in one of the more-or-less upholstered chairs.

Folks have been gathering here for years, solving the world's crises and so forth, and they have pretty much settled on where they'll sit every day.

There was one dark, colorless chair by the window where Jesse Rogers used to sit until he died.

Cairo Rogers started sitting there until he died, too.

Gordon Sexton was next. Gordon was in his 60s but was an energetic sort. One night he went to a ball game and then stopped off on his way home for some courting — I told you he was active — and when he didn't show up the next day Mottie Belle and some of the folks went to check and found him dead.

And there were several others, or so local legend has it, who sat in the chair and died.

Of course, it has been pointed out that everyone who sits in the chair will eventually die, but there is some nagging feeling around that it did seem to come rather suddenly for folks who sat in that particular chair.

"Now you know that chair never killed nobody," Mottie Belle said. "No chair had nothing to do with it."

No one sits in the Death Chair now. It rests back in a corner, beneath piles of old drink cartons, and had it not been for a flurry of recent interest, the chair probably wouldn't even be around now.

"I was going to haul the old thing to the woods," Simon Gardner said, "but I ain't never got around to it, so it's still sitting there."

The Death Chair legend gained momentum recently when a group of Bear Grass students put together a book of local ghost stories that included the story of the chair.

There are folks in the neighborhood who will not sit in the chair because they firmly believe it to be cursed, like a family member of one of the men who died after sitting there.

But for most people around Bear Grass, it is just one more local legend, like the story Gardner tells from his bootlegging days.

"We were coming down a road on our way back from hauling a load of liquor," he said. "We came up on this house, and I saw this ball of fire that looked like a grapefruit come up out of a chimney. I asked the fellow with me if he had seen it and he had.

"Then we saw two more come up. Shortly after that a man killed another man in that same house."

I suggested to Mottie Belle that she hang onto the chair and charge folks admission to come in and gawk.

She'd make a lot of money.

And that's a country tradition, too.

The Best Little Drive-in in Wilson

Wilson

The 1950s are gone — again.

They ended the first time, if you remember, when the clock struck midnight on New Year's Eve in 1959.

But the 1950s, a tough decade to kill off, would not stay dead. Those years came back to thrill us again, the second time as nostalgia. "Happy Days," "Laverne and Shirley," "Grease."

Now Laverne and Shirley live in California, and it is 1965. Amazingly enough, it also is 1965 at the Cunningham household in Milwaukee. "Grease" isn't running on Broadway anymore, and they've torn down The Creamery.

This time, the 1950s are gone for good. One simply cannot be nostalgic without The Creamery.

Don't be misled when folks in their 30s and 40s tell you the teenage years weren't like they were on "Happy Days." They were just like that at The Creamery. It was the quintessential drive-in — carhops, young bucks lounging on automobile hoods, a throbbing jukebox, girls in full skirts and bobby socks leaning out of car windows.

It was called "draggin' The Creamery." What you did was

ride around and around the parking lot. Mostly you drove because there were only 28 parking spaces. You drove to see and be seen. You had to inherit a parking space.

There always was music, loud music. The outdoor jukebox never ran out of nickels. Yes, Virginia, the man said nickels.

"Every afternoon it was like a funeral procession from the high school to The Creamery," owner Howard Whitley said. "We'd fill up in 10 minutes."

The Creamery was our switchboard — everyone checked in. You went there and sat in your car and waited for friends to join you, or you joined them in their car. And you left your car there, a message to all that you'd be back.

When you wanted to find out what was going on in Wilson, you went to The Creamery.

Where's everybody? I dunno. Did you check The Creamery?

Roy Gatchell drew the plans for The Creamery on a brown paper bag in 1946 and finally got a loan from the bank. He sold ice cream and milkshakes, and the place was adopted by the boys back from the war.

Then the high school kids took it and made it their own. Carhops were there, the first in Wilson. They were young black boys. There were Arthur and Henry and Randy (who's now a Wilson policeman). They'd hustle you a 6-cent Pepsi and you'd nurse it for hours.

You'd roll up the window on the driver's side a few inches, and they'd hook on that gray metal tray. One of the rites of passage was to swipe a tray from The Creamery. The risk of getting caught was banishment. But we did it.

George Switzer bought The Creamery from Roy Gatchell, and then Clarence Hetrick from Indiana bought it in 1954 so he could be close to his daughter at East Carolina. But the owners I remember were Carroll Baker and Howard Whitley, who bought it in 1958.

"We were 22 when we came here," Howard said. "We've spent our lives here."

So did their customers. It didn't matter if you were going parking with your girl on Airport Road or Ripley Road, first you dragged The Creamery so everyone would know who was with whom that night — unless you were two-timing, of course.

The Creamery was for city kids. The county kids went to

Cliff's, to Bruce's, to Murphy's or to the legendary Maurice's. And there were occasional rumbles between the opposing clientele.

They tore The Creamery down a couple of weeks ago, making way for a spiffy new place.

"It went down in two hours," Howard said. "I didn't even see it. But then I'm not sorry I didn't see it.

"People have been coming by since then to reminisce, to tell their kids this place was their drive-in, their Arnold's.

"Tommy Bridges (a denizen of the parking lot's famed back row) came out and got a bunch of the blocks. He is going to give pieces of them to the old-timers."

Oh, God, now we're old-timers.

A crowd gathered the day they tore The Creamery down. They watched as a bulldozer leveled their youth. They thought about Buddy Holly and white socks, and I'll bet most of them could show you the very spot on Airport Road where they fell in love. It was only an eight-minute drive away.

In Dixie Land,
Where I Was Born

I am glad I was born in the South.

I don't mean this in the "Hell, no, I ain't fergittin' " bumper sticker sense, although I usually stand up and holler with everyone else when they play "Dixie" in some honky-tonk.

This is no rebel flag-waving cheer, no screed against Yankee drivers, no call to arms to preserve another dying Southern tradition.

I've been thinking about the South a lot lately for two reasons.

First was an appearance in Raleigh by playwright Tennessee Williams. He was gently bemoaning the franchising of the South, turning the old plantation into a McDonald's parking lot.

Somber editorial writers correctly pointed out that Williams was a dreamer, that the plantations weren't all that good and how about all that pellagra anyway?

But I suspect that wasn't what Williams was talking about. If you read his plays, you know that his view of life among the fading Southern aristocracy wasn't all that hot, certainly not something to viewed nostalgically.

What Williams misses about the South — as do I — is Southernness.

There is something to be said for Sunday dinner on the grounds at your grandmother's church, surrounded by countless generations and branches of the same family, seeing all those uncles and aunts and cousins you forget from year to year, holding a plate of food seasoned with pride, fatback and love.

You are a better person for having spent a long, slow Sunday afternoon on a front porch — the little ones playing in the shade, the women talking about who married whom, and the men talking crops and fishing and church business.

Southerners didn't miss out on twilight in June when the lightning bugs were out and the kids played "Red Light," "May I?" and "Hide and Go Seek" in the dusty street, still warm from the sun.

Southerners dug fishing worms and put them in an old pork-and-bean can and called an old dog and spent the afternoon on a pond bank. You need that sometimes.

Southerners know the sting of a freshly stripped switch on bare legs, the warmth of watching a church league softball game under the lights with the cheering sections in lawn chairs down each base line, the way walking to Sunday school in May makes your chest tingle.

These are not experiences known only by me; they are commonplace to all Southerners. They are part of our lives, who we are and what we stand for.

It doesn't matter whether we are black or white, male or female, sharecroppers or doctors, old or young. It matters only that we are Southerners, and our Southernness is something we share.

That's what Tennessee Williams, a native of Mississippi, misses about the South. He now lives in Key West, Fla., a Southern place geographically but not truly the South of which we speak.

The other reason I'm thinking about the South is that I'm going to New York next week for the first time in my life. And, honestly, I'm a little bit nervous about it.

A friend from Philadelphia, hearing me make jokes about being mugged, said, with some exasperation, "You make it sound like you're going to a foreign country."

I feel like I am. I'm going to Broadway and Times Square; I'm going to Yankee Stadium; I'm going to ride subways beneath the street; I'm going to eat supper more than 1,000 feet above the street.

I feel like I am going to a foreign country. I don't know what makes people in New York tick the way I understand my fellow Southerners, so we probably will alienate each other once or twice. We have not shared enough to know each other.

The food will be different; the stores will sell different things; people will wear different fashions. They will have a different set of fears and loves.

I will feel as apart from them, and they from me, as I would anywhere in the world.

I will be fascinated by New York, envious perhaps, because it is the greatest city in the world, and I may be even a little reluctant to come home to this little one-horse part of the world. Who knows, someday I may even want to live in New York.

But one day I'm going to need something to hold onto, and I'll again walk the land where my great-grandparents lived and died, I'll catch a lightning bug in a mayonnaise jar, and I'll stand outside a country church and listen to the voices come through the open window.

And I'll be glad I'm a Southerner.

Talk Southern to Me

From time to time, this column — purely as a public service — has attempted to make life easier for our immigrants from the Northern regions.

We have discussed barbecue, how to drive in snow (or at least, how to shut up about how well they did it back home), and we have labored mightily to help our newcomers speak Southern.

Apparently we have had great success. Cynthia Poindexter may be our best student.

Ms. Poindexter lived in Raleigh and worked in Johnston County for two years before recently moving back to Pennsylvania. Now, she wrote the other day, she misses us.

"I find that I miss those special words, expressions and pronunciations that I was accustomed to hearing in Johnston

County," she said. 'I'm no linguist, but I feel that the language there is colorful, descriptive and unique.

"Rest assured that I am in no way poking fun at the people of that county, but that I only wish to celebrate their delightful dialect."

Since many newcomers have arrived of late, it is time to help them, even as we helped Ms. Poindexter. These are expressions Ms. Poindexter heard for the first time in Johnston County and never hears in Pennsylvania:

"Get shed of it" — to get rid of it, do away with it. Example: "I want to get shed of this bad cold."

"Right smart" — quite a bit, frequently. Example: "He misses work right smart; he hardly ever shows up."

"Right on" — continuing. Example: "He went right on seeing her even after she moved."

"Of a morning/evening" — every day. Example: "He delivers milk of a morning."

"Yet and still" — however. Example: "I love him, yet and still he makes me mad as fire."

"Left out of " — departed. Example: "She left out of here about two hours ago."

"It wouldn't say a word" — expression used when an inanimate object doesn't respond when it should. Example: "The car wouldn't say a word no matter how many times I turned it over" (which means engaged the ignition).

"Looking" — searching for. Example: "I'm looking my pencil."

"Bottom side upwards" — upside down. Example: "I turned the envelope bottom side upwards and everything fell out."

"Looking angry" — bad. Example. "The place where I cut my finger got all infected and was looking angry by the time I got to the doctor."

"All to pieces" — emotionally upset. Example: "I had a wreck and went all to pieces."

"Preached my funeral" — severely talked to. Example: "My mama really preached my funeral when I came in an hour late."

"Give out" — exhausted, tired. Example: "I worked so hard I am plumb give out." "Plumb," by the way, like "slap" and "slam," means "very."

"Tote" — carry. Example: "Can you tote my groceries in from the car?"

"Choicy" — choosy. Example: "He sure is choicy about what he eats."

"Pure" — a word to add emphasis. Example: "The gas tank was pure dry by the time I got to the filling station."

"Stories" — verb, meaning to lie. Example: "She stories about her age."

"Sorriness" — general unworthiness. Example: "He got fired out of sorriness."

Glad Ms. Poindexter and I could be of help. Y'all come to see us, you hear?

Besides That, They're Ugly

You should feel sorry for possums.

But you probably don't. No one feels sorry for possums. Most people think possums are ugly. And they are, amazingly ugly, what with their pointy little faces and squinty eyes. Disgusting creatures.

And dumb? If Mother Nature made anything dumber than a possum, I don't know what it is. You would have thought that by now possums would have learned at least something about how to cross a road, wouldn't you?

But no, not possums. They go charging — well, charging is too fast a word to use, chugging would be more apt — across the road and ka-thump. Scratch another possum.

And no one seems to care.

No one even calls them by their right name. The official name is "opossum." Do you know one person who has ever called a possum an "opossum?" I had a teacher in elementary school who insisted that we use "opossum." We thought she was a fruitcake. Stand around a country store and call it an opossum. Don't be surprised if people move away from you, casting sidelong glances as they go.

And the jokes. Someone sent me some possum jokes the other day. They were cruel.

Q: What is the lifespan of a possum?

A: From birth until it tries to cross the road.

See what I mean? Possums are like people from Poland. Everyone makes ugly, unfair jokes about them.

Q: How many possums does it take to change a light bulb?

A: Four, one to turn the bulb and three to watch out for traffic.

And this smart-aleck remark: "Be thankful possums don't fly, or we'd find them dead on our roofs after they got hit by airplanes."

I figured someone must have said something good and memorable about possums at some time in history. I went and checked a book of famous quotations. It has 2,816 pages and the word opossum or possum does not appear.

I've done my best to find out something good about possums. Even snakes have a good reputation in some circles (not here, though).

The dictionary describes possums as omnivorous. That means they will eat almost anything, including baby birds, garbage and slugs.

Even people who will go to a fancy French restaurant and spend a king's ransom on snails — although they hide the truth and call them escargot — will not touch a possum.

Yeah, I know. Baked possum and sweet 'taters are delicious, right? You always read that in folksy books and everyone declares it to be the truth.

My grandfather caught a possum in a rabbit box one time and he proclaimed the family in line for a real treat.

He took that ugly critter and put him in a pen and fed him nothing but cracked corn for a month.

"Cleans him out," my grandfather said.

Then he cooked him. With baked sweet potatoes. My grandmother refused to go near the kitchen.

"Boy, you're in for a real treat," my grandfather said, picking up a big piece of possum.

He took one bite. The smile on his face wilted.

"Patooie!" my grandfather exploded. Possum flew across the table.

"Well, they used to be good," he muttered. "Lelia, we got any of last night's chicken left?"

Scenes From a County Fair

Fayetteville

It was dark on the back side of the midway. A power failure, the ground that felt like a soggy sponge and a late arrival from the previous run in Greensboro had ganged up on the ride operators for The Dell and Travers Show.

It was opening night and things were not going well at all.

"Where's Mike?" an angry man shouted above the clatter of people putting together a Ferris wheel in the dark.

"Where's Mike?" he screamed a little louder, pacing back and forth.

A bare-chested young man ambled up with tattoos and long hair held back in a ponytail.

"You looking for me?" Mike asked.

"Yeah," the man snarled. "Go find me something to kick."

●　●　●

There was a beauty contest going on down at the grandstand. Forty-five high school girls, all claiming to weigh between 110 and 130 pounds (except for one girl who tipped the scales at 85 pounds and several who out and out fibbed) were competing for the title of Miss Cape Fear Fair as they paraded across the stage for the judges.

While they were there, an announcer read off their qualifications and hobbies. Not a tin ear in the bunch, all of them claimed to be in love with music. They played a large number of flutes, danced like fairies, sang like nightingales.

Not to be outdone, one young lass stoically admitted her musical interest extended no further than "listening to the radio." The audience loved her most.

●　●　●

Up in the commercial exhibits a young couple, he somber and she very pregnant, were having their pictures made by a computer gadget that prints your likeness on a T-shirt or tote bag or towel.

Her mama was in charge.

"Now move to the left," Mama directed, keeping a sharp eye on the TV monitor that showed the couple to passersby.

"No, too far," Mama screeched. "Back the other way.

"Now smile. Too much, your teeth look terrible. Try it without showing your teeth. That's better, a little more, that's it. Now hold it.

"What's the matter with you, fool? Can't you smile?" she grilled the young man.

"No, not like that, you look sick, a real smile. Tell you what, smile and I'll go home," Mama said with a deadly finality to her voice.

The young man beamed.

"Got it," the photographer said.

"Remember, you promised," the man said.

"Shut up, fool," Mama said.

● ● ●

Back at the beauty contest, the field had been narrowed from 45 contestants to 22, and then to 10. They were finally ready to announce the winners.

They picked five winners, first through fifth places. As the big winner was named, everyone gathered around her for the obligatory hugs and tears.

Except for one girl off to the side. She looked at the winner, and then, in a priceless moment seen by almost no one since all eyes but mine were on the winner, she stuck out her tongue.

I couldn't help but wonder if she were Miss Congeniality.

● ● ●

Two burly paratroopers, with tattoos promising "Death From Above" or "Death Before Dishonor," were standing in front of the "Circus of Wonders, World's Strangest People, Human Oddities, All Alive" sideshow.

It was closed.

"That's too bad," one trooper said to the other. "I really wanted to see Otis the Frog Boy."

"You didn't miss much," the other one said. "I used to date his sister."

"Did she turn into a princess when you kissed her?" the first one asked cautiously. He had a feeling he was being set up for something.

There was a long pause.

"No, she turned into a motel," the jokester said.

It was a nice fair.

Marry a Woman With Two First Names

Harry T. Saunders is a pathetic, tortured man.

Saunders — I know little else about him — lives in Washington, D.C. But that isn't the only reason he's pathetic and tortured.

Harry T. Saunders is a man without barbecue.

There will be a moment of silence as a shudder runs throughout North Carolina.

I came across Saunders' desperate plight recently when Bill Green, a Duke University administrator currently on leave to serve The Washington Post as ombudsman, sent along a letter he received from Saunders.

"Mr. Saunders cannot be satisfied in this city, so I'm relaying his query to the source. Can you help him?" Green asked.

Saunders, simply put, wants to know how to cook barbecue.

He has asked great food writers. They, of course, were no help. Those wimpy simpletons eat snails, drink carbonated water that costs a buck a bottle and prefer ambience to banana pudding. What do they know?

Saunders wrote: "I'm desperate. I really need to know from the ground up the step-by-step procedure of real, Southern, open-pit barbecue.

"There is the problem of wood, hickory or oak. What about the time involved if I used spare ribs or pork shoulders? How far should the meat be from the fire? How about a sauce? Is it a vinegar or a tomato base?

"I do want to be a barbecue afficionado, and I need a North Carolina barbecue expert to explain this wonderful madness to me."

Whoa, Saunders; first things first. While it would be easier to explain the innards of a neutron bomb or why the Mona Lisa smiles, I will be glad to do what I can.

First of all, you must move. Barbecue can be cooked only within the confines of North Carolina. Air quality makes it impossible to cook it anywhere else. In fact, I think there is a law against cooking barbecue outside North Carolina. I know I've certainly never eaten barbecue outside Tar Heelia.

And you can't live just anywhere in North Carolina. Resist the siren song of some who would spin grand and glorious tales of heavenly pigs in Western North Carolina. Do not listen when they whisper words like "Shelby" or "Lexington" in your hungry ear. Be strong, Saunders, and come East.

Imagine a football. Place one tip of your imaginary football at Chapel Hill. Place the other tip at New Bern. Then outline your football to include Enfield to the north and Pink Hill to the south. That's where you must live.

After you've been here for several years — no one ever claimed this was easy, Saunders, but you asked — or better yet, after several generations, buy yourself a hat that advertises farm products.

Get a drink crate and learn to sit on the edge and lean back and spit without leaving evidence on your shirt.

Learn to pour peanuts into a Pepsi without spilling a single one.

Love your mama, Willie Nelson, stock car racing, stewed okra and tomatoes and the joy of a good dog.

Marry a woman who goes by two first names.

Learn to live on pork and beans, Vienna sausage and crackers during hunting and fishing seasons. Seasons, shall we say, are often matters of personal choice in these parts.

Go to church, dislike all politicians except the ones who do you favors, loathe Charlotte, know how to light a cigarette with a book of matches using only one hand even though the truck window is down, and know the first names of all your grandfather's brothers and sisters and who they married.

And when you can check the bead on a jar of stumphole whiskey, and when you can repair a pickup truck with baling wire, and when you can open Pepsi on a nail head, and when you can plow straight without looking back, and when you can wear white socks and tell 'em all where to go, then you can cook barbecue.

And not before.

A Few of My Favorite Things

The Best and Worst of Eastern North Carolina, a biased, unfair, one-sided, personal opinion after 100,000 miles of backroads and four years of good times:

Best place to kill time and not feel guilty: Beaufort waterfront. The people, the view, the boats and the fresh air are a good excuse.

Hardest place to find: Bear Grass. Just try.

Best example of urban blight: Downtown Fayetteville.

Most boring highway, four-lane: U.S. 64 from Raleigh to Rocky Mount.

Most boring highway, two-lane: U.S. 158 between Roanoke Rapids and Elizabeth City.

Worst stretch of highway, period: U.S. 264 between Mattamuskeet and Mann's Harbor. The longest 52 miles on Earth.

Best place for a sandwich and a beer: Sam and Omie's, Whalebone Junction. Try the fresh fish sandwich.

Best jukebox: 42nd Street Tavern, Raleigh.

Best place to hang out and tell lies: Planters Seed and Feed, Pinetops. You can tell when owner Steve Burress is telling a whopper: His mouth moves.

Best tattoo parlors: Jacksonville

Best stand of kudzu: Along U.S. 401 between Rolesville and Louisburg.

Best fried shrimp: Donnie Smith's Cafe, Creswell.

Best motel at the beach: The Ocean House, Nags Head.

Best motel inland: The MGN Regency, Goldsboro. Contrary to some advertising claims, a few surprises are sometimes nice — such as FM radio.

Hardest town to find something in: Greenville

Easiest town to find something in: Wilmington. Numbered streets are simple and effective.

Most boring towns at night: Kinston and Williamston.

Best place to drink your beer, keep your mouth shut and mind your own business: Jacksonville's Court Street.

Hardest place to figure out how to pronounce: Chalybeate Springs.

Most overrated, semi-cultural event: Old Christmas at Rodanthe, but it makes up for it by being the dangdest party you've ever seen. Don't trip over the TV cameras.

Best pawn shops: Fayetteville.

Best bridge: Herbert C. Bonner Bridge across Oregon Inlet. But hurry, it may not last.

Best shortcut: Southern Pines to Fayetteville via Fort Bragg's drop zones. Leave Southern Pines on Pennsylvania Avenue and watch for signs.

Best town to slow down and look as you drive through: Trenton. The lake, the cypress trees and the Spanish moss are pleasant.

Best place to watch girls: Franklin Street in Chapel Hill.

Best-kept secret: Medoc Mountain State Park.

Best-looking downtown: Raleigh. The mall is terrific.

Best beach strand: Wrightsville Beach, before it washed away.

Worst beach strand: Carolina Beach, before it washed away.

Best place to walk on the beach: Hammocks Beach State Park.

Best place to take a coffee break: The drugstore in downtown Elizabethtown — 5 cents.

Best place to get eaten up by mosquitoes: Brunswick Town State Historic Site.

Best view: Silver Lake at Ocracoke.

Best-looking river: Lumber River. But then I like black water and gray moss.

Most enthusiastic town: Kenansville.

Best idea for a winter Sunday: Go see the wintering waterfowl at Lake Mattamuskeet. Spectacular.

Best suggestion: Four-lane U.S. 70-A. Quick. Please.

Best honky-tonk: Carolina Opry House, Greenville.

Best little town: Beaufort.

Best big town: Wilmington.

Best backroad: N.C. 561 from Louisburg to Ahoskie.

Best coat-and-tie joint: Sweet Caroline's, Greenville. Some of us are tired of steak or fried fish.

Best idea since the pill: Four-laning U.S. 70 between Kinston and New Bern. Barren and boring, but quick.

Worst idea since swine flu vaccinations: Four-laning the road around Clarkton, Lt. Gov. James C. Green's hometown.

Best place to kill time and feel guilty: Playing Space Invaders in the afternoon at the arcade in the Carolina East Mall in Greenville.

Best barbecue in Eastern North Carolina: You knew I couldn't resist, didn't you? It is at Doug Sauls' place outside Nashville. The chairs don't match, the screen doors slam and the nearby tobacco barns work. And the pig is heavenly.

All Kinds of Folks

Mother Tina held the naked 3-day-old baby girl before her, sitting by lamplight in the sharecropper's house.

Praying in a soft voice, the old black woman covered the tiny infant in homemade lard and told her Lord, "I can't do it anymore, but this little one will finish the job."

That was in 1915. Now, 65 years later, Ophelia Underwood has finished the job her great-grandmother Tina ordained her to do.

"No one told me what happened that night, but when I told my mama I wanted to be a midwife, she told me what Mother Tina had done and told me to go ahead," Mrs. Underwood said. "I've always felt like I was supposed to do it, that it was my birthright to be a midwife."

From 1940 to 1978, Mrs. Underwood traveled the backroads and swamps of Columbus County to deliver babies, sometimes walking, sometimes going by wagon and sometimes riding double on a bicycle with a nervous father.

She is credited with delivering 1,093 babies. As many as three generations have called her Granny, the honor given in the backcountry to the midwives they still call "Granny woman."

And she still remembers that first one, when young Willie McDuffie saw the light of day.

"Annie Bell McDuffie had had babies before, and she told me to go ahead and if I did anything wrong, she'd tell me. I didn't have any problems."

In 38 years of delivering babies, usually in sharecroppers' houses heated by wood-burning stoves, lit by kerosene lamps and using well water, Mrs. Underwood never lost a mother. There were still births, but no mother ever died.

"I was supposed to get $15 for each one, but I usually didn't," she said. "They'd give me what they had, maybe some corn or potatoes, or after the baby was born the woman might come to our place and sucker tobacco to pay me back. I usually got my money's worth from them back when nobody had any money. But after they had money they'd promise to pay but hardly ever did.

"I'd always wanted to be a midwife since I first met Dr. Naomi Muldrow from Charlotte. She was the first black woman I'd ever seen who was a doctor, and I wanted to be just like her."

It was never easy. Babies, she said, have a bad habit of deciding to be born in the middle of the night, usually when it's raining or on Sunday, just before the preacher starts his sermon.

"Sometimes I'd walk, sometimes they'd come for me in a wagon, and I've ridden many a mile on a bicycle with me sitting on the crossbar and the husband pedaling. I didn't start using a car until 1969.

"I'd get the woman up and keep her moving. I'd walk her into the field, make her sweep the floor, anything to keep her moving. When it got so bad she couldn't stand it anymore, I'd have her lie down and the baby would come."

She remembers the most frightening birth of all, when she delivered her own grandchild.

"I stuck right beside the telephone," she said, laughing. "If she'd have hollered, I'd have called the doctor and the rescue squad in a minute. It's different when it's your own."

Mrs. Underwood is the last known midwife in Columbus County. There were 28 working when she started.

"Most people want babies born in hospitals now," she said. "Back then, getting pregnant wasn't anything to go to the doctor about. You got pregnant, and a midwife delivered the baby. If there wasn't anything wrong, you didn't go to the doctor.

"My husband, Zeke, and I were sharecroppers. Many a time I've sat up with a woman all night and then gone home and suckered tobacco all day and fixed supper at night.

"I've retired now, but if it was an emergency and somebody needed me, I'd go."

And I'll bet they'd still be glad to see the Granny woman.

Karl Fleming

Vanceboro

It is noon, the last Sunday in August.

The police station is closed, a thin film of summer dust sits on the one police car parked outside. Call the sheriff if you have a problem, thank you.

A clerk in the one open business, a small convenience store, doesn't have to ask "which one?" when a stranger seeks directions to the Methodist Church.

Those who could, parked their cars in the shade outside the Methodist Church on Farm Life Road. Most have their windows down. You don't lock your car on a drowsy Sunday in Vanceboro.

Inside the church, behind the closed stained-glass windows and over the gentle hum of the air conditioning, the Methodists get up from their red-padded pews and join in that song of blind faith and unquestioning trust, "Standing on the Promises." Their voices carry into the sleepy street outside.

Preaching is over a few minutes later, and Sunday morning ends, as it has for years, with a handshake or a hug from Preacher Claude Wilson.

A few people remain inside, clustered down by the altar, surrounding a tall man with perfectly combed silver hair and an out-of-town suit.

Karl Fleming of the Maul Swamp sharecropping Flemings has completed his personal odyssey.

"This won't last forever; this should be recorded for history," Fleming said, looking at the good women of the church spreading out the butter beans, fresh corn and deviled eggs in the fellowship room behind the sanctuary. "In a few years they'll have a Jacuzzi and a hot tub back there."

Karl Fleming knows about California hot tubs, and he knows about Onslow County butter beans. He has tested both. But the butter beans were there in the beginning, and it is to those that Karl Fleming has returned, at least for this last Sunday in August.

In between were the years when the faith he was taught on those hard chairs seemed more a burden than a creed.

They were the years when his daddy, 27 years older than his mama, dropped dead of a heart attack in the Depression.

They were the years when his mama sold Bibles and bottled drinks door to door to keep that tired little family together until the TB came and she couldn't do it anymore.

They were the years when a hurt, angry, lonely little boy was growing up in the Methodist Home for Children in Raleigh.

"I used to walk along Glenwood Avenue and look up at all those big houses and try to imagine what family life was like in those places," Fleming said. "I couldn't do it.

"I was enraged. I was ashamed of being poor, ashamed of living in an orphanage. Tear a little kid way from his mother and watch the rebelliousness grow.

"Then my best friend died, and they told me that was God's will. I said forget it; I didn't want anything to do with a God that would kill my friend and let them take me away from my mother. I came out of there with a chip on my shoulder a mile wide."

But the rage drove him; the shame made him promise himself he would be poor no more and a nobody no more. He clawed his way to the top in the news business, from the civil rights struggles in the Deep South, where he grew used to mobs and shots at his back in the dark, to the riots in Watts, where his jaw was broken in three places when he was attacked by pipe-swinging men.

They were good times, too, with a new wife on his arm, a humid little book on the first sexual exploits of 28 famous people selling well and finally the position of managing editor of KNXT-TV News, where every day he decides what the news is for 3 million people in Lotus Land.

And it drove him back, back to the little Methodist Church and a plate of butter beans on the last Sunday in August.

"The old values didn't die," Fleming said, sitting with his 80-year-old mother. "The actions might be rebellious, but there is something to those Reader's Digest verities. I think what brought me back here today is a realization of that.

"Six months ago I was sitting with some friends in Los Angeles, and we were talking about right and wrong.

"They said, 'Karl, you really believe that stuff don't you,' and I thought yes, that's who I am. I came to a grudging acceptance that you can't escape who you are.

"I used to sneer at those old truths I learned as a boy, but you come to realize that all man is, is what he stands for. A friend once called me the conscience of my station. That's the highest compliment I ever received.

"It took me a long time to realize I didn't have to be a tough guy. I hope this is the beginning of some maturity for me, finally, at age 53."

And that afternoon, after everyone had told him and his mama how proud they were of both of them, and after the food had been cleared away, Fleming walked back into that little church on Farm Life Road and became the newest member of the Vanceboro Methodist Church.

"I won't go back to California a changed person," he said. "But maybe I've made an inch of progress. If nothing else, I hope I can give more love and get more in return.

"It's been a long way from that tenant shack."

Uncle Josh Hendricks

Bethel Hill

Uncle Josh Hendricks says he doesn't know "much about much," but he is — flat out — the dangdest coon hunter in the scrubby woods around this Person County community.

"Huntin' coon, that's what I do," Uncle Josh said. "People always askin' me, 'Josh, why do you hunt coons so much?'

"Now, ain't that the silliest thing you ever heard? Why do I hunt coons? Heck, I hunt coons 'cause huntin' coons beats workin'."

He laughed. Uncle Josh laughs a lot. And why not laugh when all you've got to do is hunt coons?

"You got to be smart as all get-out to be a good coon hunter," he said. "Now, you take me. I knowed I liked to hunt coons, so I decided that I'd figure it out so's I could hunt 'em as much as I wanted to.

"I farmed a long time, then I leased it all out 'ceptin' the home place, and that and the Social Security give me enough money to live on. It don't take much for an old bachelor like me to live."

Uncle Josh — everybody calls him that — claims he has been hunting coons for 70 years. Uncle Josh is 69.

"Well, now, I'll tell you how that happened," he said, just as serious as could be. "Now my daddy was probably the best coon hunter that ever lived. His name was Jacob Hendricks, and he come from Virginia.

"He hunted coons more than I do. Now, as it turns out, Daddy was courtin' my mama just on Sundays, at church and in the afternoon. Mama didn't like that too much so she told him if they got married, one of two things had to happen. Either he had to quit coon huntin' all the time or she was going with him after they were married.

"Daddy didn't see nothing wrong with a woman going coon huntin', especially my mama since she was tough as he was, so he told her to come on.

"They was quite a pair, the two of 'em coon huntin' all over everywhere. Mama told me that I was born one week from the time they went huntin' last, so I figure that I rode with my mama on coon hunts before I was born."

What does it take, I asked, to be a coon hunter?

"Now, let's get one thing straight," Uncle Josh said. "Anybody can be a coon hunter. All you got to do is go out and hunt coons. That ain't hard at all.

"But the trick, you see, is to be a coon getter. That's what I am, a coon getter."

OK, Uncle Josh, what does it take to be a coon getter?

"You got to be smart, like I said before. Coons is about the smartest animal in these woods, smarter than any dog. All a dog can do is smell. A coon can think.

"So you got to outthink him. You let the dogs smell him — a man can't smell — and they'll let you know which way he's a-headin'.

"Now, some of the boys, all they do is follow the dogs, up one creek and down the other, runnin' themselves slap to death chasin' a coon and a pack of dogs that can outrun any man.

"Me, well, I'm too blamed feeble to chase after the dogs like a fool, so I figure out where that coon's headin' and do my best to be there to say hello when he arrives.

"You got to study the coon, watch what they do, how they'll climb trees and cross over creeks and double back. Actually, the coons here are at a disadvantage. I've hunted these woods for 70 years. Some of them coons ain't but a few years old, you see. I know these woods as good as they do.

"One time I was out with some boys and we was a-huntin' coons and they took off after the dogs and I knew just as sure as I'm sittin' here where that coon was going.

"So I got there first that time and watched that coon go up this tree to hide. I could hear the dogs a-comin' and the men a-hollerin' so I went up the tree after the coon and shot him with my little .22 pistol. Then I sat in the tree and waited for the dogs and the boys to get there.

"They came a-runnin' up and there I was, sittin' on that tree branch and a-smilin' at 'em, holdin' that coon by the tail. They liked to had a fit.

"I sure do love to hunt coons."

Lynn Dudka

Chapel Hill

If love could cure, if caring could heal, if tenderness were a miracle drug, none of Lynn Dudka's patients would die.

But that is not the way things are, especially in the Clinical Research Unit at North Carolina Memorial Hospital, where Ms. Dudka works with terminally ill brain tumor patients.

"We don't have a cure; we tell them all that," she said. "What we have is treatment that can buy them some time."

What Ms. Dudka tries to do is see that those remaining weeks, months or years are as meaningful as possible.

"I'm here to help," she said. "I let them know I'm here. If they want to talk about it, I'm here to listen and talk. If they want to deny they're going to die and that helps them cope, that's fine with me. Whatever helps them the most."

She is part traditional nurse, part social worker, part patient advocate and all friend.

She came to Memorial from Duke Hospital, where her excellence as a nurse had moved her into supervisory jobs.

"I didn't want to push papers," she said. "That's not why I went into nursing. The fact that all my patients here would be terminally ill didn't enter into it. They are patients like any other; they have needs.

"They are alive, and I'm going to give them everything I can. None of us sits around saying they're going to die any minute. I enjoy them now, and when the bad part comes, I deal with it.

"Death is not the worst thing that can happen to you. There is one patient I have who is on a respirator. She cries out that she wants to die, and I want her to. What kind of life can she have? Death for her will be a release. When they're suffering, they are ready to go."

Her job is officially that of coordinating patient care for the 89 patients assigned to her and Dr. Stephen Mahaley, chief neurosurgeon at Memorial.

"But I become close to my patients," she said. "Some people in the medical profession feel you should not get involved, you should stay cold and objective, but not me. I'm human, and I care about my patients. I wouldn't be any good if I didn't become involved."

And the patients know she cares. She gives them her home telephone number so they can call when they are frightened or confused. Families call to use her as a sounding board, someone to share their grief and fear. "When they die it really hurts," she said. "I get depressed, and I hurt with them and their families.

"In the old days, nurses wouldn't talk to patients. They'd tell them they had to ask the doctor. Not me. If a patient wants to know the results of their lab tests, I tell them; if they want to see the tumor in their brains, I show them the scans. It is their life. They are the ones who are sick, and it is their money. It is their right to know the truth, but only if they want to.

"Some people die denying they have a tumor. It wouldn't do any good to grab them and say: 'Hey, you're dying. Face it.' But if they want to talk about it, I will. In fact, the question they most often ask is what death will be like.

"They're lucky in one way. Usually, there is no pain with a tumor; they lapse into a coma and simply don't wake up."

It is not the end of Lynn Dudka's love and concern when her

patients leave Memorial. While we were talking, a patient's family called her just to tell her that their son had come through an operation in Charlotte with flying colors. They called because they knew she cared. And she did.

She flashed a smile you wouldn't believe.

Jacques, Phillippe and Pauline

The wedding went off without a hitch.

There were a couple of moments there, though, when it would have been easy for the wedding of Louise Wolff and Alex Carlyle to turn into a Walt Disney movie, the kind Hayley Mills used to make with all those dogs and people chasing each other.

Louise and Alex said their "I do's" at Unity Church in Raleigh. Jacques, Phillippe and Pauline, Louise's beloved poodles, minded their manners as befitting official members of the wedding party.

Dog trainer Judy Morton, who worked with the dogs for months, was first down the aisle, the poodles walking nervously in front of her, the trio decked out with small purple ribbons in their well-brushed hair.

Alex was waiting at the altar when Louise started down the aisle, looking radiant as all brides do. She nodded at the familiar faces turned to watch her and about halfway down caught Alex's eye.

It was a brief moment, but her eyes rolled heavenward as if to say, "Please, don't let anything go wrong."

Everyone tried to ignore the three-woman television crew, but it was difficult. They scampered about the room, flashing lights this way and that, and that's probably what made Phillippe a little nervous.

First we heard a whine, Judy bent down to console the anxious dog, Louise's head snapped around and every well-wisher in the crowd wondered if this was when it would happen.

"It really wasn't a problem," Judy said later. "I just rubbed him and he was fine."

There would be other whines, though, each adding a smidgen of tension in the crowd. No one wanted this to turn into a farce.

But when Pauline sneezed, a sneeze that to many could have

been mistaken for a tentative bark, there was a small nervous ripple in the audience.

There was another collective experience. When they got to the "Do you take ..." part, Alex was asked, "Do you, Alex, take Louise to be your wife, and Jacques, Pauline and Phillippe to be your family?"

Alex said he did, and everyone relaxed.

And when they got to the "You may kiss the bride" part, everyone breathed a lot easier.

The Unity Church pastor, the Rev. Jim Rosemergy, said this was the first time he had conducted a wedding with dogs involved.

"I enjoy an unusual wedding," he said. "I believe a part of a ministry is to be accepting, so why not?

"The idea of a dogfight at the altar was in the back of my mind, and if there had been one at the rehearsal, I would have been more nervous."

And the just-married Alex?

"I was afraid someone would throw a cat in here," he said, clearly relieved, but then all grooms look relieved when a wedding is over.

All in all, it was a lovely wedding. The bride beamed, the groom looked so proud of himself, friends and family were there and when each anniversary comes around and they relight the candle they took home from the wedding, Louise and Alex Carlyle will have something to remember other than who got mad at whom at the reception.

Albert Taylor

Elm City

Uncle Jim Barnes wasn't the boy's uncle, but that's what the boy called him. That's what a respectful white boy called an old black man back then, out in the country.

Uncle Jim and the sickly boy used to go fishing, and sometimes the boy would start cussing up a blue streak, the way boys will sometimes, along about puberty when things are a little confused.

The creek-bank cussing bothered Uncle Jim. Taking the Lord's name in vain troubled the old Primitive Baptist, and he'd get on the boy for it.

"I'm scared to be down here with you, boy," he'd say. "The devil's gonna come up right now and get you."

Uncle Jim didn't know it but those creek-bank lessons were getting to the boy. Sometimes when the boy was in the woods alone he'd do a little talking to the Lord himself. There was one place he especially liked to go.

"I about wore the bark off one old stump where I'd pray," the boy would say more than half a century later. "I'd whoop and holler and shout, too."

It was a fearsome fight for the boy's soul, but the Lord and Uncle Jim were winning.

The moment came on a night in spring, at the Thursday night prayer meeting at a little country church down the road, a place called Vaughan's Chapel.

The boy gave up that night, with tears in his eyes and his heart full, kneeling at the altar for everyone to see.

But Uncle Jim wasn't there, and the boy could hardly wait until first light the next morning to find his friend.

Uncle Jim was hooking up a mule to a plow when the boy spotted him across the field.

He came flying up to the old man, yelling, "I've been saved, Uncle Jim, I've been saved."

The old man looked at the boy, his aging face breaking into a grin, and he started dancing a jig.

Uncle Jim danced all the way around that confused old mule that spring morning, clapping his hands and shouting, "Praise the Lord. Praise the Lord."

Then the old black man and his young white friend hugged each other, out there in the fields, loving each other and sharing the joy of the boy's newfound salvation.

Within six years the boy would stand in the Vaughan's Chapel pulpit and preach his first sermon. It was titled, "The Coming of the Lord."

There would be many more sermons in the 49 years that the Rev. J. Albert Taylor would preach to saints and sinners who gathered to hear him Sunday mornings across North Carolina.

"I didn't choose preaching," Taylor said as we sat on his wide front porch in Elm City, rocking in the cool morning shade. "The Lord called me to do it. I'm as sure of that as anything."

But we have to back up for a moment, back to the young

Albert Taylor, back to the days right after his conversion.

"I had some trouble with my old friends," he said. "They wanted me to run with the gang, and I knew I couldn't do that anymore. I didn't want to get in trouble.

"They used to hide in the bushes and chunk brickbats at me.

"I even had to break up with the girl I'd been seeing."

But there was someone waiting, a 14-year-old girl named Mamie.

"The first time I saw her was in church, and the Lord told me that was the girl I was going to marry," he said. "I talked back to the Lord. I said, 'No, you can't mean it, she's just a baby.' But two years later I married her. She was just 16 then, but the Lord gave her to me and I sure couldn't have done any better on my own."

There would be hard times to come. Taylor couldn't make a living preaching so he spent 20 years in a cotton mill, working all week and preaching on Sunday, he and Mamie raising their 11 children.

Then his lungs gave out and he had to give it up 10 years ago. But now, at 68, his eyes still brighten when he says, "I still do a little preaching every time I can."

Soon I had to say goodbye, laden down with an old-fashioned country dinner and "a little something to take home with you." On the way home I thought of a question I forgot to ask:

I wonder if Uncle Jim ever heard the boy preach?

"Not in church he didn't," Taylor said on the phone. "But I preached to him plenty on the side. It thrilled that old man."

Weird Harold

Rocky Mount

Meet Weird Harold, the world's baddest rasslin' hippie:

"Mean? Man, I was the meanest you've ever seen. My girlfriend used to go to the show and boo me. My mother got so mad at me one time, she wouldn't even talk to me."

And Weird Harold loved it.

His name isn't really Weird Harold, but when he was a professional wrestler the folks in the Upper Midwest loved to hate him by that name.

Actually Bob Craig, a native of Detroit, is a pleasant — although extremely large — man. He has given up big-time wrestling and now sells industrial equipment.

"Being a professional wrestler isn't something you grew up to be," he said. "I don't know a single kid who ever wanted to grow up to be a wrestler. But when you weigh 300 pounds and you're 6-4, you sure aren't going to be a ballet dancer.

"Hell, I did it because it was fun. Actually, it hurt a lot, but I thought it was fun."

Weird Harold became a wrestler after going to college in Michigan.

"I played third-string tackle," he said. "I was a terrible player who only got to play when we were winning by four touchdowns or losing by five. But I was big. I didn't have to be fast. They had to be fast to get around me. I took up a lot of space.

"This Weird Harold thing got started after I graduated. I had a part-time job in the summer as a security guard, and one time I was working a wrestling match. One of the promoters saw me and suggested I'd make a good wrestler.

"I wasn't real interested in an office job, so I decided to give it a shot. I guess I'd played football and got hit in the head too much."

To become a professional wrestler, Craig had to come up with a gimmick.

"You can't just put on a bathing suit and go out there and grab somebody," he said. "You've got to have a bit.

"Mine came accidentally. I worked for the promoter all summer long while I was learning how to fall down and not get hurt, so I let my hair and beard grow out.

"This was in the 1960s when everyone hated hippies, so they decided I'd become the wrestling hippie. Everybody loved to see me get beaten.

"Being the bad guy in a wrestling match is a lot more fun than being the good guy. I loved it when people yelled at me.

"I used to try to make them mad. I'd go in the ring and give them the peace sign and they'd yell. I'd pretend to smoke a joint and they'd really go crazy. I was that drug-crazed anti-American, dirty hippie.

"I figured those people had kids who were smoking pot and wearing long hair and they couldn't hate them, but they could hate me."

Everyone, even the most die-hard of fans, knows full well that professional wrestling is mostly show. But you do have to be in excellent shape to keep from getting broken in two.

"My best friend and I used to wrestle against each other," he said. "We both worked for the same man, traveled together, slept in the same motel room and then when it came time for the show, I'd try to kill him.

"One time he was dating my sister and we had a show to do, so my mother and my sister came to watch. We were good at it, and my mother thought it was for real. There she was, booing me and pulling for my opponent.

"Then my girlfriend joined in, all of them yelling at me. That's when I knew I was good. Everybody hated me."

So why'd he quit?

"I messed up," he said. "I fell the wrong way one time and broke my wrist. That baby hurt."

Thad Strickland

Thad Strickland is a hero, and the only person he ever saved was himself.

Strickland was working on power lines in Murfreesboro 12 years ago when something happened and he was "plugged in like an extension cord" with 2,400 volts of electricity scorching through his body.

"They went to get the doctor to have me proclaimed dead," Strickland said. "But when he got there, I was sitting up smoking a cigarette."

Strickland was hurt, badly hurt. By the time the sun came up the next day, he had lost both his arms and his kidneys had failed.

"The doctor said they couldn't understand why I was even alive," he said.

It would not be the last time Thad Strickland would baffle his doctors.

"They called my wife in after they amputated my arms and told her that a lot of adjustments would have to be made, that I'd never be the man I was before," he said. "She told them, 'You don't know my husband.' "

Amputees often spend weeks in the hospital after surgery. Strickland was there one week.

It often takes months to learn to use artificial arms. Strickland spent one day in training.

"They had me trying to learn to lace pocketbooks," he said. "I told them I wasn't trying to be smart or anything, but I wasn't going to lace pocketbooks the rest of my life. I wanted to go home and go to work."

Three weeks after his accident, before receiving his artificial arms, Strickland drove his Volkswagen from Tarboro to Washington, D.C., his wife changing the gears while he steered with the stumps of his arms.

His old employer gave him an office job, trying to do the right thing for the "permanently disabled" man. They let him sit in the office and answer telephones.

"I couldn't stand that," he said. "I've got to be working outdoors."

With the help of the state's vocational rehabilitation service, Strickland decided to become a truck driver, hauling mobile homes. Competition from other haulers — who, Strickland said, didn't care about his disability but just wanted to protect their businesses — kept him from getting the necessary permits, so he turned to landscaping.

Now he operates tractors, backhoes, front-end loaders, whatever it takes.

Strickland is an asphalt hauler, perhaps one of the most demanding jobs in trucking. Hauling sometimes 50,000 pounds of asphalt, he jockeys his 13-speed rig through traffic, making runs from the plant to the paving site.

Such haulers are self-employed. When they haul, they get paid. When they sit around, they don't. He who is fastest makes the most money.

"This guy will be going through city traffic, changing gears, talking on the CB radio all the time and if you aren't real careful he'll pass you when you aren't looking," Rich Yocco, a competitor, said of Strickland. "I haven't seen anything this guy can't do. I'll haul four loads and he'll haul five."

"If you want to do something, you'll find a way," Strickland said. "I'll try anything, and so far I haven't tried anything I couldn't do."

That isn't bragging. He water-skis, fishes, swims, hunts, runs two businesses, whatever he wants to do. His hooks are those of a working man. They are scratched and battered. If steel had calluses, his would be the hardest.

"I get irritated when people try to do something for me," Strickland said. "I want to do it. I could have spent the rest of my life drawing Social Security, but I was raised to work, and I'll end up paying more in taxes from working than Vocational Rehabilitation ever paid to help me get started in business.

"I couldn't have done it without my wife behind me. She's always saying, 'Go ahead, you can do it.' And I can."

Toby the Clown

Fayetteville

The traveling salesman goes up to the farmer's house and says he has car trouble and could he come in to use the telephone?

The farmer says there is no telephone so why doesn't the traveling salesman spend the night with him and then seek help tomorrow?

"But you'll have to sleep with the baby," the farmer tells the salesman.

The salesman says, no, he doesn't want to sleep with the baby and will just bed down in the barn, if that's all right.

The farmer agrees and leaves the salesman alone. About that time a sexy young woman comes in and the salesman asks her who she is.

"I'm the baby," she says. "Who are you?"

"I'm the fool who wouldn't sleep with the baby," the salesman says.

And the crowd roars with laughter.

"You can't go wrong with bits like that," Carroll Pippin said.

If anyone should know, it is Carroll Pippin. He has used that ancient routine thousands of times, from the stage of the old Keith vaudeville circuit to the famous burlesque houses to the tent shows that once traveled the backroads of North Carolina to the little one-man shows the old trouper still performs, 56 years after he found the love of his life.

Show business. The words still have magic. Standing out

there in the spotlight can be a powerful drug for some, and Carroll Pippin was one of those.

Ollie Hamilton's Show was based in Whitakers, up in Edgecombe County. Hamilton used to cut his tent poles on young Pippin's farm, and joining that show was all Pippin ever wanted to do.

"I was the working boy," he said, thinking back on those days. "I was a laborer. I did everything from driving stakes to putting up the tent.

"We traveled in Virginia, North Carolina and South Carolina, doing those old melodramas. We did shows like 'Ten Nights in a Barroom,' 'Kentucky Sue' and 'Peg O' My Heart.'

"It was tough. When you signed on as an actor, you'd better be one or you were gone. I've seen actors fired before they finished the first rehearsal.

"They made me the general-business man. I filled in for everyone, taking whatever role they needed. You got a script one night, rehearsed it the next morning and did the show that night."

It was during those dreamy days that the character was born who would remain a part of Pippin to this day. He was Toby, the freckle-faced bumbling yokel, a character the audience loved.

He worked the tent show circuit in the summer months, vaudeville in the winter. Finally he got a shot at the big time; the Great White Way had a place for Toby in a musical variety show.

The Broadway show was "Blossom Time," and Toby was a song-and-dance man in black face — a quick patter, a few tunes, some shuffling steps and Toby hated it. He preferred the gentility of the smaller shows; he'd had his fill of the big time and the hustlers who made it work.

There were other jobs, jobs on the James Adams Floating Theater, the original showboat. There were many years with the legendary Ringling Brothers Circus, years spent working with the most famous and most-loved clown of them all, Emmett Kelly.

Finally he'd had enough, so he returned to his native North Carolina. But while Carroll Pippin was growing old, Toby wasn't.

He helped start the now-famous Dunn Clowns, and they wear his makeup designs to this day. He has been in every Azalea Festival parade in Wilmington since the 1950s. And when he can find a good straight man, be it man or woman, he'll dust off the old vaudeville and burlesque routines to entertain a club.

Now he has a contract with a chain of department stores, appearing as Toby at grand openings and special sales events.

"I'll never stop doing Toby," he said. "I'm going blind now, but when my eyes go I'll get my assistant to tie a rope around my neck and lead me in."

Then he laughs so you won't think he's serious. But he just might be.

The old trouper can still make you laugh, and he knows it.

Take another bow, Toby, you've earned it.

Robert Lane

Edenton

They are a hardy breed, these men of the Albemarle.

For generations they have made their living on these rivers, fighting the treacherous currents on the winding, twisting Roanoke, pulling fish from the more gentle and behaved Chowan.

It is not an easy life. The Roanoke kills quickly, the Chowan lulls you until a storm blows in and it turns ugly.

"I've never lived more than a half-mile from the river," Robert Lane said, while in his kitchen a mess of fried spots and corn bread flavored the air with a heavenly perfume.

"I did go up to Norfolk one time to work in a steel mill. I lasted a week. That was enough for me."

For 31 years, day and night, in all kinds of weather, Robert Lane went about his job with quiet determination. It was a job that somebody had to do, but nobody but the man who did it ever thought about it.

The U.S. Coast Guard called Lane a lamplighter, an antiquated term in this nuclear age. His job was simple: There are 23 lighted navigation aids and 23 day markers on the Chowan and Roanoke rivers. Lane's job was to keep those markers in place, lighting the way for the river men.

But the truth of the matter is, Lane did the work for much more than 31 years. His daddy had the job for 30 years before him. So, from the time he was 12, Robert Lane was on the river.

"They were lit with kerosene back in the old days," he said. "We'd take kerosene cans out there and refill them every few days. That could get rough sometimes, that boat a-pitchin' under you while you handled them cans.

"Then it would commence to blowin' and them lights would blow out and they'd call us to go — and it was go right now.

"My daddy had him one of those one-cylinder engines — they called it a pop-pop boat from the sound it made — but he never got towed in a day in his life."

Of course, there were dangers. Lane's wife remembers one day in particular.

"I didn't like for him to go out by himself," she said. "It was a real cold day so I put jacket upon jacket and we took off about 8 a.m. We went down to the Edenton bridge and back up the Roanoke when he found a day marker (an unlighted sign) that needed fixing.

"He climbed up the pole and then the rope holding the boat broke and I took off downstream, leaving him up that pole in rough weather.

"He was up the pole and I was up the river. I'd never started a boat in my life, but I tried to, but it wouldn't. Then I tried to grab some net stakes, but I missed them, too.

"About a mile downstream I washed up in some cypress trees and bushes and I tore my hands raw trying to pull that boat to the bank. I was scared as I've ever been in my life.

"I was prepared to spend the night, but Robert finally got rescued and came for me. I don't think I've been with him since. I still don't like for him to go alone, but I don't like him to go with me, either."

Technology finally came to the river and the kerosene lamps were replaced with acetylene-fueled torches. That might have helped the lights burn longer, but have you ever tried to hoist a 240-pound tank of gas with a block and tackle when the boat is rising and falling under you?

"Now that could get to be a mess," Lane said.

Then came the batteries. The task came down to mixing caustic soda in a pitching boat.

"You spill that stuff on the boat and it'd take the paint off it," Lane said. "If you got it on your hands, it would eat your fingernails away."

There won't be any more Robert Lanes tending the lights on the river. Lane has retired, his duties taken over by uniformed Coast Guardsmen. But Lane can't help but remember the day a

Coast Guard officer wanted to inspect his lights.

"It got pretty bad out there that day," Lane said. "We were heading upriver and he asked me how far it was to my landing. I told him it was five or six miles, but that we had to go all the way up the river to check the rest of the lights.

"He said there wasn't a thing wrong with my lights, but there sure was something wrong with this river and he wanted to go in."

The Lawyer

It was an understated monument to the American Dream.

It was a buff-colored Mercedes, a big four-door job, but you had to look closely to see the windshield sticker that identified the car as belonging to a property owner at one of those posh island resorts in South Carolina.

On the rear bumper was a larger sticker, this one proclaiming that the owner spends at least a year's worth of middle-class grocery money playing ski bum.

The owner of the Mercedes stood in the hallway of the old courthouse, looking out of place among the DUIs, check bouncers and public drunks, all of them awaiting their turn before the bar of justice. He had been among them before, but not as an equal. He was a lawyer, and when he had walked through, they had parted like fish before a shark. Now they didn't move; now he was one of them. His gleaming wing tips stood out like roses in a garden of cockleburs.

I knew the lawyer. We first met a year ago, on a dreary day. We chatted, saying much of nothing for a while. He didn't seem to be in a hurry this time, and successful lawyers always are in a hurry in old courthouses.

But this time he wasn't a lawyer; this time he was a client. He was being sued by his wife.

The successful lawyer wasn't thinking this day of his shiny Mercedes or his beach house or his next ski trip. His thoughts were of another time.

"I keep thinking about the damn prom," he said. "I asked her to marry me that night after the prom. That was over 25 years ago, and now she's suing me. What in the name of God happened to us?

"We had everything. We never had to worry about money. The kid never gave us any trouble. We never had fights. I can't remember one time when we seriously even yelled at each other."

It all came easy, the American Dream on a two-acre lot, no bugs in the azaleas, no cracks in the driveway, nothing to make them turn toward each other for strength when life got tough. For life didn't get tough.

"It started about three years ago," he said. "I didn't know anything was wrong. Everyone said we were the perfect couple. I thought we were, too.

"But it changed somehow. We got to where we didn't talk very much. I didn't see much point in telling her what I did all day; she knew what I did. I didn't care much about what she did all day; I knew what she did.

"We reached the point where we were bored with each other, I guess. I tried to talk about it one time, but she didn't want to. That made me mad, and when she wanted to talk to me, I wouldn't. Isn't that something, two grown people playing silly games like that?

"The divorce itself wasn't that bad. We separated for two years, and then it was final. I thought we had it all worked out."

The details aren't important. They now are fighting over property, over money, who gets what.

Now he stands in a musty courthouse hall, kicking a cigarette butt from side to side, standing there thinking about his prom.

"I remember it like it was yesterday," he said. "I was so scared. I had never been to a formal dance. I forgot to buy her a corsage until 10 minutes before the florist closed.

"I didn't have a car so we double-dated. My buddy waited in the car while I went to get her. Walking up to her front porch was the longest walk of my life. I must have wiped the sweat off my hands and checked my fly 10 times while I was walking up there.

"She was the prettiest girl I ever saw. I was too scared to talk. We just stood there grinning at each other. But we had a great time that night. I asked her to marry me that night, and four years later, on the same date, we got married."

Someone spoke his name, and the lawyer's lawyer said it was time to go in and meet with the judge to see whether something could be salvaged so that the bashful boy with sweaty hands wouldn't have to fight it out in open court with his prom queen.

Outside the courthouse, a chilling rain was falling on the mud-splattered four-wheel drives, on the sagging sedans, on the rumpled pickups — and on the buff-colored Mercedes.

Chester

Washington, N.C.

What is this world coming to when a confessed criminal is allowed to roam the streets at will, breaking the law daily?

This criminal has popular support from most of the people in town here. A judge once ruled that not only had he broken the law, but that he was free to continue doing so, and law enforcement people should not interfere with his crime spree.

Oh sure, he's a charmer, and though a bit shaggy, he's a good-looking fellow. But his kind face and blond hair hide the heart of a true criminal. It is said that he is — or, to be more accurate, was in his prime — quite a ladies' man. His love affairs are legion, his offspring numerous.

His name is Chester, a fellow of questionable parentage, I might add. But you can say this of Chester: He may be a criminal, but he sure is loyal.

For the past 12 years, Chester — part Airedale, part collie and the rest anybody's guess — has been the loyal four-footed companion of postmen on Washington's City Mail Route No. 2.

Four postmen have delivered the mail on this downtown route since Chester signed on as their escort back when he was little more than a puppy. And still Chester helps deliver the mail in Washington.

"It is the mailmen that Chester loves," said Milton Rogers, the current carrier on No. 2. "It isn't any one of us that he follows; it is whoever is on the route."

No one is sure why Chester began making the daily 10-mile walk with city postmen. Postman J.R. Jones was the first he followed, beginning with short walks down the street and finally extending his range until he was making the whole route.

"He usually runs out to meet me after I'm about 10 minutes into the route," Rogers said. "Sometimes, if he's been left shut up in the house, he'll start whining and crying. It upsets him something terrible. And if I'm late for some reason, he'll walk down to the post office to see what the holdup is.

"A few years ago they passed a leash law here, and they tied Chester up so he couldn't get out. On the third day of that, he broke the chain.

"There was a substitute carrier on the route one day and the dogcatcher tried to pick Chester up. The sub put Chester in his car so the dogcatcher couldn't get him. They all ended up going to court over it, and the judge said that Chester had permission from the court to be without a leash. Everybody knows him here, and you should have seen the letters to the editor supporting him.

"He has never bitten anyone, but he will growl if you pull his hair. All he does is walk along and chase cats. He hates cats, but he'll never bother a kitten. He knows they are just babies.

"Chester has been really hurt a lot of times. He used to love to fight. There was one bulldog he used to fight every day for six months and whipped him, and one day two big dogs ganged up on him. And he's been hit by cars three different times, but he hangs in there.

"Following the mailman is Chester's life, his whole reason for living.

"He knows the route as good as I do. If there is a substitute on and the substitute turns the wrong way at a corner, Chester will go a few feet in the right direction and then turn around and look at him like he's crazy.

"Sometimes if it is real hot or he has something on his mind, he'll stop and wait for me to come back around. He knows the route so well that he can take a shortcut and meet me somewhere else.

"His favorite foods are hot dogs, Nabs and Oreo cookies. There is one man on the route that feeds him three hot dogs every day.

"Sundays and holidays warp him real bad. He doesn't know what's going on, so he goes to the post office."

It is Chester's mission in life to keep the mails moving. When Rogers moves his car, Chester runs out into intersections and barks like mad, trying to stop oncoming traffic so Rogers can get out on the busy streets. Then he runs, full speed ahead, to the next stop to begin his walking route again. It is frightening to watch, but after 12 years, Chester is convinced no one will hit him. He's probably wrong, but lucky.

"The old rascal is a lot of company," Rogers said. "He keeps out of my way, but I do like hearing the jingle of his collar behind me. I sure do miss him when he skips a day."

Bud Thomas

Hamilton

The richest man in town used to come to Bud Thomas' barbershop twice a week to be shaved.

"He'd tell me on Wednesday that he'd pay me Saturday," Thomas said. "And then on Saturday he'd try to make me give him both shaves for the price of one. I guess that's why he was the richest man in town."

For 50 years now, Bud Thomas has looked out at the comings and goings in Hamilton, a town of about 500 in northern Martin County. He has been, for all of those years, the town barber.

Not one of the barbers, the barber.

And he's still at it.

"When I was growing up on the farm, I knew farming was hard work," he said. "I looked at barbering and said that looked easy. I'd never get tired of that."

So he packed up and went off to Richmond for barber college, where in six weeks — for the princely sum of $125 — Bud Thomas became a barber, learning his trade on the heads of Richmond's winos and bums.

"I was homesick after three days, but I'd already paid the money in advance, so I stuck with it," he said.

But there was already a barber in Hamilton back in 1929. So after taking a job in Apex that lasted but one week, young Bud went back to farming.

"But the fellows used to come out to the house to get me to cut their hair and got after me to open my own shop," he said. "So I did. It was in one room built on the side of a service station.

"I'd plow with a mule all day, then walk to town to open the shop at night and then walk home again. The boys used to like to come here and sit at night. They didn't have anything to do and had plenty of money. All I could think about was having to get up the next morning and catch that mule."

Finally, there seemed to be enough business to stay open all the time, so Bud came to town for good.

"I have seen the time when I'd do 18 hours standing at this chair," he said. "I had my dinner and my supper brought to me, and I'd cut hair.

"All the store clerks used to rush down here after 10 on Saturday night so they'd have a fresh haircut on Sunday. I have been here as late as 3:30 on a Sunday morning cutting hair."

Although he charged only 15 cents for a shave and 30 cents for a grown-up's haircut, lots of times people couldn't pay.

"I've swapped food for haircuts," he said. "I had four children to raise and food was the same as money to me. I've even swapped labor on my farm for haircuts.

"I'd take food today if I could get it."

Bud's shop is a little quieter now. Longer hair has hurt some, and fathers don't take their sons to the barbershop anymore, he said. Now their mamas take them to the beauty parlor and even though he doesn't say much on the subject, Bud doesn't seem to care for that turn of events.

It took Bud 15 years to get his own place, and he's been in his current shop — the one with the two real leather and porcelain barber chairs and the 35-year-old RCA radio and the waiting chairs he bought used in 1930 and his original tools the barber college gave him — for 26 years.

At 75, he still works every day, but his wife, Eve, does get him to go hunting or fishing most every Wednesday. Last Wednesday he caught 61 trout, thank you.

"I don't want to retire," he said. "If I did, I'd end up working on the farm and that might be worse for me.

"I'd like to be working right up to the last day."

Lash LaRue

Sanford

When Al was a young fellow he used to say prayers every night, like all good boys.

"I used to ask the Lord to bless my mama and please, let me grow up to be a cowboy," he said.

"I guess that's why I was so good at it. It was something I'd always wanted to do."

And he was good at it. Boy, was he good at it. There were lots of good guys on those Saturday afternoon shoot-outs, but for me and my friends, the only one who counted was that mean-looking, dark-eyed man with the whip, the man in black.

Lash LaRue.

I know journalists are supposed to be objective, but I am not objective when it comes to Lash LaRue. I was a fan of his then and I'm a fan of his now. And when I spent two hours with him, it was a childhood dream come true. I even got to pick up his whip.

Lash was in Sanford visiting his sister, Lee Baine. Dressed in black, as usual, his steel-gray hair neatly combed, his silver beard trimmed, his dark glasses in place, he was the perfect image of the middle-aged gunfighter.

But it wasn't always so. There was a time when young Al LaRue just about killed himself learning to use the whip that would make him a legend.

"Tom Mix was my idol when I was a kid," he said, that deep voice growling. "I used to ride a broomstick and imagine it was the fastest horse in the West.

"Bob Tansey (a Hollywood producer) had this character named Lash that he wanted to use in the movies, so I lied and told him I could use a whip, but I couldn't do it.

"We made movies in five days then and on about the third day Bob called me over and asked me what the problem was with the whip.

"I pulled up my shirt and showed him what I'd done to myself with that whip, trying to learn. I was covered with slashes. Finally they brought in a man named Snowy Baker from Australia to teach me to use it.

"After that it became pure instinct. It was like an extension of my arm. I had complete confidence in a whip. I could bring a man down from 30 feet away or pull him off a horse. It was natural to me."

No one had any idea that the man in black would become a star. He wasn't even mentioned in the credits of the first Lash LaRue movie, "Song of Old Wyoming."

"Fan mail started coming in from everywhere," Lash recalled. "They didn't even know my name. The mail was addressed to the man in black with a whip.

"Hollywood never did accept me. It was the people who made me a star."

There was always something different about Lash LaRue. He was the anti-hero, the John Garfield of B-westerns.

When the likes of Johnny Mack Brown or Roy Rogers or Hopalong Cassidy rode into town, you knew from looking at them that they would win, simply because they had white hats and were the good guys and everyone knew that good guys triumphed over evil.

It wasn't like that with Lash. You knew he would win, but you knew he'd win because he was tougher and meaner than any bad guys around. He seemed to be one of them: The outlaws feared him; they understood him.

His days in Hollywood were not all pleasant. He never caught on with the film moguls. He was a rebel.

"In Hollywood, you either conform or they destroy you," he said. "If it hadn't been for the fans, there never would have been a Lash LaRue."

There was never big studio money behind Lash. He started small and stayed that way, but his films have become classics of the genre.

And there were some good times for a young man from Louisiana.

"I loved every minute of it," he said. "There I'd be, chasing bad guys on a horse, firing guns, playing cowboy.

"That was what I'd always wanted to be and here I was doing it.

"When I got my opportunity, I was ready. I'd studied drama in college, I could ride and I could shoot. I once even outshot a pistol champion, so I was able to do what I appeared to be doing.

"How could any kid who'd wanted to be a cowboy not enjoy being Lash LaRue?

"It was a dream come true."

M.T. Maness

Swansboro

M.T. Maness has been the police chief in this old port town for 35 years. His philosophy is simple:

"If you have to beat them in the head, do it. But if you don't have to, then don't do it.

"I've wore out heads until I didn't have a billy club left and there's some people who hate my guts, but there isn't anyone who doesn't respect me or who will say I've abused them."

Most of those head knockings were in the old days, back when Swansboro had a reputation as a place where fishermen worked hard all day and fought hard all night, back when the town fathers brought in M.T. to clean up the town "so women folks could walk the streets again."

"My daddy used to farm that island over there," Maness said as we sat in the Rip Tide Restaurant, looking out across the White Oak River.

"Every time I'd come to Swansboro I'd get in a fight and it would cost me $3.85 in court costs."

Maness left Swansboro when he was 14, running away in the midst of the Depression, riding the rails and following the wheat harvest to Montana. He came back in 1939 and did what most young men of the time did — made a living as a shrimper.

"Right after I got back from the war they asked me to be police chief temporarily, and after doing it temporarily two times I told them either hire me full time or forget it," Maness said.

"They hired me at $30 a week and that was 24 hours a day, seven days a week. I didn't have a day off for the next 17½ years — not one day.

"The town was three blocks long and four blocks wide. I picked up the trash on Wednesday and collected taxes to keep the town going on Saturday. I put in the sewer lines one block at the time by hand. I installed the first water meter. And when I wasn't busy I cut grass for widows with a swing blade.

"Finally the swing blade got to be too much, so I bought the town's first mower and later the first town tractor with my own money.

"I even bought the town's first five police cars out of my own pocket."

As for the police work, the town settled down once word spread that Maness was taking his job seriously. "They told me to clean up the town, and I did," he said.

Maness has mellowed in recent years, doing what needs doing to keep his town going, like raising money for the annual town

Christmas and Easter parties for the kids, and training young officers.

"I've had a lot of young officers working for me who have gone on to police work in other towns and counties," he said. "It is hard to get good officers because of the pay.

"Last year I got a $1,200 raise and I turned it down. I told the town to give it to my lowest-ranking officer. He didn't deserve it any more than I did, but he needed it a lot more. That's twice I've done that.

"Some of these young officers go at it a little hard sometimes, writing tickets. I tell them these people aren't criminals, they're the people who pay our salaries. They don't have a quota for tickets. If they want to write tickets, I'll go out there and show them how it's done. I could write 50 a day, but just this morning I stopped two people and let them talk me out of tickets.

"I've been in trouble a few times. One man used to go to the town all the time and complain about my cutting the grass for some of the old women. He raised holy hell about it. He thought it was beneath the dignity of the police chief to be cutting grass, so I told them I'd do it on my own time and pay for the gas.

"I'm 66 now and I could retire with $150 more retirement each month than I make now, but I'm not ready to quit.

"I want to stay here to irritate the hell out of my enemies."

Hugh Battle

Rocky Mount

Hugh Battle was trapped in terror, a prisoner inside his own body.

"I used to sit there and talk to him," Evelyn Battle said. "It was so frustrating, not knowing if he was hearing or understanding me. It was like talking to someone dead."

But Hugh Battle, paralyzed, unable to move, speak or even open his eyes, could hear his wife talk.

"There were times when I prayed to die," Hugh said. "I came out of it because Evelyn was there with me."

Hugh, now 60, never had suffered serious illness, so he didn't think much about it when that cold hit him in August 1979.

"It was the kind of cold that half the people in Rocky Mount have at anytime," he said. "In fact, I was over the worst of it, just a hacking cough."

He was coming back from a day of jury duty in nearby Nashville when overwhelming fatigue struck him.

"I had never been so tired in my life," he remembered.

It was 5:30 p.m., Aug. 8, 1979.

By 6 p.m., he was wobbling like a drunk when he tried to walk.

By 7:30 p.m., he could barely walk.

By 8:30 p.m., he could not stand up alone.

By 2 a.m., he was paralyzed from the waist down.

By daylight, he was paralyzed from the neck down.

About 10 a.m., he spoke the last words he could speak for many days when he looked at Evelyn and said, "I'm choking."

They then taped shut his eyes to protect them because the paralysis had reached them.

The disease, called Guillain Barre syndrome, had claimed another victim. It was to be 586 days before Hugh Battle would return to the two-story white house in Rocky Mount. It would be 586 days of nightmares, terror, tubes, anger, frustration and then small glimmers of hope as the ravages of the disease some call French polio began to loosen their grip. And there would be a homecoming.

"I don't know how long those first days lasted; I couldn't tell if hours or days were passing," Hugh said. "I could hear people talking, but it felt like my head was attached to a very short telephone pole or a log. I knew my body was there, but the only time I had any sensation was when they moved me. Then every joint in my body ached.

"There was a terrifying awareness I was in a bed unable to do anything for myself. I could hear the doctors and nurses talk, but I couldn't understand the medical language. It was as if I was in solitary confinement in my own body.

"I couldn't answer questions, I couldn't complain. I was dreadfully afraid I was going to die and not be able to tell anyone I was dying.

"It was as if you were having a nightmare and then you woke up and realized it was true, you were going through it."

The total paralysis lasted a month, with Evelyn not leaving his side.

"It was my job to keep Hugh Battle in this world," she said. "They become very depressed and withdrawn. I kept talking and talking. I told Hugh that when he came home I would never talk again."

First, the eyes opened and there was rejoicing.

"The most important thing was to be able to see a smile," Hugh said. "Can you imagine never seeing another smile?"

Then, after a year, came speech — his first words were "Tell my wife I love her" — and the movement, little by little.

Now Hugh is home, in a wheelchair, becoming stronger as time passes, learning to care for himself. The terror is gone, and now the work to reclaim his body begins.

The first step, getting his priorities in order, has been taken.

"When you're lying there in bed, helpless, you think a lot about what's important to you," he said. "A lot of those things that were important suddenly turn to trash.

"You realize, when you're getting better, that you're living because a lot of people over whom you have no control worked very hard to save you.

"That makes you humble."

Sonny Simpson

Tarboro

His first one was a child molester.

"I had love and compassion for the man," Sonny Simpson said. "I didn't like what he'd done, but I had compassion for him.

"There was a lot of resentment from people because I was willing to stand by him."

Sonny Simpson is a preacher without a pulpit. There are no pews in his church, and when it comes time to baptize someone, a bathtub takes the place of the River Jordan.

For the past two years, Simpson has carried on a quiet — but by all accounts successful — jail ministry in Tarboro, walking the cold, steel halls, preaching his gospel to killers and sneak thieves.

"A lot of these fellows haven't had time for God on the outside," he said. "But when they get to jail they don't have anything but time."

He didn't go to jail that first time to be a preacher. Some

friends knew him as a quiet Christian, a man who cared. And when one of their family members got in trouble for molesting two young girls, they thought Sonny might be able to help.

He did. He gave the man a Bible and the belief that someone cared, and he prayed with him.

"When it came time to go to court, he asked me to be with him, so I went," Simpson said. "I didn't want to, but I felt I had to. And there was a lot of resentment."

Soon the word spread in the Edgecombe County Jail. If you needed someone to talk to, someone who would listen and care about you, call for Sonny Simpson.

"I get calls all the time, day and night," he said, "and I go. That's the least I can do.

"I come down every Saturday, and at first most of them don't accept me, and I don't push it. It usually takes several visits and a word from other inmates that they can trust me.

"Sometimes on Saturday, depending on who is here, the jailer will get all of them that want to together and we'll have a traditional service, reading the Bible, preaching, praying and singing. Other times, if the jailer doesn't feel it would be safe, I'll visit from cell to cell, just talking to those who want to talk. And usually at our services, we'll have half of the inmates attend.

"Maybe what I'm doing is accomplishing something. Sometimes the spirit of the Lord is so strong you'll have goose bumps. I wish that spirit was as strong in some churches I've been to.

"You can't always tell who is serious and who is just using you. A lot of these guys can fool you, and I've had them leave here and go out to become preachers.

"But when it doesn't work, it hurts a lot. I'll see repeaters come back who I thought were saved and that hurts me, but I don't give up on them. I just tell them they have to start all over again. If the Lord is willing to forgive them, who am I to hold it against them?"

Lee Parker

Lee Parker is 87. He still goes to his office in Raleigh's Insurance Building every day.

When times are slow he can lean back in his chair, look out of his ninth-floor window and remember ...

He was 23, a farm kid from Ahoskie, fresh out of law school at Wake Forest but with no plans to be a lawyer. What he wanted was a job, a chance to see some of the world and maybe, just maybe, a little adventure. He got all he asked for, and more.

"I heard they were hiring at the tobacco market in Wilson, so I stopped the first man I saw and asked him for a job," Parker said. "Within 30 days I had a job, a Pullman ticket to San Francisco and a ticket on a ship bound for China."

Parker had been hired by the British American Tobacco Co. His job was "to put a cigarette between the lips of every man in China."

For the next five years, from 1916 to 1921, Parker traveled the back roads of China, from the Mongol tribesmen of Manchuria to the decadence of Shanghai, trying to do just what the company ordered.

His travels were many, his adventures hair-raising and you can get the full story in his delightful little book *China and the Golden Weed*. This one jaunt by the boy from Ahoskie boggles the mind:

It began in Wuchau, where he lived. The destination was the mountain town of Kweiyang. No American had ever been there. Soon Parker would know why.

They set out on the river, heading west toward the towering mountains. The river was at flood stage and after a day and a half, after they had left the leper colony behind, they reached the rapids.

A boatman cut a chicken's neck and splashed the blood on the bow of the boat to appease the river gods, and they set off to go up the rapids. The boat's engine roared, the boat did not move, the water was too fast.

"It was pandemonium," Parker said. "The water eddied and rose in great masses of foam. The noise of it echoed from canyon wall to canyon wall. Our boat was like a bug caught in a current. It shook and quivered and was lost in great walls of spume. It was lifted up and banged down. It made a full half-circle before it righted itself. And always there was the roar of the water mingled with the sing-song of the coolies heaving on the cable (to pull the boat up the rapids)."

Not bad for an Ahoskie boy.

Finally they made calm water and boarded a flat-bottomed

passenger boat packed with peasants and livestock. Once they got to the next town they had to wait for a caravan of 100 or so to form so they could all chip in and pay armed guards to protect them from the bandits and warlords of the mountains. They had 25 armed guards when they headed west again.

This time it was by a canoe, paddled by two boatmen. That stretch took 10 days, and three people drowned. Everyone was delighted it was such a safe trip.

In Hochin, heart of the opium-smuggling trade, Parker and his group made arrangements for seven days of travel by sedan chair to their destination, travel unchanged since the days of the pharaohs.

There was fever, desertions by coolies frightened of the bandits, a successful 10 days selling cigarettes in the mountains, and then it was time for the trip home again.

That's when the bandits struck.

They met the white man's canoes and pretended to be soldiers checking papers. They were not. They wanted money, which they knew Parker had because he had sold his cargo of cigarettes.

But Parker was smart; he had hidden the money on his servant, figuring the bandits would never search there.

"I was scared," he said. "I knew I was licked, but I wasn't going to give in. I stood up in that narrow canoe and told them if they wanted to search me, they had to come on that little canoe to do it, and I knew it would tip over.

"Then I sat down with my back to them and had a cup of tea. They couldn't see my hands shaking. I was bluffing the whole way. They couldn't see my yellow streak, but it was there."

They made it safely, the first expedition in and out of those mountains. There would be other trips on other days until after five years, Parker came home on vacation, fully intending to go back.

"Then I fell in love," he said. "And she wasn't about to go to China with me."

So how'd it work out?

"Well, she fixed breakfast for me this morning," he said, "55 years later."

Joel Jackson

"He was a poet, and they are never quite grown up." — J.M. Barrie

We met only a handful of times, but each moment gleams like a jewel in my memory.

His name was Joel T. Jackson and he died May 23. He was 35.

He left before I had a chance to say goodbye.

It is difficult even now to write about Joel. There was something magic in that old cowboy; a lover of people, a lover of good times, he was the original good old boy.

I will leave it to others to remember Joel in other ways; his gentle lady, Terry, will remember a husband; his four children a father; his co-workers in the Wake County library system a talented, loving professional; the schoolchildren of Wake County a wizard puppeteer.

I choose to remember another Joel Jackson, a good-time Joel in a smoky old barroom, buying a round every time it was his turn.

The first time we met was one of those Saturday nights when writers like to get together and do what they do best: drink beer, tell lies and sing along with the jukebox.

I was standing at the jukebox in the 42nd Street Tavern, looking for a song that would make the night last forever.

There appeared at my shoulder a tall, gangly, bearded man with more skin than hair on top. He watched me punch up a Waylon Jennings tune.

"You like Waylon?" he asked, and I nodded.

"Me too," he said. "Let's have a beer and talk about it."

We sat in a booth for hours that night, all the way to closing time, talking of Willie and Waylon and the outlaws we fancied ourselves to be.

"Old desperadoes" he called us and we laughed, the way the boys will do in a country music bar as they slide toward closing time.

He told me about going to see Waylon — I forget how many times — and how he had every Waylon Jennings album ever made and hey, why didn't we come to the house one night before long and we'd play every last one of them.

I did — and we tried to.

It was a damnable night. I had a flat tire in one of those neighborhoods where the last thing you want to do on Saturday night is have a flat tire.

I walked in his house with skinned knuckles, looking grimy and feeling miserable.

He looked and laughed, pointed out the beer, slipped Waylon on the stereo, turned it up loud and laughed again.

He could do that — create joy in those around him. He made first-time friends remember forever.

Later that night he joined my wife and me out on the porch for some quiet talk about writing and kids, two things he loved deeply.

The last time was perhaps the most precious of all. He came by the house and invited me to ride out into the country to meet a friend.

We piled in that battered old car of his and took off down a road in summer twilight, the green greener, the air like a lover's kiss, singing Waylon's songs at the top of our lungs, two grown men making fools of themselves and savoring the moment.

Joel died just seven hours after Waylon himself came by his Five Points home to say goodbye. Joel knew he was dying — he'd been dying when we met years ago — but he grinned when Waylon walked in.

Joel died with friends around him, friends who came from all over the United States to be there at the end, giving him a little of what he had given them.

Those of us who were blessed to know him said goodbye in a pretty church. Lawyers were there, and children in blue jeans and a doctor or two, poor folks and rich folks, and they all stood up and wept together when Waylon sang: "Then a good month of Sundays and a guitar of gold, had a tall drink of yesterday's wine, left a long string of friends, some sheets in the wind and some satisfied women behind.

"Ride me down easy, Lord, ride me on down, leave word in the dust where I lay. Say I'm easy come and I'm easy go, and easy to love when I stay.

"Put snow on the mountains, raised hell on the hill, locked horns with the devil himself. Been a rodeo bum, a son of gun and a hobo with stars in his crown."

He's a good cowboy, God. Take care of him.

Some Days Are Like That

Pine Knoll Shores

I am big on self-pity.

My theory is that if you can't feel sorry for yourself, how can you ever expect anyone else to feel sorry for you?

Some people are better at feeling sorry for themselves than others. They can walk into a room feeling so sorry for themselves that self-pity oozes from every pore, and in five minutes someone is getting them a cup of coffee to cheer them up.

Then there are people like me. My chin can be hanging down, my lip all aquiver with imagined outrage, and everyone will use it as a cue to tell me how much worse they have it than I do. That is not what I want to hear.

And there is a third class of folks, people who tell you such tales of woe that you can't help but giggle. I used to think that my friend Bill Morrison, our resident critic and professional victim, was the only one around. Then I met Charles and Judy Harker.

Did you ever have a vacation that went wrong? I bet it didn't go this wrong:

Charles and Judy are from Washington, D.C. They decided this would be a good summer to visit the North Carolina beaches and drop in on some friends in the state.

"It started about an hour out of Washington," Charles said. "That's when we realized neither one of us had taken the dog to the kennel and, in fact, had left him in the yard. We called our neighbors and asked them to do it.

"That's when they told us about the fire. The last thing I did before I left was put the yard furniture in a little storage building out back, and I apparently dropped a cigarette and the building burned to the ground and the dog ran away when the firemen showed up with the sirens going.

"I came back to the car to tell Judy and slammed the car door on three of my fingers.

"We sat there for a few minutes while I tried to calm down and get my hand working again. We kept the car running so the air conditioner would work, and the car overheated and the air conditioner blew out.

"We got down here, and the motel we were supposed to stay at had never heard of us, no reservation, no nothing."

That was Day One of the Harker Vacation Saga. There was more to come.

"We called home to check on things — why I don't know — and we found out the dog was all right," Charles said. "He was safe and sound and in the dog pound, and I had a citation for letting him run loose waiting for me when I got back.

"Plus, our neighbors had to pay $25 to get him out."

I won't bore you with the trivial tragedies that Charles and Judy faced. Things like Judy getting sunburned so bad that it became sun poisoning, Charles cutting his toe on a pop-top and both of them getting so mad with each other they didn't speak for two days.

Those sorts of things happen on vacations. No, we will stick to only major calamities. And we will try not to laugh.

But it will be difficult. Personally, I thought the story about how the muffler on the car fell off and the fellow in the next car ran over it and blew a tire and Charles had to pay not only for a muffler but also for a stranger's tire was funny.

And when Judy told me about buying a $10 straw hat to keep the sun off her sunburned head and how it blew off and into the ocean within 60 seconds of the time she paid for it, I must admit I laughed out loud.

"It is a good thing we both have a sense of humor," Charles said. "I cannot think of a single week of my life when so much went wrong."

You may wonder how I met Charles and Judy. We were in the parking lot of a restaurant, and Charles wanted to borrow a lug wrench. He had a flat tire.

"I took everything out of the trunk when I started packing for vacation," he said. "And I forgot and left the lug wrench at home.

"I think it is in the storage shed, the one that burned down."

And the Fish Weren't Biting, Either

Remember those mornings when you arise, full of good thoughts and a smile creasing your eye — and then you remember what you did the day before?

Remember the chagrin when you recall that heinous deed, that knot in the pit of your stomach when you know you have really done it this time?

There is no one to blame, you know that, nowhere to hide, not even a plausible reason.

The only excuse you can muster is a lame, "Well, it seemed like a good idea at the time."

This story is true. And this was one of those days.

It was about a month ago. August. Hot. Muggy. The leaves did not move, the air was as still as a painting. The heat came from all sides. The oven was on bake.

It was a day for two kinds of people, fools and fishermen.

It was the heat of the day, right after lunch, those long afternoon hours when there isn't much to look forward to but getting off work, and that is so far away as to be depressing.

The men in the factory on the banks of the Roanoke River were taking a break, crowding by an open window in a futile hope of stealing a bit of coolness from the scalding air that is a Southern trademark.

Below the factory rolled the river, a treacherous beast much of the time, stilled this hot day to a gentle meandering. In the middle of the river was a boat. And on the boat was a fisherman, a beer can in one hand, a fishing rod in the other, a picture of contentment.

It was too much for the workingmen. Here they were, slaving away while just outside their window a fisherman had the gall to flaunt it in front of them. And then to make matters worse, the fisherman began to taunt them.

Too hot to work, he said, look at you guys working while I'm fishing. Ha ha. Don't you wish you could be down here?

Pop another top and my, isn't this beer cold and delicious? The fisherman was a cruel man.

Stick it in your ear, the workingmen taunted in return, hope your boat sinks, buddy.

It went on all afternoon. As each hourly break crawled around on the clock, the workingmen went back to the window to see their friendly antagonist.

The sun got lower. So did the fisherman's beer supply. It happened that the workingmen were watching when the fisherman decided to call it a day and rose unsteadily to start his boat motor.

Tapukata puk puk, went the engine. Tapukata puk puk. Try again, a little harder. Tapukata puk puk. Grit your teeth and really pull now. TAPUKATA PUK puk.

It would not start. An hour went by; still it would not start. Stand up, get a solid footing and yank. What had been a cooling sheen of sweat became a eye-stinging torrent. Skinned knuckles, sore arm, damnable internal combustion engines. TAPUKATA PUK PUK.

Revenge is sweet. No more cold beer waved at the workingmen, no more cruel taunts. They hooted and catcalled. They rubbed it in. They laughed. They called their friends to the window. Look at that, Ralph, ain't that the funniest thing you've ever seen?

There is, in each of us, a breaking point. For some it is a six-putt on the 12th green. Whap goes the putter around the nearest tree.

And so it came to pass that the fisherman lost his cool in full view of his tormentors. An eerie calm overtook him. No more curses, no more pulling that stupid, ornery, cantankerous motor. All of that was gone, leaving an ominous tranquility.

He kneeled as if in prayer, loosened the bolts holding the motor to the boat and smiled as it slid gently in the waters of the mighty Roanoke.

He felt so much better. He felt so wonderful that he picked up his cooler and sailed it into the river. My, this feels good. Splash went his fishing gear. Ka-plunk went the tackle box. Lovely.

Now the boat was empty. Aw, all the fun was gone. But his spirits lifted suddenly. He began rocking the boat from side to side, feet planted wide. Whee, this is fun, let's see how long it will take to turn it over.

Not long. Dumped into the river for his efforts, the fisherman swam back to the now-capsized boat and climbed on the bottom. Then he began to stomp it.

Goodbye anger. Goodbye frustration. Goodbye boat.

But she was a sturdy craft, well-built. She would not break. So the fisherman jumped back in the water, found the anchor line, pulled out his trusty knife and slashed the line with a delicate swipe.

Then he swam ashore, to the silent wonderment of the workingmen, a fisherman finally at peace.

Until the next morning.

Miss Susie Drips With Culture

Tarboro

It was a grand night, of that you can be sure.

The crowd at Tarboro Elementary School was abuzz with excitement. "Oh, how wonderful," some said. "Isn't this just the most splendid thing?" others said.

They had spoken of it for weeks and here it was, the night of nights. There was a tingle loose, and it ran up and down backbones.

For tonight, in a long-awaited performance, Susie Pender would sing.

Everyone knew Miss Susie. She was one of the two music teachers in town, and some say she was just as good as any of them Yankee teachers in them conservatories up North.

Miss Susie herself was twittering with excitement. She had been teaching the town's young all these years, and the highlight of each year's recital was her solo. This year would be no different.

No expense had been spared to turn the elementary school stage into a place fitting for such High Culture. A bare stage might be all right for foot-tapping music, but when it comes to the good stuff you've got to have a fern or two and a fountain.

And Miss Susie's stage crew was Tarboro's best.

They found some ferns to give the place a touch of class, even a bench or two, sort of your down-home Greek Classical look. And you should have seen the fountain.

They took a washtub and some rocks for the base of the fountain and then ran a water hose from offstage into the washtub.

Everyone said it looked real good. It worked well in rehearsal.

All the young artists went on first, just singing and playing up a storm.

The crowd loved that part. Those little dickenses got up there and squawked, squealed, blushed, stammered, squired and made everyone feel just wonderful, the way kids always do at a recital.

Ah, but the culture lovers in the crowd were growing restless. They had smiled and applauded in all the right places, but where was Miss Susie?

They may have been country, but they knew good singing when they heard it and Miss Susie was good enough for them. But she coulda made it on Broadway.

Miss Susie hit stage in full voice. She rattled the rafters. She cut loose. It was wonderful.

Miss Susie was in full flower that hot night. Clasping her hands to her ample bosom, she freed that mighty voice and it soared with the eagles. Oh, Lord, it was inspiring.

The fountain was burbling away, just as it was supposed to do, but trouble was brewing down at fountain control.

Miss Susie had chosen for her finale the famous Nelson Eddy-Jeanette MacDonald number from "Rose Marie," the one that goes, "When I'm calling you-oo-oo."

She was at the highest part, her neck just trembling, her eyes closed, her hands clasped tight.

That's when the fountain went berserk.

I won't tell you who did it. I'm not sure what the statute of limitations is on public humiliation. But my friend Dow Pender of Raleigh knows who did it. So does his wife.

Someone turned that water hose on full blast. What had been a gurgling spurt became a rush. What had been a water hose lying on the floor became a spitting, snapping, flying, water-spouting dragon.

It sprayed everyone, but mostly Miss Susie. It flew with a mind of its own. Everyone who wasn't laughing sick made a dive for it — and missed.

Miss Susie just stood there, dripping and disbelieving.

It was a great moment for High Culture in Tarboro.

And Now for the
Important Stuff

I like to think of myself as a patient man.

Slow to rile, laid back, Mister Mellow. That's me.

No sweat, I say with a yawn when faced with one of life's little irritations.

But I have had it with blow dryers in bathrooms.

I hate those things.

The scene is the men's room of a chain hamburger joint, one of those look-alike places by the road where everyone smiles a lot. The place will remain unnamed because, although they smile a lot, those hamburger chains have hit squads.

It is lunchtime. The place is crowded with hungry men trying to wash their hands before eating, like their mamas always told them they should.

It also is as hot as blazes outside, a real sweaty day.

Being the simple old fool I am, I decided it would feel good to wash my face as well as my hands. Mama told me that, too.

So, somewhat refreshed, with wet hands and a wet face, I

looked around for the paper towels.

That's when I heard that telltale roar.

I turned toward the sound. I couldn't see well because of all the water in my face, but between my squinty lids I could make out that a crowd had gathered by the machine.

Four men were waiting in line just to dry their hands.

So I mustered what dignity I had left, wiped a sleeve across my dripping face, and stalked out.

I hate those machines.

Did it ever occur to anyone that you might want to dry your face in a men's room?

Did it ever occur to anyone that you might want to wipe off your glasses in a men's room?

Did it ever occur to anyone that you might want to blow your nose in a men's room?

Did it ever occur to anyone that you might really want to dry your hands in a men's room?

Did it ever occur to anyone that every human being on Earth, with the exception of the man or woman who invented the cursed things, hates blow dryers?

Does the man or woman who invented the thing have one in his or her bathroom at home?

I'll bet the grocery money he doesn't.

First of all, the machines don't work. You stand there, with hot air blowing on your hands, rubbing them gently to prevent chapping (chapping, in a bathroom?) as the directions say, and they always cut off just before your hands are dry.

So you hit it again, and now the air is really hot. By the time your hands are dry they feel sticky. I don't know about you, but I do not like coming out of a bathroom with sticky hands.

They claim you can dry your face with the thing if you point the nozzle upward. Try it. Your hair blows backward, your eyelids flutter and the thing blows out air that smells bad. And it takes a long, long time, while you stand there, pretending this is not weird.

Before you bring it up, yes, I have used toilet paper.

But when I'm spending money for a hamburger, I do not relish spending the rest of the day picking little pieces of toilet paper off my face.

There are other problems. Many people can simultaneously dry their hands with paper towels, but with blow dryers it is one at a time, leaving everyone else to stand there dripping in unison.

And after a machine has blown through half a dozen people the temperature in the bathroom is approaching the boiling point.

I have tried to be fair about this thing, as fair as I can be.

What I did was ask everyone I know to say something good about blow dryers.

No one could think of a thing.

They waste energy, are inefficient and make customers mad.

They'll probably be around forever.

Just This Once, Lord

Golf is mean.

Golf is the most contrary, unforgiving, cruel and maddening way to spend a day that has ever been devised by man.

The Scots invented it, and they've got a lot to answer for. It would take a stern, rock-ribbed, humorless race of people to invent such a miserable game.

Who else would have dreamed up a game in which, if you are relaxed and comfortable when playing it, you're doing it all wrong?

Who else would invent a game in which no matter how hard you concentrate, no matter how long you've played it, no matter how good you think you are, a person sneezing 20 feet away at the wrong time can make you look like you're chopping cotton?

Who else would invent a game in which the temptation to cheat is so strong that honest and true folk will "accidentally" kick their ball out of a bad spot or forget how to count if they think they can get away with it?

The Scots did not invent golf as a fun pastime. They invented it as penance. It is a test of internal strength. If you can play golf, you can do anything.

A golfer is an optimist who will never face reality. He truly expects his next shot to be perfect no matter how bad the last shot was. He never gives up in his belief that somehow, magically, his game will come together.

It never does, but he goes on believing in the rightness and fairness of life.

A flat surface hitting a round ball offers thousands of interesting possibilities in the physics of flight. Unless it is hit just right, the ball can shoot off in any number of directions — some worse than others, but all of them wrong.

And the surfaces of all but two golf clubs are not even flat. They are sloped, adding infinitely to the ways to mess up.

Golf makes people mean. There is no greater pressure on your ego than standing on the first tee on a crowded course, with a bunch of other golfers watching you, and trying to hit that devil straight.

All I can think of is how many times I've duffed such shots and please, Lord, let me hit this one ball long and straight, and I'll never ask for anything else. And if it can't be straight, at least let it be long. Or vice versa.

Just one out of two, Lord, that's all I'm asking.

And every person watching you secretly hopes you'll mess up. They've done it themselves, plenty of times, and it makes them feel better to see someone else do it, too.

Usually I screw it up. My feet move or my head moves or my knees move or my arm isn't straight in the backswing, or I tee the ball too high and pop it up or I tee it too low and it dribbles out 10 feet and stops, or I do it all perfectly but God just decides this isn't my day and I have to do it all over again with them still watching.

One of the sweetest things about golf, which just goes to show you how mean golf makes you, is taking a first-timer out on the course.

What usually happens is that he does pretty well for a beginner, ignoring all the free advice you give him and still knocking the fool out of the ball.

And then he comes back for the second time — relaxed, comfortable, confident, visions of his own set of clubs dancing in his head — and falls apart. He didn't believe you when you told him it was hard. Now he believes. Superiority, no matter how relative, is wonderful.

They make golf harder than it has to be. Just in case you accidentally hit the ball, they dig holes and fill them with sand for it to land in. They make the fairways wind around woods where wild things live and eat your ball. They make you hit over water sometimes. They won't even keep the greens flat, so you have to putt on a sloping surface.

But with the same frequency a blind squirrel finds an acorn, sometimes — for reasons you can't remember — you hit a good shot.

That sucker takes off like a mortar round, drifting high, straight and long. It's so good you can feel it in your feet. You turn around, ready for the plaudits.

That's the one nobody else ever sees.

A Lie Beats a Whipping Anytime

Lying, we have been told all our lives, is a terrible thing to do.

No matter what you've done, don't lie about it.

Go ahead, George Washington, cut down the cherry tree, but then 'fess up to Pop and all will be forgiven.

Sure. I tried that once. If memory serves, the object was a new 1949 Ford convertible. My best friend at the time was a red-haired vixen named Tootsie, and we were playing hide-and-seek.

Since I was one of those kids who tended to peek when others were hiding, Tootsie came up with the brilliant idea that I had to get in the back seat of that spiffy new convertible while she went and hid. She theorized that I wouldn't be able to cheat as well from there.

Silly girl. I merely took out my handy little Barlow knife and, with surgical precision, cut a one-inch square hole in the canvas top and peeked away.

When confronted by my steaming father — I had never seen a pencil-thin mustache quiver with rage — I knew my explanation had to be good. So I played George Washington and confessed.

He liked to have killed me.

I learned an important lesson that day. There are times when it is not only permissible to lie, but when it is the smart thing to do.

People lie all the time. One of my personal favorites is the guy who looks you straight in the eye and says, "Yes, I take Playboy, but only for the articles. I don't even look at the pictures."

Right.

"What do you think of my new hairstyle?" your wife asks. Tell her she looks like Leon Spinks in drag and I guarantee you will be eating green bologna on stale bread for months. So tell a lie.

"That style is quite a change for you" is a good way to put it. "You're lucky, not everyone can wear that style."

Of course, don't tell her that the reason not everyone can wear that style is that it would make most of them look nauseating.

A friend shows up at your house with a new date.

"What do you think of him?" she asks, grinning from ear to ear and casting longing glances in the direction of some Neanderthal cretin who would make a fundamentalist agree that at least this one man is descended from the apes, and probably descended last Tuesday.

"He's really something" is a good way to put it. "I'll bet he's interesting to be around," you say while the monster is peeling a dog in your den.

Those are examples of little white lies, the social fib that makes smooth the road of life and keeps you from getting your lip split by a crashing right cross.

There are times, however, when you must steel your courage and tell a whopper. But for the big lie to work it must be so big that no one would question it. Example:

You've been out with the boys, hoisting a few, and now the boys are hoisting you through the door. There, waiting in the living room, is the Wrath of the Angels, and she is not smiling.

Hoss, it is time for creativity.

"It was really scary," you say before she has a chance to start screaming. "There was this little girl, she was a blind, crippled orphan studying to be a nun and she walked right out in front of this speeding truck.

"I ran out and grabbed her and pulled her to safety."

And then, as if it were an afterthought, you quickly add, "Then the truck crashed into a telephone pole. Boy, you ought to see what happens when a beer truck wrecks — spilled beer all over me.

"I think I'll go take a shower. Phew!"

One suggestion, though. Don't use it but once.

Haven't We Had This Before?

The issue today is old food.

Old food lives in many guises. Sometimes you see it in the dog's dish — a dark lump, a hardened mass of something faintly evil that even the dog wouldn't eat.

Sometimes you run across it in the dark, shadowy world that lives under the sofa, that dusty netherworld of lint, old pencils, forgotten notes from school and other small, unidentifiable bits of life's leavings. Once it may have been a sandwich crust, or perhaps half a cracker, dropped in a moment of ecstasy when the lovely young couple from Tarzana won the microwave on "The Newlywed Game."

But those are harmless chunks of old food, petrified memories of meals past.

The old food of which I speak goes by another name, hiding in that haven of little dishes, that chill coffin with the white light, the family fridge.

They are called leftovers. Who would eat something called old food?

It has happened to us all. You straggle in from work, mind-blitzed and hungry, so blown out by the rigors of modern survival that kicking off your shoes somehow seems complicated.

But you are prepared for a good meal.

"What's for dinner?" you ask the half of the family who has kitchen duty that night.

"We're having leftovers," you are told. So far, so good. You remember some nice chicken from a day or so ago and you remember leaving one breast, two legs and three wings — yes, Virginia, chickens now have three wings, or so the chicken packer at my supermarket would have me believe, along with an odd little piece that would be unrecognizable to a still-walking fowl — and the thought of chomping down on used bird is not altogether unpleasant.

But it is not chicken that graces your plate. It is a lumpish brown thing. This is certainly a leftover, you think. No one would ever create such a vile thing on purpose. But the nagging question is leftover from what ... or where ... or worse yet, from when?

I'm going to tell you where that stuff comes from. There exists in our fair kingdom a leftover food conspiracy, a cartel of food swappers who pass food from home to home the way con men move hot stock certificates.

As soon as you leave the house it begins.

"Betty, this is Sue. Look, I've got two helpings of two-day-old meat loaf, nine tablespoons of peas from Tuesday and a roll and a half. I'll let it go for some leftover instant mashed potatoes and some brown Jell-O."

Now if Betty is an old hand at the food game, she knows she can parlay the meat and the peas into a 19-course meal of leftovers. She already knows that Peggy has been serving chicken stew for three days and is getting desperate. Properly approached, Peggy will be more than happy to pass off the now-gray stew and perhaps even throw in an hour of baby-sitting, or at least the lamp she bought at Sue's yard sale.

One of the biggest problems with leftovers is how to divide them up come mealtime. There is not enough of any one item to serve all of you. Someone will get the chicken, three kinds of beans (one tablespoon each) and the Mexi-corn, while someone else gets the piece of pork fat, two biscuits and all the rice.

Being that these are hard times and all of us are eating leftovers, you might try this scheme. Each person gets to eat the food that matches the color of the shirt or blouse he or she is wearing.

That would not only help divide the food fairly, but the dribbles down the front wouldn't show half as much.

Happy eating.

The Phantom of the Kitchen

I have always wanted to live in a haunted house.

Not one of those really scary joints where green gook runs down the walls and creepy things reach out and grab you in the dark, but one that was haunted by friendly ghosts.

I think I've finally made it.

But my house is not haunted by the ghost of some former resident come back to claim his home, but rather by phantom kitchen utensils.

And from talking to other people, I find I am not alone. It is possible that even you are haunted but have never realized it.

Here's how you can tell:

You walk into the kitchen, open the silverware drawer and there, staring you in the face, is a strange spoon.

It is not your spoon, you know that. So where did it come from? How did it get there? Does someone in your house, as you have long suspected, take in dirty dishes? Was it stolen? Was it abandoned?

Or is it a ghost spoon?

No one ever knows. They just show up, these phantom utensils that populate our kitchens.

I remember a green plastic bowl in particular. One day it was there, nestled in the sink, encrusted with some unidentifiable something.

No one knew where it had come from; guests usually don't bring their own bowls when they come to dinner. It was just there.

We didn't use the bowl at first; we don't like to get too friendly with strangers.

We washed it like a good host and left it sitting on the counter for a few days, figuring it would be claimed. But it would not leave. Finally, someone stuck it up with the other bowls to make it feel at home, but off to the side and a little to the back, so we wouldn't accidentally use it one day. Using someone else's bowl seems somehow an invasion of privacy. Like Mama used to say, you don't know where that thing has been.

We got used to seeing the bowl around, sitting back there in the corner. One day, when every other dish in the house was dirty, we said the heck with it and used it.

Everyone noticed the new dish, but no one had the faintest idea from where it had come.

The green bowl became a valued member of our household; we began to depend on it, to think of it affectionately, the visitor in our home who had decided to stay. And then we made our mistake; we began to take the green bowl for granted.

I think we hurt its feelings, for one day, while everyone was gone, the green bowl left our house.

I don't know how it left, but it did.

What happened to the green bowl, we asked one another. I don't know, we answered one another right back.

We missed the green bowl, it had become a part of us, but now it was gone, perhaps to spread joy in another home. That's the way phantom utensils are, here today and gone tomorrow.

But when the green bowl left, I do wish it had taken a few things with it.

Things like the very last glass of six different sets of glasses that clutter up my kitchen.

Why does it work that way? You go out and buy a set of glasses. Soon they all begin to break, shattering one after the other until there is only one left.

But that last glass, the reminder of your clumsiness, refuses to break.

You could look at the other glasses, and they would dissolve before your amazed eyes.

But the last glass?

You could run over the last glass with a tractor, and the tractor would bounce.

I have a phantom spoon, another visitor, but this one is so ugly I have thrown it away four times, and each time it somehow finds its way back from the city dump to my silverware drawer, like the party guest who won't leave.

If the phantom green bowl comes to your house to live, tell it the chipped yellow bowl it used to sit with said hello.

Pabulum is Yucky

It is amazing that we babies aren't flaming wimps when you consider the way we are treated by our parents. Sometimes you wonder if the big folks have both oars in the water, if you know what I mean.

It isn't that they don't love us little folks, it's that they drive us bozo with their weird questions. And they start fresh out of the chute, so to speak.

The scene goes something like this: You are racked out in the crib, checking your toes and pondering the gold crisis when Mommy comes in, grabs you and plops you down in a cold-bottomed high chair.

She opens one of those little jars that has the creepy smiling baby on the front and begins to ladle out the vilest concoction you can imagine, fun stuff like creamed liver or strained beets.

Did you ever see her eat that glop? Of course not. She's sucking down a Schlitz and chewing on a Slim Jim, telling you how yummy this mess is. She'll shovel it in your mouth and then hit you with the biggie:

"Isn't that good?"

"No, Mommy, it isn't good, it tastes like sweat socks boiled in fish heads," you think. But you don't say that. You don't say anything at all because you can't talk. So why does she ask for a culinary critique when you haven't uttered one meaningful sound in your life? Because she is weird, that's why. And if you did answer, she'd whap you one for talking with your mouth full.

But there is something you can do. You give her a big toothless smile, push with your tongue and give her a "goo, goo." Properly done, you can dribble that mess down your bib and with practice you can dribble it down her blouse.

She'll think that's cute, and while she's getting a towel you grab her Slim Jim and gum it to death. She'll think that's cute, too.

Remember: Baby does not live by Gerber's alone and we're too short to slide a quarter in the machine to buy real food. Besides, diapers don't have pockets.

The next question you'll face is one fraught with peril, so put down your rattle and pay attention.

Aunt Smelly has come to call and Mommy wants to show off the new baby. She picks you up, pats you on the fanny to make sure you're presentable. Then she'll say something like, "Show Aunt Smelly who you love."

Now all babies know that the expected response is a smile and a hug for Mommy. But just for kicks, if you are a man baby, say, "Well, I am very fond of Loni Anderson, but of late I have been smitten by Mariel Hemingway." If you are a woman baby, say, "Redford has a nice bod, but I'm drawn to the quiet magnetism of Al Pacino."

To really mess up her head, when she asks you the other question that always follows, "Do you want to go home with Aunt Smelly?" take a long look at her, raise yourself to your full 24 inches and say, "Are you kidding? I'd sooner go to Iran."

If you have trouble getting the words out, kick Aunt Smelly right in her lilac sachet. And then, to be safe, babble and grin. She'll think that's cute.

I would like to be able to tell you that it gets better as time marches on. But take it from me, the only thing that gets better with age is good wine and beautiful women.

About the time you start toddling, you get, "Can you show

Uncle Squeeze how old you are?''

Sure you can, but don't. If you are 3, hold up two fingers. Ignore their hints. Hold up four fingers, then seven, then one. Lie on the floor and wave all 10 toes and fingers at them. They'll tire of the game long before you do, so keep flashing those numbers at them, but never the right one.

For that you wait until the game has gone on for 15 minutes after Uncle Squeeze has left the house. Then toddle up and flash three fingers at Mommy. It will make her crazy, but she'll think you're cute.

No matter what your age, from kindergarten through graduate school, there is one question everyone who speaks English will ask you at least five times:

"What do you want to be when you grow up?"

When they ask you that, give 'em your biggest smile and say sweetly, "I want to grow up to be just like you."

They'll eat it up.

And they'll think you're cute.

Old People Are Sneaky

It is a wonderful example of the oft-lamented generation gap.

A reporter for a college newspaper — kindness toward the hopelessly young will not permit me to identify the reporter or the newspaper — wrote: "Although she is 51, she seems to be in her prime."

You don't really mean it? At such an advanced age she can still walk by herself and even speak in complete sentences? Isn't medical science wonderful, keeping those old codgers in their 50s mobile and lucid after all these years? What will they think of next?

Oh, the silliness of youth. But that's the way they see old people, as tottering old veggies, sitting around waiting for the grim reaper to call.

If they only knew. Having spent most of my younger days in the company of some good old people, I'm here to tell you that old people are sneaky. Here everyone thinks they're senile, and the old folks are laughing at 'em.

The best part about being old is that you can do or say anything you want and get away with it.

For instance, if I go around grumbling and grousing and pretty much telling the world and everyone in it to take a hike, I get labeled as an ill-tempered person.

But when old folks do it, they get smiled at and called a lovable curmudgeon.

For example, a terrible show comes on the tube. If I sit there and doze off while watching it, someone is sure to wake me up and tell me if I want to sleep, then please go to bed and quit bothering everyone else.

But if an old person who is equally bored by that mindless pap says to heck with it and decides to catch a few winks, everyone in the house is ordered to hush-hush, lest Gramps be disturbed.

Family reunion time. Here come all those good-looking young family members. Folks my age get a handshake and a howdy and a look that says, "I know I should know you, but frankly, who cares?"

But Gramps is sitting there in the best chair in the house surrounded by lovely young things who take turns plopping down in his lap and covering his head with humid kisses.

He grins. I grimace.

Here it is, suppertime. The family is eating leftovers. I have two choices: I can eat it and shut up, or I can go hungry.

"Gramps, we're having leftovers, but I'll be happy to fix you something else, anything you'd like to have, just name it." And they mean it.

Parents get hit up for loans. Grandparents get hit up for advice. Giving advice is a lot cheaper.

What old people can do with children is amazing. I have seen homes where it would take a squad of Green Berets to maintain order among the squabbling young.

A grandfather can sit there with nothing more than a twinkle in his eyes and hold them spellbound for hours.

And look what old people can do to your children. Two weeks in the summer at Gramps and Granny's can spoil a child for life.

"Johnny was just wonderful," we are told when we come to reclaim the little monster, who is at that moment planning yet another unspeakable thing to do to the sofa.

"Here, let me hold the baby awhile," Granny says, and the baby coos like a room full of pigeons.

"This nasty baby needs changing," Granny says, and hands the child back to Mama, as if she's never heard of changing diapers. Who me?

I guess I should go ahead and apologize in advance to all old people for writing this. So I will.

Sorry folks, I'm afraid I've spoiled your fun. Oh, well, you've been getting away with it for far too long anyway.

How to Know If You're Ugly

"O, what a tangled web we weave when first we practice to deceive," Sir Walter Scott once wrote, and that seems as good a way as any to get into a discussion of a serious problem that has come to my attention.

As president of the Wake County Ugly League (membership cards for the truly deserving are available on request), I have charged myself with the weighty task of being the arbiter of ugly hereabouts.

I would like to point out that I am not merely claiming the title; no indeed, I am the appointed representative of The Ugly of Uglies himself, the legendary Bobby Wilkerson of Henderson, founder of the Ugly League.

Now comes distressing news that there are among you, even as you read this, ugly people trying to pass for pretty.

I know you wouldn't have thought it, but it is true. But being a kindly despot, I am willing to assume that they are doing it out of ignorance.

They don't know they're ugly.

That's a sad state of affairs. So on this Halloween, a national holiday for ugly people, I would like to give you some tips, a few easy ways you can tell if you are ugly.

For instance, when you had your class picture made back in elementary school, did they always make you stand at the back of the group so that nothing more than the top of your head and one ear showed?

When you were a kid, playing all those kissing games like Post Office, was it you they always sent to get more drinks and chips and when you got back they had moved on to other games, like Pin the Tail on the Governor?

Did your mother have to tie a piece of bacon around your neck so the dog would play with you?

If so, rejoice and be proud, you were ugly then and you can bet you're ugly now.

If you are a man and spend an hour getting just as spiffy and dressed up as you can before a big night out with your lady, does she walk in just as you're finished and say, "Oh, you're not going to get dressed up, huh?"

When you go to class reunions, do people walk up and say, "Well look at you, you haven't changed a bit"? What they're saying is, you were ugly then and you're ugly now, unlike the handsome fellow who lost his hair and his waistline and now looks like 40 miles of bad road.

When you went trick-or-treating on Halloween, covered from head to foot in the most gruesome costume you could find, did people still recognize you?

When they have those father-and-son or mother-and-daughter things at school, does your offspring forget to tell you about it, or suggest that maybe you'd rather spend a quiet evening at home? When your child would rather be thought of as an orphan than be seen with you, you are probably as ugly as homemade soap.

Did your wife ever suggest that you grow a beard — a big beard — and then comb your hair forward?

If any of these situations seem familiar, then you are probably ugly and shouldn't go around claiming that what you have is a face with "lots of character."

Don't be ashamed to be ugly. It has its advantages.

For one thing, when you first peek at yourself in the mirror you know that's as good as you're going to look all day and you don't have to spend hours primping.

Ugly people can do what they want in this world while pretty people have to live up to their looks.

Let a cute kid grow up to be something really awful, like a senator or a dentist, and people will say, "I don't know what happened, he was such a cute little child."

But let the ugly kid do something equally disgusting, like becoming a newspaper columnist, and people say, "Well, what did you expect? Remember what he looked like?"

And remember our motto: Beauty is only skin deep, but ugly goes all the way to the bone.

Make someone happy this Halloween. Walk up and tell them they are ugly. They may beat you up now, but they'll thank you later.

People Who Love Liver . . .

There are too many laws, people say.

That's true. There are too many laws, and the sad thing is there isn't anything anyone can do about them.

I'm not talking about the dumb laws that make it illegal to do things like curse a rooster on the sidewalk in Benson on Sunday. I'm talking about the laws of living. They're the ones that will get you in the end.

For instance, we've all heard of Murphy's Law: Nothing is as easy as it looks; everything takes longer than you expect, and, anything that can go wrong will, at the worst possible moment.

But there are other laws just as valid and just as infuriating:

The Garden Club Law: The dog will forget it is housebroken as the first member of the garden club arrives for the monthly meeting, and you'll find out just as you say, "Why don't we go into the living room?"

The Boss Law: Beer cans will always be rolling on the floor of your car when the boss asks for a lift home from the office.

The Deep Throat Law: If you go to a porno movie in the afternoon, you will see someone you know just as you walk out.

The Lunch Law: You will always wish you'd ordered what the other person did.

Mom's Law: When they finally do have to take you to the hospital, your underwear won't be new or clean.

Munchie Law: Your stomach never growls when you're alone.

Reporter's Law: Your only pencil will break just as they get to the good part.

The Hollywood Law: No matter when you finally leave your movie seat to go to the bathroom, you will choose the worst possible moment.

The Yellow Line Law: The only time in your life you ever cross the yellow line when it is in your lane will be in front of a highway patrolman's house just as he is leaving for work on Monday with a headache after having a spat with his wife.

Reader's Law: If two people buy books, the other person gets the one you wish you'd bought.

Wonder Bread Law: Bread always falls butter-side down.

Detroit's Law: Cars never break down at service stations, except on Sundays when they're closed.

Boob Tube Law: There is never anything good on TV tonight. It was on last night.

Finagle's Law: Once a job is fouled up, anything done to improve it will make it worse.

Hiccup Law: They always begin three minutes before a funeral, wedding or introduction to the most important person you've ever met.

Puff's Law: Cats that hate everyone love people who are allergic to them or terrified of them.

The Liver Law: People who love liver never marry their own kind, and vice versa.

The Spot Law: Women never notice that embarrassing spot on their dress until after the party.

The Ostrich Law: Anytime things seem to be going well, you've obviously overlooked something.

The Desk Law: Clutter and debris expand to fill the space available.

The Telephone Law, Part One: The telephone will ring 20 minutes after the children have left the house, and there is a gleam in your spouse's eye. The call will be important and take a lot of time.

The Telephone Law, Part Two: The telephone will ring when you are the farthest point possible from it. It will not be important.

Rogers' Law: Things are never as bad as they seem, or so you thought.

● ● ●

Laws from John Trasti of Harnett Central High School:

The shortest distance between two points is still under construction.

No two people think alike ... until it comes to buying wedding presents.

● ● ●

From Dan Dye of Raleigh:

Gas Hog's Law: Your car will run out of gas exactly halfway between the last gas station you passed and the next one down the road.

Gas Hog's Law, Exception: The next station is just around the next curve, but you don't know it and walk back to the last one you passed.

Deep Throat Law 2: While doing the laundry, your wife will find the X-rated theater ticket stub that you absentmindedly stuffed in your pocket.

Shutterbug's Law: Your kid does the cutest thing just after you shoot the last frame on your roll of film.

Golfer's Law: You can lose only new balls and find only old ones.

Carolina Gardener's Law: The only plants that will still be green in your yard by the end of August are crabgrass, wild onions and dandelions.

Girl Watcher's Law: The prettiest girls will walk by your place on the beach when you leave to get a cold beer. But don't worry, your wife will tell you all about them.

Lest We Forget

"Poor is the nation that has no heroes, but beggar'd is that nation that has and forgets."
— Lt. Col. William Jones III, *Maxims for Men at Arms*.

Elizabethtown

One of the things people do on vacation is pay attention to state historical markers.

You know the ones, those 1,200 silver-and-black plaques by North Carolina highways that offer some historical morsel a few yards or miles away.

I saw one in Elizabethtown the other day that read, "Battle of Elizabethtown. Whigs broke Tory power in Bladen Co., August, 1781, driving them into Tory Hole, 50 yards north."

The Tory Hole is more a steep ravine than a round hole. What's left of it is just behind the stores on Broad Street, a dark green gash running from the top of the high bluff where the town sits down toward the Cape Fear River. It is hard to tell how far it goes, but at the high end the walls are sheer and the bottom is lost in the shadows.

The Revolutionary War was not going particularly well in Southeastern North Carolina in 1781. George Washington's Continental Army was far to the north, and the British were in control of Wilmington.

The area around Elizabethtown was patrolled by 700 loyalists, American colonists who did not want independence from England. They were the Tories, most of them Highlanders from Scotland.

They were led by the fearsome Col. David Fanning, reputed to be the meanest and most effective Tory fighter of all.

Facing him was Col. Thomas Robeson, leader of 180 guerrillas who called themselves Whigs. The Whigs were hiding in the Cape Fear swamps, afraid to come out and fight Fanning. They waited three weeks, hoping to catch isolated Tory patrols, waiting for local men to join them. Neither happened.

Robeson took his band and headed north and west, as far as Raleigh, looking for recruits. They were gone for six weeks, and as James Cain, a veteran of that march, recorded, "They found many friends and were kindly received and hospitably entertained at almost every place where they made an appearance, and three general musters were called to supply them with reinforcements, yet they could not find a man who was willing to join them and march against the Tories ...so great was the terror of the name of Fanning."

In fact, by the time Robeson got back to Bladen he was down to 71 men. The others had deserted. He called his dwindling band together and proposed one last suicidal battle, to either run the Tories out of Bladen or die. He asked them to step forward if they would follow him. All did, but one.

Cain's description: "They were all mounted and had guns, but many of their horses were wore to the bone and all the bones seemed to stick through the skin.

"The knees, elbows and shoulders of a great many of the men were exposed and some had not even a change of clothes.

"These 70 men, scantily supplied with ammunition, without clothes and without provisions, broken down by a long march, set out early one morning to give battle."

It took three days of forced marches with no food to get in position across the river from the Tory camp where 400 men slept.

The Whig attack began when the night was darkest. They stripped and piled their clothes on their heads and waded into the black river. The tall men remembered the river as chest deep. The short men fought to keep their noses above water as they held their guns and powder high.

Robeson split his tiny force into three groups once they reached the other side and circled around the sleeping Tories. Now the Tories had their backs to the river and to The Hole.

A Tory sentry spotted the ghostly troops, fired one shot and fled. Before the Tories could realize what was happening, the Whigs attacked, firing as fast as they could and screaming their battle cry, "Washington!"

The Tories panicked. They thought, in the darkness, smoke and turmoil, that Washington's large army had arrived, which was what Robeson wanted them to think.

Many of the fleeing Tories fell screaming into the dark ravine between them and the river. When it was over, 17 Tory bodies were pulled out of The Hole.

Not a single Whig was killed, and the Tories did not come back to Bladen.

The Gray Ghosts of Shiloh

Shiloh

A gray mist of legend always has surrounded the high ground in the North River Swamp, the ground known as Guerrilla Island.

It is difficult to reach; often the water is waist deep. Only experienced swamp men dare to seek it. When they do get there, they find traces of trenches, some old brick and remnants of a well.

"People had always talked about the Camden Guerrillas," said W. W. Forehand, a Camden County insurance man and Civil War historian. "But we never knew who they were."

The story of the band of farmers-turned-guerrillas goes back to late 1862 and early 1863, when Camden County was under firm Union control during the Civil War.

The blue-clad troops were under the command of Gen. Edward A. Wild, a fierce soldier who prided himself on his terror — bragging in his reports about how many homes had been burned, how much livestock his troops had stolen, and the prominent civilians he held hostage.

"No one today can imagine what it must have been like to live through that," Forehand said. "And no one can imagine what it did to this county."

What it did was divide Camden County. We've all heard how the Civil War was a war of brothers fighting brothers, and Camden is a living testament to that.

"There were a lot of Union sympathizers down around Old Trap," Forehand said. "They were called 'Buffaloes.' They even formed a unit called the First North Carolina, and they were stationed right here at home, wearing their blue uniforms. A lot of those boys were poor, and $14 a month and a blue suit was something to them."

But not all the men left in Camden, those not off on distant battlefields, were "Buffaloes."

"I don't know where all of them came from," Forehand said of the pro-Confederacy troops left behind. "Maybe some of them were from the battle of Hatteras and had been pardoned, and a lot of them were young boys.

"But in July 1863, Willis Sanderlin formed the Camden Guerrillas."

There were about 50 of them. Some like Peter Smith were only 17, and some like Edward Ives were in their 50s.

They established a camp in the North River Swamp. They built cabins, dug a well, began making ammunition and gathering supplies, preparing to launch their futile, but heartfelt, attacks against the Union troops ravaging their homeland.

The guerrillas lasted but six months, confounding Wild's men, attacking at night from the gloom of the swamp, hitting fast and hard, and disappearing as quickly as they came. They would flee into the swamp on a bridge of trees cut down in what seemed to be a random pattern, but if you knew which way to go the felled trees led straight to Guerrilla Island.

They lived off the remains of what Wild's men had not taken, supported by locals who shared what was left.

Wild finally sent 400 men into the swamps in search of the guerrillas. He tracked them to their sanctuary and found abandoned weapons, campfires and supplies. But no guerrillas. They had fled into the deep swamp, and no Yankee would ever find them.

"Most of them headed west," Forehand said. "They ended up fighting out the rest of the war in other units and surprisingly, only three or four of them were killed, contrary to what Wild had said. He gave the impression most of them were killed."

Wild's men found something else that day on Guerrilla Island, a complete roster of the guerrilla band. He immediately ordered the homes of every guerrilla burned to the ground.

That roster — which showed that while many of the Old Trap men were fighting for the North, other Old Trappers were fighting with the guerrillas against their own brothers, uncles and cousins — disappeared, only to turn up in 1980 when Forehand located it in Florida.

"That's when we finally knew who the guerrillas were," Forehand said. "We found out that most of the people around here were kin to them. They were our fathers."

Fannie Fought for Her Home

Smithfield

She was a lady of gentle breeding, daughter of a country doctor in New York, educated in a posh private academy, editor of the campus literary magazine, hardly the image of country grit.

But when times got tough, Fannie got tougher.

Born Francis Secor, she came to Smithfield as a teacher in 1859. She had been hired to teach the children of the wealthy Mitchener and Rand families of Johnston County.

She made her home with Agrippa Mitchener, a widower with two children. She had lived there for a year when Agrippa asked her to marry him. She was 20; he was 35.

They were social leaders in the county. Their wedding was described as "one of the brilliant social events in this section." These were the halcyon days of Southern plantation gentility, but tragedy was waiting for the young Mrs. Mitchener.

Within a year, her husband would die. Within two years, North Carolina would be plunged into the Civil War, effectively trapping the Northern lady in the South.

The war years proved her mettle. She ran the plantation with determination, growing crops and storing them for better days. By war's end, she had 60,000 pounds of cotton in storage on the plantation.

The war was ending by the spring of 1865. Sherman, the scourge of Georgia, was approaching. Although her sympathies and loyalties were to the North, Fannie was worried about what might happen to her home. She asked Gov. Zebulon Vance for protection, and he sent a squad to protect the plantation, 12 soldiers led by a Lt. Carter.

Carter and his men hid the silver, jewels, china, meat, lard, brandy and wine from the household and attempted to hide the stored crops.

There wasn't much he could do with the cotton, but he hit on a plan to hide the corn inside the huge columns in front of the house. He had holes drilled in the top of the hollow columns and managed to store 16 bushels of corn.

Soon Sherman was at hand. The battle of Bentonville was over, and nothing was in the way between there and Raleigh. Lee was trapped at Appomattox. The end of the Southern experiment had come.

You could hear the approaching army when Carter mounted his horse and rode down the lane between the tall trees, paused for a moment, waved his hat and rode off.

Fannie was left alone to face a mighty army.

The first Northern troops to arrive were led by Henry Gildersleeve, who oddly enough had been a classmate of Fannie. He promised to leave a guard on her plantation so it would not be harmed. The Mitchener plantation even became the headquarters for Gen. Schofield.

Schofield was asleep in the mansion when he received word that Lee had surrendered. A lantern was hung on an upper balcony to alert the troops that Lee was finished.

The troops left the next day, heading for Raleigh. But no guard was left behind; once again Fannie was alone.

A group of Northern soldiers rode up to Fannie's plantation later that morning and, without warning or reason, destroyed her storage barns, farm equipment and confiscated her horses.

That was more than Fannie could take. She had been promised safety; she had opened her home to the generals; she had maintained her Northern loyalty; she had worked to hold her home together during the war and to have it all come down to this. A senseless, useless destruction of private property.

Fannie would never forget that day.

She would marry again, and be widowed again and marry a third time.

She would move to Smithfield, travel extensively, give birth to a daughter, but still the day they burned her cotton would not leave her mind.

She filed a claim against the government for $14,365 for her cotton, although she was a wealthy woman and really didn't need the money.

She pursued that claim year after year, a special bill was introduced in Congress, she went to court, contacted witnesses. She had been wronged, and she fought back.

Finally, just before the turn of the century, after fighting the United States government for more than 30 years, Fannie got her money.

Her war had finally ended.

He Wept for His Little Anne

Warrenton

It was 1862, the Civil War was raging, and Confederate Gen. Robert E. Lee was concerned about his wife and four daughters in Virginia. Mrs. Lee suffered from rheumatism, and daughter Anne, 23, was sickly.

He advised them to head south, so they went to a health spa and vacation spot owned by the Jones family between Louisburg and Warrenton on what is now U.S. 401.

Anne became sick shortly after they arrived in the spring of 1862. It was typhoid fever, and the young lady died despite all Dr. Frank Patterson, the spa's physician, could do.

The Jones family offered the family burial ground to the Lees, and since it would be difficult in those war-torn days to return the body to the Lee home in Northern Virgina, Mrs. Lee accepted.

Gen. Lee could not be at the funeral, nor was he there in 1866 when a disabled Confederate veteran, Zewald Crowder, unveiled the stone marker he had carved as a memorial.

But Lee did visit the grave of his daughter. Author Manly Wade Wellman chronicled the 1870 visit in his book, *The County of Warren.*

That visit is perhaps the most touching part of the story:

Willie White was a 26-year-old veteran of the Confederacy. He was waiting at the train station the night of March 29, 1870, waiting for his sister, Mary, to return from Petersburg, Va.

It was a chilly, moonlit night when the train pulled in, but when Mary stepped down, Willie didn't notice her. He was looking at a white-haired old man and a young woman.

It was a face no Southerner, no man who fought for Dixie, ever would forget. It was Gen. Robert E. Lee.

Willie politely introduced himself and asked the general whether he could show him to his hotel. But Lee, by then old and sick and not wanting to attract attention, said he had come without making reservations. Willie invited the general to stay at his house, and Lee, accompanied by daughter Agnes, accepted.

O.P. Shell drove the general to the White home, where the awed family made him comfortable.

Word spread quickly through Warrenton that Lee was in town, but everyone respected his wishes not to be disturbed. No one came to call that night or the next morning. But when Lee was ready to drive out to the grave of his daughter, his carriage was filled with freshly cut flowers quietly left by the people of Warrenton.

Then, as Lee rode through the streets of the small town on the way to the grave, the people gathered by the roadsides, standing there silently, coming to get, as Wellman lovingly put it, "a glimpse of a living legend of grace, valor and nobility."

Lee departed the next day, leaving his signature in the Bibles of the White family children, a lock of his hair for Ellen Brownlow and an autographed picture for Maria Alston, two women who had helped erect the granite marker at Anne's grave.

Lee died later that year.

His daughter's grave still is there. Look for the marker along U.S. 401 between Louisburg and Warrenton. There you can stand where Lee stood and where he wept for his little Anne.

•   •   •

The Lee family was not the only famous Confederate family to spend part of the Civil War in this area.

Mildred Lee, the general's youngest daughter, attended St. Mary's College in Raleigh during the war, and Varina Howell Davis, wife of Confederate President Jefferson Davis, spent several months in Raleigh, first in a hotel and later on the St. Mary's campus.

Thanks to Raleigh's Martha Stoops, who is researching and writing a history of St. Mary's, here is the story:

President Davis decided Richmond was too dangerous for his family in early 1862, what with Gen. McClellan's Union forces advancing up the Virginia peninsula. Yorktown and Norfolk had been evacuated, and Williamsburg had fallen.

On May 10, 1862, Varina Davis left Richmond with her four children, seeking safety in Raleigh.

She moved into the Yarborough House, a fashionable hotel of the time. Mary Boykin Chesnut wrote in her diary on May 29, 1862: "They tell us Mrs. Davis was delightfully situated at Raleigh; North Carolinians so loyal, so hospitable."

Davis' son Billy became ill in June, so sick that Davis sent the family physician to Raleigh to nurse him back to health.

Richmond was saved by the Seven Days Campaign in late June, and Mrs. Stoops reports that Mrs. Davis got the news at the hotel while walking the floor with young Billy:

"When the news of our great victory over such long odds came to Raleigh," Mrs. Davis later wrote, "everyone was breathless with excitement.

"The telegraph office was separated by a narrow alley from my room in the hotel ...as a telegram to me from the president was recorded, every word was shouted to the crowd.

"At the end of the message someone said, 'Don't hurrah, you will scare the sick baby.'

"The crowd could not remain silent long and after they reached the middle of the street they shouted themselves hoarse. One old man called up, 'I say, madam, we will pray for your poor baby, don't be downhearted.' "

Shortly after that news, Mrs. Davis accepted the invitation of Dr. Albert Smedes, founder of the college and the great-great-grandfather of Raleigh Mayor G. Smedes York, and lived on the campus until late August when Richmond was declared safe again.

Mrs. Stoops said: "The St. Mary's girls had mixed feelings about Mrs. Davis. They admired her beauty and the air of distinction with which she wore her simple but fashionable clothes.

"She was tall with thick dark hair worn sleekly groomed from a center part. Her unusually large and expressive dark eyes were considered memorable; they could blaze with anger or shine with friendly interest or amusement.

"Varina Davis possessed a flashing intelligence but was subject to mercurial shifts of mood. She spoke beautifully in a well-modulated voice but was inclined to sarcasm and was a compulsive talker.

"St. Mary's students considered it an honor to have known the first lady of the Confederacy, but some of them remembered the sting of her barbed witticisms.

"Mrs. Davis seems to have had pleasant memories of her stay in North Carolina. In 1895 she recalled: 'Dear old Raleigh. When I rented a part of Dr. Smedes' house and took board in his school, I was greatly depressed and heavy with anxiety, but in him and his, and in the dear people of hospitable Raleigh, I found friends whose regard made a home feeling which I am sure would now come back to me if I should revisit that dear and well-beloved town.' "

The Earth Was in Shock That Day

Wendell

They are almost gone now.

If they were teenagers when it happened, they're in their 80s now, a fading group of North Carolinians that will never forget the last two days of September 1918.

They were called the Old Hickory Division, the famed 30th Infantry Division from North Carolina, and they led the charge that broke the back of the Hindenburg Line.

Alvin Bridgers, an 87-year-old retired coal merchant in Wendell, remembers it all too well.

He was 23 when he was drafted, a farm boy from Lee County working for Du Pont in New Jersey.

"I wanted to be with North Carolina boys," he said. "So I came home to North Carolina and was drafted from Lee County."

Bridgers was a private first class, attached to D Company, 120th Infantry Regiment. He had been fighting in Belgium when the call came to go to France. The final push against the line of fortifications named for German military hero Paul von Hindenburg was ready to begin.

It was dawn, Sept. 29, 1918.

"A big gun somewhere in the rear area sounded the signal to begin the attack," Bridgers said. "Our objective was the mouth of a narrow-gauge railroad tunnel about a mile away. They told us that it had been attacked 13 or 14 times so far and no one had taken it.

"Capt. John Mays read us our orders that morning. He told us that our orders were to go as far as one man was left standing. We had to have the Hindenburg Line.

"The firing began all at once. Everybody got all mixed up. The privates didn't know where we were going to start. We were like dogs being driven.

"Everybody started shooting, and then everybody got lost. Seven of us stuck with Capt. Mays, and we started forward toward the tunnel.

"The earth was in shock that day. There were big shells and small shells falling everywhere. The Germans had said the line could not be broken, and no one knew what to do or which way to go.

"About 10 that morning, the seven of us were in a shell hole with Capt. Mays. Machine guns were all around us firing over the top of the hole. A shell hole was as good a place as any that day – some of those holes were the size of a house.

"We knew we were gone. Capt. Mays told us that everyone was on his own. He said: 'It looks like we are gone, boys, I hope to meet you again in heaven.'

"But as luck would have it, a smoke bomb landed nearby, and we crawled out of the hole in the smoke and stayed in it as we went forward.

"We lost heavy that day. There was no cover out there. What the artillery hadn't destroyed, the gas had killed. We lost 100 out of the 234 men we had when we landed.

"We didn't have much trouble after that. We got to the tunnel, and one fellow named Henry Stroebel could speak German. He yelled out to the Germans dug in at the tunnel that they might as well give up because the whole American Army was out here. He didn't tell them it was just the eight of us.

"A few of them came out at first, and then they began to come out in groups. They were ready to quit. They'd had enough of fighting."

By the time it was over, 242 Germans surrendered to the little band of scared Americans.

Bridgers and a friend named Henry Fowler marched all 242 of them back to the rear lines, picking up bodies along the way.

"They could have run anytime and we couldn't have stopped them, but it was over for them," Bridgers said. "They'd had enough. The Germans were really pretty nice people.

"By noon, we had broken the Hindenburg Line. We had it, and the 30th had done its job."

For his actions that day, Alvin Bridgers was awarded the Distinguished Service Cross and the Silver Star, America's second- and third-highest awards for bravery. He was also awarded the British Military Medal, England's second-highest award for bravery. Every man in the little band from D Company was similarly decorated.

Within weeks, it was all over. The armistice was signed Nov. 11, and the guns fell silent over Europe.

"We used to get together," Bridgers said of the men who fought beside him in France. "But they're all dead now.

"I'm the last man alive who was there that day at the tunnel."

A Duel in the Carolina Seas

Kinston

They were knights on piston-driven steeds, carrying the standards of their warring nations into battle.

They had come from as far as 3,000 miles away, each from a different world, to meet that one day in combat.

There was a cocky kid from Brooklyn, Harry Kane, a 24-year old second lieutenant, a fly-boy.

There was the 29-year-old cold professional, Horst Degan, a daring German submarine commander.

They would meet each other off the coast of North Carolina on July 7, 1942, in a blaze of high explosives and screaming warriors. Only one could win this duel; fate had decided this one would not be a draw.

Kane, now a Kinston salesman, was a pilot with the 356th Medium Bombardment Squadron. Members of the unit had flown their Lockheed Hudson bombers from California to Cherry Point, to what was then called the Eastern Sea Frontier. Their mission was to do something — anything — to stop the slaughter of American merchant seamen in what for years had been called the Graveyard of the Atlantic. There was no reason to change the name now.

In the first six months of World War II, Hitler's U-boats, those oily, silent killers from the sea, had sunk close to 600 ships along the East Coast, hundreds of them off North Carolina's shores. The war was closer than it would ever be again. Often you could see burning ships from the beach.

Kane's mission that day was to fly from Cherry Point, out over Cape Lookout and southwest to Charleston, S.C., looking for submarines to sink. The pickings had been slim so far. Germans had sunk 585 ships; Americans had sunk two submarines.

Nothing happened on the first leg of the five-hour trip. It was quiet to Charleston, so Kane and crew made a wide turn and headed northeast toward home.

"We'd been told to fly at 100 feet," Kane said. "We didn't do it that day. There were broken clouds, so we took her up to 1,500 feet. We were in clouds more than not. We used the clouds to hide so we could maybe see subs without them seeing us."

The bomber was about 25 miles east of Avon, out of sight of land, when suddenly, through his left window, Harry Kane saw something on the still sea below.

"We all looked out the window the next time we came out of the clouds, and we all saw something on the water about seven to 10 miles away," he recalled. "We didn't know it was a submarine then."

Kane slowly brought his two-engine bomber around, staying in the clouds whenever possible, throttling back to keep the engines as quiet as he could. But all the time he was bringing that steel-clawed bird lower and lower, creeping up for the attack.

The plane dropped, engines barely turning over, all hands straining to see.

It was a German submarine.

"I slammed the throttle all the way forward," Kane said. "We were doing 220 miles an hour, 50 feet off the water, coming at him."

The sub finally spotted the roaring plane and tried to crash-dive, seeking the safety of the sea. The tactic had worked so many times before.

But not this day. America was fighting back, and Harry Kane and the men of the Army Air Corps were leading the charge.

"He was about 40 to 50 feet underwater," Kane said. "And I let the depth charges go."

The first depth charge missed, short of its target. But the second one didn't miss. Neither did the third one.

"There was a huge explosion," Kane said. "We circled around and saw oil in the water, and then we started seeing heads popping up. They had faked sub sinkings with oil before, but they don't fake it with men in the water. I counted 15 heads in all."

Kane and his crew had several alternatives then. They could have flown on, leaving the submariners in their watery fate, or they could have shot every one of the survivors with their seven .30-caliber machine guns. But they did neither.

Instead, the American airmen dropped their life jackets and rafts to the struggling enemy sailors below, not worrying that the plane was 25 miles out at sea and that they might need them.

"They were beaten," Kane said. "They couldn't hurt anyone anymore. We couldn't leave them to drown like rats.

"They were like us, they'd had a job to do and they'd done it."

By radio, Kane and his men sought assistance for the vanquished foe. A Panamanian freighter congratulated the Americans but refused to help. A Coast Guard cutter came to search but couldn't find the men in the water.

Kane had to leave then. The sun was low in the sky. The trip was to have taken five hours, but it was closer to eight now. Only five minutes of fuel were left when the plane landed.

And that night, as the men of the 356th Medium Bombardment Squadron celebrated their first kill, the first time a plane had sunk a sub, 15 German sailors struggled for life in the Graveyard of the Atlantic, 3,000 miles from home.

● ● ●

Horst Degan was one of the rising stars in the galaxy of German U-Boat commanders in World War II. When Germany began production of a newer, more deadly submarine, Degan was chosen to command the first one off the line — the ship called U-701.

He had graduated from naval training in 1933, in a class that would go down in German military history as the best ever in that warrior land.

Degan took command of the U-701 in the summer of 1941,

when no one would have bet on the outcome of the war. He would win plaudits as a "daring and reckless" commander famed for his "bold daylight attacks."

U-701's first cruise was off the coast of England. Degan and his crew sank a British freighter on that maiden voyage. On its second cruise, off Iceland, the U-701 sank four British warships.

But then came the cruise when Degan was to meet a bomber crew from North Carolina. He wouldn't be so lucky this time.

U-701 left Brest in May 1941, its mission to sink ships off North Carolina. It left with bands playing — the hope of German world supremacy, off to take war to American shores.

The trip lasted 22 days, with the U-701 hunting while crossing the Atlantic. The crews of four ships never knew how close they came to dying as Degan stalked them en route before deciding, for various reasons, to pass them up.

The days were pleasant on that late spring crossing. Most of the time, the off-duty crewmen sunbathed on the deck. But as the coast drew closer, Degan, the professional, became cautious. He ordered the sub below, and it traversed the last 100 miles or so submerged.

The sub arrived off the U.S. coast on June 11, several days before a new moon. So Degan hid on the bottom for five days — waiting, like a wolf in its lair, for dark nights to do his killing.

Degan's hunting ground stretched from Emerald Isle, N.C., to Norfolk, Va. On June 16, he attacked a freighter but missed with two torpedoes. On the 17th, he was chased and depth-charged by a Coast Guard cutter but escaped. On the 19th, he fought a blazing surface gun duel with the same cutter, and sank it within minutes.

On the 27th, he damaged a freighter. On the 28th, he sank the tanker William Rockefeller off the North Carolina coast. Hunting, and luck, were getting better.

In the first week of July, as America celebrated Independence Day at war, Degan hid off Virginia Beach, so close he could see bathers through his periscope, and then followed an American ship through a maze of mines in the area. Four ships went down in two days. There was joy among the U-701's crewmen. They were doing their jobs, and doing them well.

July 7, 1942. Fresh air was low in U-701, so Degan brought the sub to the surface to replenish the supply. He and three other men stationed themselves in the vessel's tower to watch for enemy aircraft.

One of those four men was the sub's executive officer, the second in command, a lieutenant named Konrad Junker. Degan did not trust Junker. That very morning he had severely reprimanded the young officer for not being alert on lookout. Junker would die for his mistakes.

Suddenly, in early afternoon, Junker screamed, "There, airplane!"

It was Harry Kane and crew, screaming down at U-701 at 220 mph, loaded with four 300-pound depth charges.

"You saw it too late!" Degan cursed as he hit the Klaxon to signal a crash dive.

The sub was at 40 feet and diving fast when the pressure hull was crushed by the depth charges Kane had dropped.

Lights went out in the sausage-shaped craft that was to become a coffin. All the instruments were shattered. Water was rising fast. The sub hit bottom 60 feet down, listing 20 degrees to starboard.

Everyone who could, made it to the control room. There were 15 of them. They grabbed what life jackets and escape lungs they could find, opened the tower hatch and headed to the surface.

Less than half of the crew made it.

As they drifted, they slowly died, one after another, some men going mad before their death. Two survivors thought they could swim to shore, 30 miles away. They couldn't, and they drowned.

One by one they slipped away, some saying a quiet goodbye to their comrades, others screaming in defiance as they went under.

Soon only seven men were left alive. They were covered in oil and sick from the salt water. Degan was unconscious most of the time, kept alive in the strong arms of his quartermaster.

By late afternoon on July 9 they had been in the water for 49 hours. The Gulf Stream had taken them 100 miles out to sea. They had found a coconut and a lemon floating with them. Each man got one bite of coconut, one suck of lemon.

As the afternoon neared an end, they were spotted by a Navy dirigible, and within an hour they were on their way to the U.S. Naval Hospital at Norfolk.

"A few days after we sank the sub I got orders to go to Norfolk to the hospital," Kane said. "I didn't know why. I was a second lieutenant; they didn't tell me anything.

"When we got there, they took me to a big room that was surrounded by FBI agents carrying machine guns. We walked in, and there, sitting in a chair in the middle of the room, was a bearded, sunburned man. He looked pretty bad.

"He was introduced to me as Horst Degan, the commander of U-701, the sub we had sunk on July 7.

"He stood up, gave me a smart salute and said, 'Congratulations. A good attack.' "

But it would not be their last contact. Kane and Degan began corresponding in 1980, with a series of letters that has heightened hopes the old foes will once again salute each other.

"If divers ever get down to the U-701, I've already told them to bring up Degan's binoculars, the ones he wore when he was looking for me in the sky that day," Kane said.

"I want to present them to him myself."

No Name Tag for Leonard Pone

Wilmington

Ike Thompson was the only one who mentioned Leonard Pone all day.

They talked about what a great bunch of guys they were, how they'd fought and lived together on the mighty USS North Carolina, and wasn't it just great that after all these years 180 former crewmen would come together to celebrate the ship's 40th birthday?

They wore name tags so former shipmates could sneak a peek and say, "Sure, I remember you."

Some did, some didn't.

But there wasn't a name tag for Leonard Pone. Ike Thompson was the only one who mentioned him.

Part of the weeklong reunion was a re-enactment of the day the ship first came under enemy fire, and it was a good show. But they left out Leonard Pone's part.

The ship's log for that day doesn't even mention him by name.

During the re-enactment, four World War II vintage warplanes streaked low over the battleship as the ship's Klaxon sounded.

Old sailors, their legs responding to orders their ears had not heard in about 35 years, thundered onto the deck and raced to their guns to show their kids and their wives how it used to be, how it was when they were young and there was a world to save.

Leonard Pone had been with them at 3:36 p.m. on Aug. 24, 1942, when it happened for real, when wave after wave of Japanese dive bombers and fighters began a two-hour attack on the ship.

This time, Leonard Pone wasn't there.

The old sailors manned both of the 40mm guns on the ship's fantail, sweating and grumbling about how heavy those helmets were.

But no one manned the 20mm gun that Leonard Pone was on in 1942. The gun itself isn't even there anymore.

They swung their guns around, just like they used to, aiming at the attacking aircraft.

They didn't sound silly when they shouted orders to each other:

"Here he comes, Ike, get him, get him!"

"Bring it around, here comes another one!"

"Stay with him, stay with him!"

And when the re-enactment was over — after the seven simulated bombs had exploded to remind them of the seven Japanese near-hits, and after they had recalled how on that Aug. 24 at least seven and possibly 14 planes had been downed by the young crew — it was then that Ike mentioned Leonard Pone.

"He was standing right over there," Ike said. "He was on a 20mm gun when we were strafed that day.

"He was a good kid, from Brooklyn, and he had just gotten married before we left.

"He was killed that day, the first man killed on this ship."

Around us were sweating, smiling old salts, guys like Clinton Rood from Melbourne, Fla., who joked and said: "I didn't know it was this much fun. Every time they blew the horn, I had to go below."

But Ike Thompson kept thinking about Leonard Pone.

"We were all young then," said Ike, now 61 and living in

Houston, Texas. "Doing things like this brings back a lot of memories, but they're not pleasant memories.

"Don't let these boys kid you, you're scared to death all the time."

Just for the record, there were nine others killed on the North Carolina during the war.

They were George Conlon, Everette Brenn, Albert Geary, Carl Karan Jr., Elvin Means, Ingwald Nelson, William Kelton Jr., Oscar Stone and John Watson.

But memories of fear and death are not the memories you bring to reunions; those are not the stories you tell to enthralled youngsters. You remember the good times, mostly.

The other memories come back all by themselves.

At night, alone, that's when they'll all remember Leonard Pone.

War Comes to Holly Ridge

Holly Ridge

There were but seven families living in this Onslow County town when it all happened; the Hineses, Davises, Rochelles, Thomases, Sanderses and two sets of Hansleys — 28 people in all.

There were two stores and a run-down train station. Surrounding the village were thousands of acres of piney woods.

Holly Ridge "wasn't even a wide spot in the road," said town councilman Kenneth Howard. "It was still a narrow spot. We had cattle grazing out on Topsail Island, and men on cow ponies herded them. About the only people you ever saw were farmers and fishermen. It was a wild and woolly place."

That's the way it was at Christmas 1940. By Memorial Day 1941, just five months and 10 days after the papers were signed, 1,000 buildings had been constructed and 20,000 people had arrived. They didn't call it Holly Ridge anymore. They called it Boom Town.

The U.S. Army had arrived, and Holly Ridge would never be the same.

The Army selected Holly Ridge as the site of Camp Davis, an anti-aircraft artillery training base, just as World War II was peeking over the horizon. By the time it was in full swing, close to 100,000 people were in Holly Ridge — soldiers, camp followers, civilian workers, con men, bootleggers and families. It was one of the largest cities in North Carolina, and it happened nearly overnight.

"We still have deeds recorded for lots that were 20 feet by 20 feet," said Phyllis Hines, a descendant of the original Hines family. "People would put up a tent and sell anything you can imagine out of it. They sold groceries and dry goods and bootleg whiskey, anything they could sell to make money.

"There are some people living near here now who came here then — some ladies, shall we say, who were very popular with the soldiers."

Honky-tonks were everywhere, the most famous of which was called The Bucket of Blood.

"It was a two-story place," Howard said. "The bar was downstairs, and you can imagine what was upstairs."

The impact on Holly Ridge is hard to imagine. From 28 to 100,000 people within a year, from a forgotten backwater to a major metropolis.

Camp Davis was huge. There were 3,200 acres in the camp and an additional 5,000 in nearby firing ranges. More than $20 million was spent at the crossroads community within months.

In the spring of 1941, war was coming and men had to be trained. Troops arriving at Camp Davis — including two all-black regiments — found newly built service clubs with cafeterias, libraries, lounges and dances with women from Wilmington.

There were four movie theaters, bands, drama groups and glee clubs. Eight churches were built practically overnight.

The camp hospital had 56 buildings. There were three fire stations and two miles of fire hose that could be connected to 223 hydrants.

The laundry employed 450 people. There were 16 wells, four water towers and 50 miles of water mains. The camp had 30 miles of paved streets, 22 miles of sidewalks and 830 streetlights.

And every bit of that, plus two airports, was constructed in five months and 10 days.

The people of Holly Ridge were stunned.

"People slept anywhere they could lay their heads," Howard said. "Construction workers were everywhere. They slept in tents, in their cars, in people's houses, even on boats in the Inland Waterway."

It was like that all through the war. The soldiers called it Boom Town; the merchants called it paradise. Fortunes were made, and so were babies. The future had come to Holly Ridge, and it was payday every day. People were dying in Europe, but they danced in Holly Ridge.

But it was not to last. Folks driving through Holly Ridge today, on their way to Topsail Island, see mostly shabby, abandoned stores and lonely chimneys peeking from the pine forests.

Camp Davis disappeared as quickly as it was built. Peace destroyed Holly Ridge.

Medal of Honor for a Country Boy

Eastover

Geddie Herring was sure he was going to be court-martialed.

All those months, while he had been lying in a hospital, the young lieutenant was sure someone was going to find out about those extra beer rations he had stolen for his crew on the landing craft he commanded.

But that wasn't why they sent word they wanted to see him at Navy headquarters in Washington.

They wanted to give him a medal, the highest award for heroism this country can give.

They gave Geddie Herring, a 23-year-old country boy from Roseboro, the Congressional Medal of Honor.

There have been 38 million Americans in combat since the Civil War. Of those, 3,405 have won the Medal of Honor. North Carolinians have received 29. Of those, only five recipients still live here.

For Geddie Herring, the path to the Medal of Honor began Feb. 17, 1945. In six months the Japanese would surrender. The war was almost over, but there was one island yet to take.

As long as this nation remembers its battles, the battle for Iwo Jima will not be forgotten. Neither will the heroism of a Roseboro man, a 90-day wonder Naval Reserve officer.

Herring was commanding a landing craft that had been refitted as a gunboat. His job, with 11 other ships, was to lay down covering fire so Navy frogmen could clear the beaches for the invasion that was to come in two days. Intelligence said it would be an easy job, a milk run.

But intelligence didn't know everything. They didn't know there were 10,000 Japanese on the island, fully prepared to die. The Japanese knew they would not be relieved, and they knew they would not surrender. And intelligence did not know there were big guns on the island.

The ships in Herring's group were approaching the beach, preparing to lay down their withering rocket and 40mm cannon fire when the big Japanese guns opened up.

"It all happened in 45 seconds," Herring said. "The first shell hit the forward gun and killed that entire crew. The second shell took out the other forward guns and killed that crew. The third shell hit the bridge.

"There were seven of us up there. Everyone was killed but me."

Herring was wounded. His right leg was broken. His right arm was shattered at the shoulder. A large piece of shrapnel was sticking out from the wound. He was bleeding heavily.

In 45 seconds, 40 of his men had been killed or wounded. He was the only man left on the deck of his ship, a burning deck, littered with the crumpled bodies of his deck crew.

And he was in charge. He had to do something to save the 14 remaining crewmen, who had been below decks when the steel rained down.

"The ship was foundering," he said. "And we were heading straight for the beach. I looked out, and there wasn't a soul standing. The canvas covers on the ammunition were burning. There were bodies everywhere, some on fire. I didn't know I was hit until I turned and my arm just hung there and I saw the blood.

"My first thought was, 'You SOBs, you had your chance, and you didn't get me, and you're not going to get me now.'

"I reacted the way I'd been trained. I really wasn't scared, I was mad. I tried to fire the rockets, but the firing mechanism had been broken.

"I was able to hop on one leg — thank goodness the broken leg and the broken arm were on opposite sides so I was balanced — and I made it to the ladder so I could go down to a telephone to the engine room."

Herring made it down the ladder and got the ship moving out, but it was going in a big circle, turning broadside to the artillery fire that had hit all nine ships in the operation.

Unable to control the damaged ship by himself, Herring finally got a seaman on the helm, and he hobbled outside where he could see and direct his battered ship to safety.

Propping himself against a box of ammunition, the rapidly weakening Herring organized his crew to tend to the wounded, put out the fires on the ship and steer it to safety.

He had lost 40 men; he would not lose the other 14.

"My only thought was that somebody had to save the ship and the crew," he said.

"I never think about it much, but it did make me wonder why the Lord spared me.

"There were seven men in a 10-foot circle, and you're the only one left. It does make you think."

They Could Be Young Again

Emerald Isle

The waistlines have grown larger, the hair sparser, but not everything has changed.

Max Gates is still the quietest one; Alex Gwozd and Clem Szalkowski still pick on each other as fiercely as ever; Tommy Kamas is still the handsomest, and Chet Crumbo still thinks he's their fearless leader.

"It was like the last 35 years never happened," Mrs. Lee MacKay said. "From the moment they met, they've been talking like they'd never been apart."

The nine men who gathered in the backroom of an Emerald Isle seafood restaurant, some from as far away as Provo, Utah, shared that most personal of experiences.

They fought, and won, a war together.

They were the crew of a B-24 bomber in World War II.

They were pilot Chet Crumbo, now the vice president of a sand and gravel company; co-pilot Tommy Kamas, a Texas oil executive; navigator Grady Martin, a poultry expert at N.C. State University; nose gunner Eddie Clarke, an airline engineer in Boston and the only one still flying; tail gunner Max Gates, an Indiana dairy farmer; upper gunner Lee MacKay, a contractor in Utah; engineer Alex Gwozd, a retired Brooklyn cop; wisecracking radio operator Clem Szalkowski, a wine salesman; and ball gunner Kit Pearce, a big man in nuts and bolts down in Atlanta.

"As you can see, not a one of us is on welfare," Crumbo bragged. "This was a special crew. We were closer than most crews. We never had a moment of trouble."

Well, there was a little trouble. One time Lee told off Alex, so Chet had him write a 500-word essay on military discipline.

"So he copied it right out of the regulations and when he had 500 words he quit right in the middle of a sentence," Chet said, laughing.

The 35 years have produced 29 children and 31 grandchildren among the men. Only one of them has been divorced, and that was 33 years ago.

They met first in Pueblo, Colo., in mid-1944. By Thanksgiving, they were flying bombing runs from Italy into the crumbling remains of Hitler's fiery dream.

"We used to fly into Vienna to bomb refineries," Chet said. "There were 16,000 anti-aircraft guns around Vienna. One time we took 152 hits and not a man was hurt.

"Of course, we didn't make it home that time."

No, they didn't. They flew for almost four hours on two engines, Chet and Tommy taking 15-minute turns at jamming their feet on the rudders while Grady frantically searched for a pass through the Alps since the plane was without oxygen and couldn't fly over the mountains.

Grady found the way through; Alex got an engine going, and Chet — flying with his head out a window because mist had frozen on the windshield — brought the plane in on a Yugoslavian beach.

They were nine miles behind enemy lines and were rescued by Tito's partisans, who led them to an abandoned airplane they managed to get off the ground.

"But since we had lost all our codes, we couldn't signal who we were, and the British tried to shoot us down," Chet said.

They came together at Emerald Isle because it was as centrally located as anywhere. But they came together, first of all, because ... well, they love one another.

It was getting late by the time they broke out the champagne that came from the isle of Capri, where they used to go for rest and relaxation during their off-duty hours.

There were toasts — some short, others maudlin — and then they broke into song.

"Off we go, into the wild blue yonder," they sang, middle-aged men and their ladies, joining, forgetting some words, but finishing strong, cheering themselves and their crusade.

They were boys when they met, some still in their teens, and for one night 35 years later, they could be boys again.

Do You Ever Think of Little Charlie?

Clement

The Marines called him Charlie Two Shoes. That was as close as the American boys tried to get to Tsui Chi Hsii.

There were a lot of kids like Charlie, the waifs of China, poor and homeless after World War II. Charlie was raised for several years in the barracks with the Marines stationed in Tsingtao.

"He ate with us, slept with us and wore uniforms cut down to fit him," said ex-Marine William Bullard of Sampson County. "He was like a little brother to us. His shoes were spit-shined, his uniforms were neat, and he'd snap to attention just like we did when an officer came in the barracks."

Charlie lived with the Marines for several years. They educated him in a nearby missionary school and filled his heart with the glories of the place they called "Stateside."

But the world was changing. Mao's Communists were taking control in China; the time for Americans was ending.

"At night you could see the big guns going off to the west," Bullard said. "And then they began pulling us out."

Charlie was there at the airstrip when his buddies left. They had thought about stowing him in a duffel bag and sneaking him out, but ideas like that never come to be.

They all had tears in their eyes, but mostly little Charlie Two Shoes.

"You'll send back for me afterward, won't you?" asked the little Chinese boy in his cut-down Marine uniform.

Sure we will Charlie, they told him, sure we will.

But they didn't. There were a couple of letters in the next year or so, but then the Bamboo Curtain slammed shut.

"I used to think about Charlie and wonder what happened to that little fellow," Bullard said. "But there was no way to get word in or out of China."

But now, 32 years later, Charlie Two Shoes might be on his

way to join his buddies of so long ago.

"When I pulled that letter out of my mailbox I sat there without opening it and cried for 20 minutes," Bullard said.

It was a letter from Charlie.

"Do you remember your old buddy in China?" the letter began. "Do you ever think of little Charlie ...thanks to God and the deed of pure friendship between our two great countries we are able to get in touch now ...in all these times my heart was like on fire from day to night. I was always thinking of my old buddies ...I pray for the day for us to meet. Do you think it would be possible? I could never forget how you and my other buddies support me to school and treat me as your own brother."

It is more than possible, Bullard said.

"I want him here, and I'll do it if I have to mortgage everything," he said.

"It is hard to believe all of this. I wondered so many times what had happened to Charlie. When you promise a kid something, they don't forget it."

Of course, Charlie Two Shoes isn't a kid now. He is a middle-aged man with a wife and three children, a graduate of an agricultural college in China. But he still thinks about America and his friends, the Marines.

"Buddy, my faithful brother, you can never know how long and terrible these past 32 years have been," Charlie wrote. "You can never know how many times I have dreamed of you and my other buddies and awoken with tears."

A Warm Place in a Frozen Wind

A story for Thanksgiving:

There is a nameless wind that shrieks out of Manchuria about this time of year.

It blows straight and hard, down from the plains of China, bringing a fierce cold that stabs through Korea like a frozen ice pick through a warm stick of butter.

The wind was blowing on Thanksgiving Day of 1965.

It brought the first slash of winter with it. It might have been mild the day before, but when the wind blew out of Manchuria you forgot that autumn ever was.

Two soldiers left the village of Paju-ri in a jeep that

Thanksgiving morning, glad, in a way, to be working. It is easier when you're working, when you don't have time to think of all those other Thanksgivings, the ones that are sweeter in your memory than they ever were in reality.

Holidays have a way of doing that to you when you're half a world from home. You remember not the real Thanksgivings, but the ones they show you in pictures: a happy family, a fat turkey, and funny Uncle Ed telling his old jokes. No matter that you don't have an Uncle Ed, or that real Thanksgivings were never like that. Those are the ones you remember when the wind blows out of Manchuria and you're a long way from home.

The soldiers drove north, skirting the Imjin River, just a routine job. It would take about three hours to make it to Uijongbu and back again.

On the way back from Uijongbu, almost home, the jeep broke down in the village of Yongju-gol. The two soldiers were about five miles from camp. It was late afternoon. They knew that at that moment the men in their unit would be sitting down to a Thanksgiving dinner, and they knew they'd miss it.

They stopped in a bar, a concrete blockhouse called The Seven Up Club. It was a famous bar for the men of the 1st Cavalry Division. Of all the scuzzy bars in Korea, this was the one they would tell stories about when they got back to the States. When you talked about The Seven Up Club, they knew you'd been there, you understood what a year in the First Cav was all about.

Usually the place was full, cavalrymen drinking and talking to the bar girls — or, to be honest, hookers. This day it was quiet. The oil heater was bouncing from the roaring fire, the jukebox was quiet. Two girls sat at the bar talking to Mama-san, that ageless gnome who ran the place.

The two soldiers sat down, wondering if they should call for help but hating to do it because they knew that someone else would miss dinner if they did ask for a wrecker. They knew they'd missed it already, so why make someone else do the same?

They sat, nursing that vile beer called OB, figuring they'd kill some time and then call for a ride.

Mama-san and the girls were curious. What were these two doing here, in the late afternoon, when the wind was blowing, when all the other Americans were sharing that curious holiday Koreans never understood?

They asked, and the soldiers told them about breaking down,

about not wanting their buddies to miss that most special of meals, about Thanksgiving. We'll be here only a couple of hours, they said, and then they'll come get us.

Mama-san left the barroom and went upstairs, where the girls spent those furtive moments with lonely cavalrymen. She came back in a few minutes, carrying an Army-issue can.

She opened the can and sat it on the stove to heat. It didn't take long.

She brought it over to the soldiers, using her flowing dress as a pot holder. She sat it down on the table and handed each man a pair of chopsticks.

On the side were the words "processed turkey."

"You eat, GI," she told them in pidgin English.

The soldiers looked at each other and at the offering, turkey for a Thanksgiving dinner. They invited Mama-san and the girls to join them, and they did.

It was an unlikely Thanksgiving dinner — two soldiers, two hookers and a madam, outside the Manchurian wind, eating processed turkey with chopsticks, 11,000 miles from home.

"Sorry you missed dinner," their friends told them when they got back to Paju-ri early that night. "It was great."

The two soldiers smiled. It would be a Thanksgiving they would think about warmly in other years, when they were home, when funny Uncle Ed started telling his old jokes.

Blood on a Jungle Trail

Spring Lake

Meet Charlie Morris, a 49-year-old man with a quick smile and a firm handshake and the scars of 26 wounds on his lanky, country-boy body.

He is a professional solider.

His credentials are impeccable: He served 22 years on active duty, most of them as a paratrooper. He has fought in two wars, served in Europe, the Caribbean, Asia and the United States. He reached the highest rank attainable as an enlisted man — sergeant major.

He wears the Congressional Medal of Honor, the highest award for bravery this country can bestow.

He also wears the Distinguished Service Cross, this country's second-highest award for bravery.

"All my life, I have looked for a challenge," Morris said, sitting in a living room littered with unpacked moving boxes, a familiar setting for professional soldiers.

"I got out of the Army after the Korean War. I had a good job working at a glass company. But after seven years, I came back in the Army.

"Why? Well, I missed being able to influence young people. I wanted to do more with my life than produce a product."

He did.

We go back to June 1966, Republic of Vietnam.

It was dawn, time to go to work for Morris and the 40 men of the third platoon of A Company.

"We'd been in the jungle two hours when I started seeing signs of humans," Morris said. "There were worn spots on the jungle carpet, broken twigs, that sort of thing.

"I held up my men, and two of us moved forward. From a mossy bank 10 yards away a machine gun opened up. Smitty got it in the shoulder, and I got it in the chest, left hand and leg.

"I was blinded for a moment and fell to my knees, and the guy was still shooting. My vision came back, and I fired with my M-16, and at that range I don't miss. I crawled up and threw a grenade, and that took care of the rest of the crew.

"By then the platoon was taking fire from the front, the left and the right from automatic rifles, machine guns, recoilless rifles, mortars and rockets.

"I told Smitty to get back and I'd cover him. I was on my belly and I'd fire a burst and roll, fire a burst and roll. They were missing me by two inches."

The battle was on. By the time it was over, three men were left in one piece. Thirteen were dead, 25 wounded. The platoon was pinned down for eight hours by constant fire from a force 10 times its size.

They came from all sides that day, in five waves. One by one, the American troopers, including the medic, fell.

Morris, leaving a trail of blood behind, crawled from man to man, performing first aid. One man had a leg and arm shot off. With Morris' care, he lived to become a Detroit lawyer.

"There are long, dark periods of that day I don't remember,"

Morris said. "I'd be hit again and black out and come to doing something and not knowing how I got there."

He squirmed among his troops, passing out the dwindling ammunition, tending their wounds, stripping the dead for ammunition and equipment, firing one-handed as he dragged himself along on useless legs and a useless arm. The wounded were hit repeatedly.

"All I did was my job," he said. "I gave them the skills and the leadership. They (the soldiers) gave the heroism, those teen-age boys."

Finally, Morris could move no more. He was lying behind the lifeless body of one of his young troopers, using it to prop his rifle so he could shoot. He had three rounds left when it grew quiet.

"I heard some rustling and out of the corner of my eye, I saw the most beautiful person, male or female, I've ever seen," he said. "It was this big, black, sweaty soldier with a stained helmet, easing out from behind a tree. Our relief was there.

"The company commander came up, and I saluted him from flat on my belly.

"That day totally influenced the rest of my military career. I saw what young American boys can do when they have the training and discipline and are properly led.

"Don't talk to me about the poor quality of American soldiers."

Torture at the Hanoi Hilton

Jacksonville

None of us will ever really know what it was like for the hostages in Iran. Living in terror night after empty night, finally tasting sweet freedom.

J. Quincy Collins knows how it feels.

The hostages spent 444 days in the hands of the enemy. Collins, a 49-year-old Charlotte insurance executive, was held captive for 2,721 days by enemy forces.

It was Sept. 2, 1965. Capt. Quincy Collins kicked the throttle of his F-105 jet fighter and screamed into the sky from the runway at Thak Li, Thailand, heading for the famed Ho Chi Minh Trail and a bridge in the jungle.

It was an uneventful flight. He peeled out of formation to

make his last bombing run. Then his graceful jet shuddered in the sky.

"Suddenly there was smoke and fire in the cockpit," Collins said as we sat in a Jacksonville restaurant.

"Every red light on the panel came on. It showed me that everything that can go wrong had. I felt one more explosion. I didn't know if it was the bombs exploding or I had been hit again. There was fire and smoke everywhere.

"I didn't have to think what to do. That's what my training did for me. I was traveling down at a 45-degree angle at 600 to 700 knots. I was 1,000 feet from the ground when I reached for the ejection handle. That is the last thing I remember.

"When I came to, I was leaning up against a tree wearing nothing but shorts. My leg was broken and sticking out at a 45-degree angle. Four Vietnamese were squatting down in front of me. I was looking down the barrel of four guns. They were grinning at me as only the Vietnamese can grin.

"They tied me to a pole like a captured tiger and wrapped me in a net. My leg was broken, and I had to fight to keep it from falling out of the net while they carried me through the jungle. They put me in a jeep, and off we went.

"A lot of things flashed through my mind. I had visions of the last time I had seen my kids, my wife and my family. I could remember each time clearly.

"I could hear the roar of falling water, like a big waterfall. I figured they were going to take me there and throw me over and that would be that. I thought I was going to die and it would be over.

"Then they took a right turn, away from the water, and I had a new lease on life. I knew then I'd be a prisoner of war."

Collins was taken to a place called the Hanoi Hilton. It was a grim joke.

It was a prison built in Hanoi by the French when they ruled Indochina. After the French left, the prison remained behind as part of the Democratic Republic of Vietnam, and it housed some U.S. prisoners taken by the North Vietnamese during the Vietnam War.

"We had been trained to give only our name, rank and serial number," Collins said. "That was fine, but the first thing they asked me was my blood type. To tell them was to already violate what I was supposed to do as a prisoner of war, but I needed the blood. I told them.

"They had me already.

"The next thing they wanted was a complete family history — the names of my family, everything. I held out. I figured that was part of my job, to hold out."

He was tortured almost daily.

"They tell you that they're going to get the information they wanted," he said. "And then they send you back to your cell and let you sit there, wondering what they're going to do to you.

"Then later you'll hear them coming down the hall, jingling those keys. You just know they're coming after you.

"Sometimes they are, but sometimes they aren't. Sometimes they want you to think they are. They always jingle those keys.

"Every person has to decide for himself how much he can take. If they take you to a point with torture and you break down, they always take you just a little further to make it hurt more before they stop.

"I wanted to hold out as long as I could, to make them work for what they got. If it got to be too hard to get, they might stop.

"I was in solitary confinement in what I called the outdoor toilet when one of the other prisoners whispered to me not to hold out too long on the Blue Book (the personal history). He said it wasn't worth it. So I made up a complete history and memorized it.

"Not knowing what they're going to do is the toughest part. That's how they can break you; you never know what's going to happen."

Collins considered suicide. "I was that low," he said. "What keeps you going is the people with you. They keep telling you to hang on.

"You play fantasy games in your mind, imagining what things are like at home — and they aren't always good fantasies.

"You imagine your wife with someone else; you imagine your kids on drugs; you imagine horrible things when you're down. We thought of every conceivable thing. But the main thing we thought was, 'What does it matter, I can make a new life.'

"We used to make bets on when we'd get out. One guy would bet on next Easter, another by Christmas. Some would bet it would be five years in the future. A lot of people lost a lot of champagne and money.

"When the bombing started at Christmas of 1972, we knew the end was coming. We knew they couldn't take that.

"Every night you could set your watch by the B-52s coming over. The earth would shake, and the plaster would fall off the walls when they unloaded.

"It was like being inside a blast furnace, one horrendous rush of noise. We'd look up, and sometimes we'd see a B-52 get hit. That was an eerie feeling.

"Then the bombing stopped, and we started smiling. We knew it was almost over. The (prison intercom system) said the Americans were giving up, Vietnam had won, and we knew then we were going home. We knew it was a lie."

The Vietnamese began fattening up Collins and the 21 other men in his group and gave them new clothes and shoes.

"They took our group away from the others, and we figured we'd be the first ones to go home," Collins said. "They began to give us much better food and even had us stand on a piece of toilet paper while they traced the outline of our feet. We knew they were going to make shoes for us."

The shoes made and the clothes fitted, the men were herded aboard a bus and taken to an airport runway.

"I saw an Air Force colonel standing beside a table," Collins said. "There was an Air Force flag and an American flag beside him, and the wind was blowing slightly to make them wave.

"It was the most gorgeous sight I've ever seen.

"I marched up to the table and saluted the colonel and signed a piece of paper. There was a Vietnamese there we called The Rabbit because his ears stuck out. I looked down at him and said, 'The best part of all this is that you've got to stay here.'

"I walked toward the airplane and I looked up and there was a big American flag on the tail. I was just crying. It was the prettiest airplane I'd ever seen.

"We got on the plane, and there was the ugliest flight nurse in the history of aviation. Then she hugged me, and I got my first whiff of perfume in 7½ years. She was beautiful to me then.

"When the plane took off down that runway, we waited until the landing gear slapped up. Then we cheered."

There would be briefings on board, a hero's welcome at Clark Field in the Philippines, ice cream, Cokes and fresh milk by the gallon, two baby bottles of Mai Tai's smuggled on board in Hawaii and finally home to the United States.

"I don't think we knew what heroes we'd be," Collins said. "We didn't know how badly this country needed heroes when we came home. We felt we'd be looked up to, but not to this extent.

"In time, they forgot us.

"That's what happens to heroes."

Veterans of a Different Time

Fayetteville

There was Johnny Reed, with his black, shaggy mustache and hair curling around his collar. He smoked Marlboro Lights, one after another.

And there was Amos Creech. He didn't have much hair left, just a sandy memory in back. He smoked Camels, one after another.

"You going out to the cemetery next week?" Amos asked Johnny.

"Hadn't planned on it," Johnny said, looking like he wondered why he should be going to a cemetery then or any other week.

They both ordered another beer. Not much was said for a while. The clatter of the pool game in the back was the only sound in the bar.

"I'm going to go out there," Amos said. "Might as well, have for a long time. Nobody much else goes, but I keep going."

"What are you talking about?" Johnny asked.

"Armistice Day is next week," Amos said. "I'm going out to the cemetery for the flag raising."

Johnny hadn't known about the flag raising, and if you'd pressed him, it might have been tough for him to remember what Armistice Day was, or when it was.

They don't call it Armistice Day anymore. Few remember that it was at the 11th hour of the 11th day of the 11th month of 1918 when the guns fell silent in The Great War, the one that only later came to be known as World War I.

Now they call it Veterans Day, the day each year when America pays homage to its military veterans. But if you don't look closely, you'll miss it.

"I never thought much about being a veteran," Johnny said. "I haven't joined any of those clubs like the American Legion or the VFW. They're for the other vets, I guess."

The other vets. The guys from World War I and World War II, those are the ones Johnny was talking about, not the new vets, the guys who fought in Vietnam. They don't even call it Vietnam, they call it "Nam" — rhymes with ham.

Then Johnny and Amos got to recalling the days they came home, when their own wars ended.

"I got off a troop ship in Brooklyn," Amos said. "The war had been over for six months — I'd been on garrison duty in Germany — but you'd have thought it had ended that day.

"People were great. We'd walk in a bar, a whole bunch of us, and the place was ours. People bought us drinks and patted us on the back, they told us we were heroes. Hell, we weren't heroes. I was a cook, for crissakes. I never did shoot a gun at anybody, but that didn't matter.

"When I got home to Arkansas, they had a bunch of people at the train station to welcome us back. We'd all been in a National Guard unit together before the war, and a lot of us came back at the same time. You really could tell the war was over."

Johnny didn't have much to say about his homecoming.

"Wasn't nothing to it," he said. "I got off an airplane at Travis (Air Force Base) in California. They treated us just like they had when we left. They yelled at us and made us pull barracks details, and then three days later I got my orders to report to Fort Jackson, S.C., where I got my discharge. I never saw a parade."

They didn't have parades for the likes of Johnny Reed and the millions who fought beside him. He was a Vietnam veteran, and that made a difference.

"I tried to tell my daddy that it was different in Nam," Johnny said. "He'd been in the Marines in the Pacific in World War II, and he couldn't figure out why I didn't feel like he did.

"I don't know why it was different. But it was. Guys coming back from Nam just wanted to get out and go home and forget about it.

"I didn't have nightmares or flashbacks and all that stuff. I just didn't care. I don't ever think about it."

Johnny won't be at a Veterans Day ceremony today. Few

from his war will be. Most of those present will be old warriors, the other veterans that Johnny spoke of.

"I guess one difference between veterans like him and me," Johnny said, nodding toward Amos, "is that they won World War II.

"And we lost in Vietnam. It wasn't our fault, but we lost anyway."

No Yellow Ribbons for Bryan Ellis

Let's not forget Bryan Ellis.

North Carolina did not have one of its sons or daughters held hostage in the U.S. Embassy in Tehran. We could not have our own welcome celebration when the 52 flew home to freedom, cheers and yellow ribbons.

But Bryan Ellis was one of us, a North Carolinian by birth and rearing, and he should not be forgotten in the outpouring of thanksgiving that has surged across the land.

Ellis, a 29-year-old helicopter pilot, was from Swansboro. He was killed when a howling mob attacked and burned the U.S. Embassy in Islamabad, Pakistan, Nov. 21, 1979, 17 days after our embassy in Iran was seized.

He died as a soldier, on the job until the mob broke down his door. His charred body was found in the rubble on Thanksgiving Day.

Ellis, who served 11 years in the Army and was a chief warrant officer, was buried in Swansboro on a breezy Dec. 3, 1979.

Young Bryan always had wanted to be a soldier, as his father and stepfather were. As a child, he would build mock battlefields for his toy tanks and plastic soldiers, complete with bomb craters.

He played some football in Swansboro and met Brenda, who would become his wife. When he finished high school, he joined the Army.

He was a chopper pilot in Vietnam, one of the most dangerous jobs — and certainly the most glamorous — for a solider in that war. He was decorated for a mission on which he made a flight to pick up a team of Navy commandos.

In April 1979, Ellis arrived for his assignment in Pakistan.

His job was to be personal pilot for the U.S. ambassador. Brenda and son Chris were soon to follow. Army wives are used to that.

Ellis flew a mission on Nov. 20, 1979. It would be his last. He had the next day off and was in his third-floor apartment at the embassy when the mobs attacked shortly after noon. Brenda was at the international school in Islamabad where Chris was a student.

The first assault on the embassy was minor by terrorist standards. A mob of about 150 jeered and broke the windows in a guard shack near the gate.

But they came back, their ranks swollen to more than 1,000. A few police officers arrived, but they were far too few. The mob took the police officers' guns away and turned them on the besieged Americans.

Soon the horde was inside the embassy grounds. The Americans hastily barricaded the building, and everyone began destroying sensitive documents. They retreated slowly, heading for a third-floor steel vault.

Ellis volunteered to return to the second floor to aid a group of women and children. That group safe, he then volunteered to stay in his room, unprotected by the steel vault walls, and man an observation post in his apartment.

He was on the telephone with an American woman in Rawalpindi, 15 miles away, reporting what was happening. She was in contact with U.S. officials, relaying Ellis' reports.

His last words were, "They're coming to the door."

Then there was a silence. The phone went dead.

Everyone escaped from the vault when Pakistani soldiers landed helicopters on the roof later that day. Chris and Brenda were rescued from the school, and all of the Americans were airlifted to safety.

For a while, they hoped Ellis had escaped and was hiding out. For a time, they even hoped that the body in his fire-gutted apartment was that of a Pakistani rioter. It wasn't.

There was another American killed, too, Marine Cpl. Steven Crowley.

They brought Bryan Ellis home to Swansboro, gave him a military funeral with honors. Jets streaked across the sky, a bugler played "Taps" and an honor guard fired the soldier's last salute.

Brenda got her husband's medals — the Legion of Merit, the Distinguished Flying Cross, the Bronze Star, the Soldier's Medal for Bravery, the Navy Medallion, the Air Medallion and, for giving his life for his nation, the Purple Heart.

Ellis used to sing a song when he flew combat missions: "Nearer My God To Thee." A choir sang it at his funeral.

The Life and Times
of an Urban Redneck

Cherry Grove

There is a drive deep within us all, a drive to somehow, if only for a moment, go home again.

We go back to places we used to live, to see how they have changed, to look at the old house, the old school, the old barn.

Sometimes we make a mistake and take others with us. But it doesn't mean the same to them as it does to us. The present and the future can be shared, but not the past. We must live alone with our past.

I lived on Carl Richardson's farm at Cherry Grove during the mid-1950s. I've been back twice in 25 years, once a hurried visit when they buried Mr. Carl.

Two weeks ago I went back again, alone this time, on a hot Columbus County day.

Names and memories flashed back from mailboxes as I drove the 2½-mile side road that was my world for four years.

There was Tracy's house. Tracy and I both loved a girl named Macey. Everyone thought it was cute that Tracy and Ma-

149

cey, with their rhyming names, were fifth-grade sweethearts. I didn't think it was cute. I was jealous.

There was a pond behind our house. One of the creeks that fed the pond was a favorite nesting place for ducks. One time I shot a duck with a .22 rifle and stood and watched as that duck slowly flapped away its life in the shallow water. I never hunted again.

Linda used to live in a sharecropper's cinder-block house on a sunbaked hill a hundred yards down the road. Linda was the first girl who ever said she loved me, and it was she who made me realize, in a blinding, heart-pounding moment, that girls were not just boys with long hair.

The house where Mr. Carl and Miz Lillie lived is falling in now. Weeds are growing up around it, and it looks so small.

Mr. Carl was one of the last of his kind, a kindly patriarch, a gentleman planter. Time had outgrown that old gentleman, but he didn't pay any attention. I remember his hands being baby smooth, his white hair never ruffled, and he never wore anything but white shirts.

He drove a big Buick from field to field, checking on his crops, holding his beloved granddaughter Dixie on his lap, while Miz Lillie really ran things. Had he lived a hundred years earlier, people would have called him "Colonel."

On my visit, I saw that our little house had been fixed up a lot. The first time I ever saw it, there was hay stored in it. There was no bathroom until Daddy finally put one in.

I saw the spot where our tobacco barn had burned to the ground when lightning struck it one stormy afternoon. A barnful of cured tobacco went up in flames that day, and it was the only time I ever saw my Daddy cry.

The left rear corner of the house was where the propane gas tank used to be, the gas tank I ran into that day when I was 11 or 12 and tried to drive Daddy's Henry J.

Across the road was the tobacco field where I turned over a drag filled with fresh-cropped tobacco because I was pushing the mule too fast. No one would help me clean up that mess because it had been my fault, and I was told I had to learn to be more careful with our life's support.

I remember crying from frustration, anger and shame. But I picked up that tobacco, and I never turned over another drag.

Up a trail was another memory, of the time when a friend and

I fell off a horse, and she broke her arm. I felt guilty for a long time because she had wanted to ride in front and I wouldn't let her.

Other memories came back. I learned to pole a skiff through a swamp on that farm. I remember sitting on a back porch with Miz Lillie one summer day and churning butter by hand; I remember learning that you have to be careful when weeding corn because a good hoe is sharp and young cornstalks are tender; I remember learning to kill tobacco worms by throwing them to the ground; and I remember learning how to tell when green pepper is ripe and how to get eggs from under a hen (very carefully).

Thanks for going home with me again.

Just a Little Off the Top

We approached the building with all the bravado of young swains on their first prom dates, full of bluster to mask the foreboding. We knew the time had come, and there was nowhere to hide.

Until now there had been the possibility of escape, a quick dash through the pines, hit the highway, flip out a thumb and leave all this insanity behind.

But in a very few moments our chances for escape would drop to nil. We'd be marked once we'd had an Army haircut.

There were five chairs in the Fort Jackson, S.C., barbershop, manned by five bruisers who looked, to our scared eyes, like five gorillas — or professional wrestlers.

The 250 of us in D Company, 5th Battalion, 5th Training Regiment ("Delta Five-Five, SIR!") had been awake for what seemed like most of our young lives. Those of us from North Carolina had spent all day Monday being processed like so many sides of fresh meat. We were sworn in as defenders of the flag shortly before 5 p.m. and spent a goodly part of the night riding a clattering train from Raleigh to Columbia, arriving at 3 a.m. Tuesday.

That got us there just in time to pull KP in the biggest, greasiest kitchen in the Western world until about 8 a.m., when we began intelligence testing.

Fresh from 24 hours of no sleep and massive culture shock, we would now be tested to see if we had enough sense to come in out of the rain. I fell asleep taking my test and as a result was assigned to the West Texas desert where it never rains, except for one month of the year, when it floods.

But the testing finally ended that Tuesday afternoon, and we marched off, or as close to marching as a bunch of punchy Carolina farm boys and New Jersey junior Mafia types are likely to do at that stage of their military careers.

We looked like a parade of drunken ducks.

Each of us had saved a really funny, clever joke to pull on the barbers, one they had never heard before. "Just a little off the top," I'll quip and they will all laugh and take pity on me. It seems that the other 249 trained killers in Delta Five-Five had the same idea — and the same joke.

We marched in five at a time. Being part of the group waiting at the door was the worst. In the chair you couldn't see the atrocities being done to your noggin. Standing in the doorway made it hard to ignore.

It was a massacre. There were at least six inches of hair on the floor, a many-colored shag carpet of sorts. There were no mirrors, no cool green tonic awaiting our scaled necks and scalps, just those five bruisers. They got bigger as I waited. Today they are just this side of King Kong.

"Next!" one of them bellowed. Windows shook for miles. Children ran for cover. I wanted to go to the bathroom.

We scurried in, climbed in the chairs and tensed.

"Close your eyes," my barber growled. I did. If he had said, "Stick needles in your nose," I would have done it.

The clippers sounded like a sawmill in overdrive. He placed the clippers at the middle of my forehead and roared backward with the swiftness of Richard Petty at Daytona. It gave me a nifty case of whiplash.

"Sit up straight," he growled. It was getting late, and because he was at "R," time was drawing near when he and his buddies would get off work, drink a case of beer and stomp a pickup truck to death for the fun of it.

The first pass done, he aimed the clippers at my ample ears and swept back again. Hair fell everywhere. This was war, remember, and no Commie-pinko, sissie dropcloths here on Freedom's Frontier.

The whole thing took less than 60 seconds. In one minute my

greasy ducktail was gone, and I had emerged with all the sex appeal of a sickly slug.

Picture a wino with a two-day stubble and you are close. I looked worse.

And then, after getting all 250 of us through there in less than an hour, the rotten Army took our identification pictures.

You want to demoralize a bunch of people in a hurry? Keep them up for a couple of days, take all their clothes away, issue them baggy boxer shorts, shave their heads and yell at them constantly. And then make them pay for the haircut. Works every time.

All of this came back the other day when I read a little story in an out-of-town paper.

"From now on, Army recruits won't have to endure skinhead haircuts and will be treated with the same respect and dignity accorded all soldiers," the Associated Press reported.

It just ain't fair, I thought. Then I realized the catch.

" ...the same respect and dignity accorded all soldiers."

Nothing has changed.

Love Is Fickle and So Are Cars

Every now and then you run across some fellow who tells you, "Yep, been driving this car for 10 years, got over 200,000 miles on it, ain't had to do a thing but grease it twice."

That usually happens when you're busy trying to decide which child to hock to pay the garage bill for the most recent atrocity your car has inflicted on your bank account and emotional well-being.

It has been said that Americans are a people in love with their wheels. If so, then it is probably the most tempestuous love affair since Cleopatra and her asp.

Buying a new car is an instant love affair, easily the equal of a prom date with the dashing quarterback or the perky cheerleader.

You sit there behind the wheel, smelling all that new plastic, no gunk on the windshield, not a ding in the door — it is a time of quiet joy.

You leave the price sticker stuck on the window until it turns brown. As long as it is there, it is still a new car and everyone knows it.

But love is fickle and cars even more so.

I have owned 10 cars in my life. Of those I can say there has been one goody, one possible goody and eight four-wheeled nightmares.

My first car, like my first love, is one I'll never forget. And for the same reasons. They both done me wrong, as the old song goes.

It was a lovely baby-blue Ford, one of the solid ones, or so the greasy salesman said. The plan was to drive the baby-blue dream from North Carolina to West Texas, hauling the four of us across country.

It was a lovely Sunday afternoon when we left. I had owned the car less than 24 hours. We pulled out with great fanfare, the blue baby humming.

It hummed for 75 miles, then it clanked, gasped and rolled to an oily stop.

It took two days in a sleazy motel and three-fourths of the entire travel budget to get on the road again. The next four days were most memorable for the amount of bologna we ate.

But the blue monster wasn't through. We still had to get back from Texas. The return trip was highlighted by four days in an equally sleazy motel in Mississippi while a new engine was installed.

The Ford was replaced by a spiffy little Chevy II that after 18 months was in such bad shape the salesman had to come by my house to look at it before he could tell me how much trade-in he'd give me. I would have gotten more money if I'd spent an afternoon picking up bottles.

Who could ever forget the 1960 Corvair that had plywood floorboards after rust ate through the car? It had a heater that would cook a pot roast faster than a microwave oven but an evil habit of spewing vast amounts of carbon monoxide into the car, so you had to drive with the windows down come snowstorms or rain.

Puffy was the name we gave a green Opel station wagon that once tried to cut off my finger when I closed the back door from the inside. Puffy was lovable and would take you anywhere — at 19 miles an hour — downhill. You had to pack a lunch to drive up a medium hill.

Puffy, however, was most known for her windshield wipers. They worked independently of each other and at different speeds, and then only when you reached under the dash and banged on the motor every half-minute. You haven't lived until you've driven through rush-hour traffic in the rain in my beloved Puffy.

How memories come back. I loved the Spitfire most of all and I'm here to tell you that everything that fell off it was of the very best British workmanship. The wheelbearings made so much noise they sounded like a marching band when we chugged past.

I once owned a Lincoln — for two weeks until the man who sold it to me for $200 came to get it in the company of some very official-looking uniformed Texas cops. They seemed real anxious to get their hands on the car.

But even worse than having a car that's a clunker is having one that is very good, but you hate it.

It was a white 1968 Ford, and Henry never made a more dependable one. It had turned to rust but kept on running like an obsessed politician.

I mean, how can you junk a car, no matter how tired you are of it, when it still works perfectly, even if it does look like something used to haul migrant workers?

But I finally put my sensible nature to rest and traded it in on a car that needed a complete valve job within 48 hours after first we came to be a couple.

I am now driving No. 10. So far it has performed flawlessly. I love it best of all. It gets good gas mileage, looks great, rides well, will haul a lot of stuff.

And it is probably, as these words are being written, crumbling to dust in the parking lot.

She'll Always Be the Baby

For all the babies in all the families, but mostly for Melanie, the baby is mine ...

You've been waiting for today, your 16th birthday, for a long time, and it may come as a surprise to you to know that you're probably the only one who ever really believed it would arrive.

Oh, we all knew in our minds that you would grow up, of course, but deep in our hearts we never really believed the baby of the family would ever be anything else but the baby, the little sister.

The firstborn is often pushed to grow up, sometimes pushed too far, too fast, but it is different with the baby. We want the baby to wait awhile, what's the rush, stay a little girl a little bit longer.

That isn't being fair to you, but when you're the baby of the family, that's the burden you bear. Everyone wants to treat you like a baby forever.

The only ones who ever think being the baby in the family is a soft job are the ones who aren't. They think you've got it made.

You're the baby, they tell you, you're Mama and Daddy's favorite, you can get away with anything. You're spoiled.

But you know that being the baby in the family isn't easy. You're the little sister, tagging along because someone told you to. Watch out for your sister, we order the oldest, she's younger than you. Take your sister along, we tell her, she won't be any trouble.

So the oldest becomes a built-in baby sitter, and the baby becomes a built-in victim.

You were a handy target when your sister was angry at us and there was no one else she could yell at and get away with it. You were a handy target when your sister's friends needed someone to pick on so they'd feel all grown up.

And you were a handy target when your sister's outgrown sweaters and jeans were just too good to throw away.

How you must have resented that, and who could blame you? It must have seemed to you that you didn't have an identity of your own, that you were doomed to go through life being someone's little sister and your Mama and Daddy's baby.

You were the last one to do everything, you got the old bike, the old record player, you got the teachers after your sister had already had them.

When they heard your name at school they'd ask, "Aren't you her sister?"

But to your everlasting credit, you didn't give in to all of that. You remained your own person despite all of us. You were determined to be you, not the younger half of someone else.

We tried not to make comparisons, but we did sometimes, and I know now that must have hurt you. You probably even made some comparisons yourself. I hope you were happy with what you saw. I was.

I wish I could tell you that you won't always be the baby in the family, but in all honesty I can't.

For you represent something special to us. Your sister was our firstborn, with us in the hardest days and she will forever be in our hearts, a living, loving symbol of our beginnings. That's the luck of the draw.

You may marry, you may have children of your own, you may travel the world, but in one little corner of this world, in two hearts, you always will be the baby.

For while your sister was there when we became parents, you were the one who brought that part of our lives to the time and place of change.

So don't blame us if we try to hang on, perhaps longer than we should, if we try to hold onto the joy of family just a little bit longer.

And you aren't spoiled — too much, anyway.

A Clean Man Is Hard to Find

I think I'm in big trouble.

Here it is, the time of the year when man's only hope for survival is to hunker down and wait out the misery of winter, and I am longing for spring.

You remember spring, don't you — flowers and birds twittering and balmy breezes? Remember the way your stomach tingles when the weather is so good you can hardly do anything but stand outdoors in short sleeves? And remember spring cleaning?

I don't care much for blossoms and twittering and breezes and stuff like that, but I am crazy about spring cleaning.

In fact, I love cleaning, period. No, let's be specific here. I love clean. I'd much rather someone else do it, but if they won't, I will, with disgusting eagerness.

I don't think I'm compulsive about my clean fetish. I don't think I'm sick or anything. There are those of my acquaintance and blood who do, but what do they know — they're slobs.

I simply think of myself as very, very tidy.

I love spring cleaning because you get to throw things away.

No one loves to throw things away more than I do. I love having a pile of stuff out by the street or a load of clothes for the Salvation Army box.

There are pack rats reading this who are going into shock, but I think the disposable society is just lovely.

Mostly I like things neat and in their place.

Do not eat slowly when it is my turn to do the dishes. Pick at your food too long or, worse yet, put down your fork for some engaging conversation, and you'll find yourself chasing your plate to the sink, trying to grab the last few morsels before the plate hits the soap.

I am a ton of fun at a party. Don't turn your head and leave a half-full glass of anything within my reach. By the time you finish flirting or whatever, that glass will be in the dishwasher, and the table where once it sat will be polished to a high sheen.

I have been known to make up a bed when the occupant was just going to the bathroom.

I will run a washing machine for two handkerchiefs and last night's socks.

I wear out ashtrays, washing them daily in awfully hot water.

I know where it came from, this urge to be tidy. But a lot of people had the same experience I did, and they came out perfectly normal slobs.

It began in the Army. I figured out the Army right away. No mystery for me.

A tidy soldier got Saturday afternoon off and could go chase women.

A messy soldier had to work on Saturday afternoon and maybe, if lucky, got one beer at the PX.

To me, the choice was simple.

I kept a complete set of six pairs of shorts and T-shirts and socks, never worn, just for inspections of my footlocker.

I had a toothbrush whose only job was to clean imaginary dirt from the bottom of the boots I never wore anyway.

I shined the back of my brass belt buckle. I really did.

Understand this: I am not overly proud of my tidiness, although there is a certain satisfaction to sitting in your spotless abode and silently making fun of other people's houses, but I am far too kind to ever mention it to them.

In fact, if I had my druthers, I'd druther relax and live like my friends, comfortable in what is usually called that "well-lived-in" look.

It doesn't bother me a bit to trip over winter coats in July, grilles in January and litter boxes a year after the cat died. It doesn't bother me a bit — at their house.

Alas, I am trapped, a victim of my own cleanliness. I work far harder than a lazy person should, gripe about others' sloppiness far more than is kindly, but when you get through with the albums, please put each album back in the proper paper sleeve, put it in an album jacket, sleeve opening up to keep dust out.

But I'm getting better; I haven't taken the ashtrays out of my car and run them through the dishwasher in weeks.

A bed unmade after the second cup of coffee, however, still gives me the hives.

Wimping Out in Macho Land

Greenville

I was going to ride that bull.

I said it Tuesday night when I was talking with friends.

I said it Wednesday night when I packed my cowboy boots, my pearl-button shirt and my cowboy belt with the big buckle, along with the jeans and sneakers I normally wear while roaming Down East.

And I sure enough said it when I carefully placed my battered old cowboy hat, the one with the red Willie Nelson bandana hatband, on the front seat beside me.

I kept saying it Wednesday afternoon while I drove to Greenville, listening to country music on the radio the whole way.

I was gonna ride that bull and write about it.

I was sure I was going to ride that bull when I dressed in the motel room Wednesday night. Why else would I take so much time to make sure the jeans were neat, the boots clean, the hat sitting just so on the back of my head?

Why would I take such care experimenting to see how the hat looked best if I weren't going to ride the bull? Standing there in front of that full-length mirror in the motel room, I decided the hat looked best on the back of my head. Too bad it was too dark to wear sunglasses. They looked tough.

There was no doubt I was going to ride that bull as I drove

toward the Carolina Opry House on U.S. 264 just east of Greenville. I already was figuring out how to describe how I rode it
without bragging. Then I decided to go ahead and brag. I was
going to ride the bull, and I wanted the world to know it.

There were a lot of us out there at the Opry House to ride the
bull that Wednesday night, cowboys and cowgirls, duded up like
nobody's business.

I love cowgirls. Give one a pair of designer jeans (no,
cowgirls do not wear everyday jeans), a pearl-button shirt open to
one button below where Mama would allow if she were there, a
pair of high-heel boots and a sassy hat sitting just so on the back
of a curly head, and you've got yourself a picture to remember on
cold nights.

We were there when the place opened, 50 strong, ready to
play cowboys and cowgirls, and ride that bull.

It's a big place — seats 700, someone said, although rumor
has it that nearer to a thousand have crowded in on weekends.

You don't sit around in cowboy country. You pose. Remember
how the outlaws stood at the bar, mean-looking, casual, ready to
reach for a six-gun or a shot of red-eye whiskey?

I had it down pat. Hands in back pockets look sharp.

Finally, I went in search of the bull I was going to ride, that
mechanical beast from "Urban Cowboy." I found it, just beyond
the ladies' room, down some steep steps.

The bull sits in a corral, surrounded by padding.

Cowboys and cowgirls stand around the corral fence, beer in
one hand, elbows on the fence, seeing who'll be next.

I figured I might as well be next. It was time to ride the bull. I
was ready.

Then they turned that sucker on. It has four speeds, with
settings of three, five, seven and 10. I figured I'd try seven.

The first cowboy up asked for seven. A ride lasts eight seconds. The cowboy lasted three, dumped on his blue-jeaned behind
to the catcalls of the cowboys and cowgirls around the corral.

Then the second cowboy got up. He had red hair. He asked for
a setting of 10, wide open and let 'er rip.

About halfway through his ride, he turned loose both hands
and rode until it stopped. The crowd cheered.

I'm going to ride that bull, I told myself.

No you ain't, myself said back. You're going to get out of here alive tonight.

There are worse things than busting your head, myself said. For instance, you can get out there and make a fool of yourself in Macho Land. That's worse, isn't it?

I had to agree, especially when a woman rode it to a stop on seven and then her boyfriend was dumped on five.

I walked back up those steps by the ladies' room, one of the thousands who were going to ride that bull — until they saw it.

Life sure is rugged for a macho man.

Hot Wheels in the Slow Lane

Technology began, it can be argued, when the wheel was invented.

And in all likelihood the wheel will be the death of mankind.

Which is poetic justice, I suppose; the one invention that did the most will end up doing us all in.

Those weighty philosophical thoughts are brought to you courtesy of the pain that is racking my frail little body today.

And it is the wheel's fault.

There were eight wheels in all, four on each skate. At one time, I could have sworn that all eight of them were going in different directions.

This latest discovery began one Thursday night when my eldest and I decided to "do something."

"How about a movie?" she suggested.

"Nah, going to a movie isn't doing something," I foolishly said. "That's just sitting there. Let's do something."

I'm such a simpleton. I should have chosen a movie.

We decided the thing to spice up a Thursday night was to go roller-skating.

It is funny how good that sounded sitting in the living room.

I had tried roller-skating only one time before, 10 years ago. It was not my finest hour. I took one spill that was so jarring that my hip pocket ended up about even with my ear.

Skates in hand for another try, I did fine getting them laced on. Then I tried to stand up. I found that if you turn around, get on your knees and slowly unfold you can reach a standing position.

Then all you have to do is walk — not roll, walk — to the rink — with eight wheels on your feet, while around you whiz those detestable little crumb snatchers who love to yell "Watch out!" as you career your way to the rink, lunging at the last second to grasp the railing.

I finally reached the rink. There I stood, holding onto the railing like a man terrified.

"How do you start these things?" I asked myself.

I leaned forward. Then I started to fall, saved only by my friend, the railing.

I tried to push on my left skate. My right skate went out from under me.

I decided the only prudent thing was to pull along the railing. That worked. At least I was moving.

I was moving straight toward the wall and a cute little blond child of about 6 who was doing tricks.

She'll be fine — someday — when the swelling goes down.

Slowly but surely I began to figure it out. Eventually, I was actually skating. I called it skating. Everyone else called it hilarious.

"Relax," said the skating pro.

Relax? I'm getting ready to fall on the hardest floor known to man and this yahoo is telling me to relax?

I never actually fell. There was that one time when I creamed another kid, ricocheted off him into the wall and grabbed the trusty railing just in time, but I didn't fall. The kid shouldn't get in my way, I tried to explain, but you just can't communicate with a 3-year-old with terror in his eyes.

I got very thirsty doing this. I saw where they had put the snack bar and headed in that direction. Then I realized that to slake my thirst I had to skate across an open floor — no railing — buy a drink and skate back to a table, drink in hand.

I made it to the door, anyway.

Then I stuck my head in and yelled, as plaintively as I could, "Do y'all deliver?"

By evening's end, I actually did skate around the rink a couple of dozen times. It wasn't pretty, but by the end of the night I could yell "Look out!" and you've never seen people get out of the way so fast.

Now I'm trying to learn how to walk again.

Nice Guys Finish Last, as Usual

Rose Hill

Everyone who knows me or has followed this column for any time at all knows what a humble man I am, how I never brag on myself, how much I hate fame and the spotlight.

So I find it difficult to explain just how brilliant I really was in this year's Duplin Wine Cellars third annual Grape Stomping Championship in Rose Hill.

Let's put it this way: I was fantastic.

Rarely in the annals of sport has there been such an exhibition of grape pounding.

And what did I get for my troubles? How did the wine-makers treat my championship form with respect? Did I get what was coming to me?

Probably.

All I can say is this: I won, fair and square, no tricks, no con, just flat-out foot power, and I do not have a trophy.

Other people have trophies. Other people got bottles of champagne. Other people were congratulated.

For the third year in a row, I was humiliated.

What I ended up with was splinters in my toes and bruises on my feet.

I knew something was up when I arrived, decked out in my finest garb, trying to bring a little class to Duplin County. The first thing I saw was my nemesis, the bare-chested Zorro.

Zorro, or someone dressed in his costume, stole my trophy last year after I won the stomp.

This year was to be a grudge match, me and Zorro, "mano a mano," the Spanish say, may the most macho win.

The official results were that I stomped 2 ¼ inches of grape juice in two minutes. Zorro managed a miserable 1 ½ inches.

He was embarrassed, as well he should have been. When last seen, he was sneaking off on foot. I think his horse even abandoned him.

I beat Sherry Jones, Miss Duplin County. I beat Cynthia Gentry, Miss Poultry Jubilee. I beat Jo Carol Jones of The Goldsboro News-Argus. I beat Lou Griffin of WWAY-TV. I even beat Charlene Simmons, a paratrooper's wife.

While news reports said that one Robert Crawford won the

main event, that isn't the way it really happened. Crawford stomped 1 ¾ inches of juice. Good for amateurs, but not even close to what the pros can do.

I thought that maybe this year David Fussell, who runs the place, would do the decent thing and let me enjoy my victory and the plaudits of the 1,500 people who gathered to watch.

But no, not Fussell.

There I stood, basking in my rightful glory, when out of the sky came four skydivers. The crowd thought it was part of the show. I knew I had been had again.

I watched with growing fear as they drifted to the ground.

One of them was this big, ugly, mean-looking dude, a sergeant in the 82nd Airborne Division.

Him I could have handled. The black .45 in his hand convinced me otherwise.

This cowardly paratrooper ran up, grabbed my trophy at gunpoint and scampered away, staying just long enough to crush my foot when I tried to sneak up behind him and reswipe my trophy.

I know sneaking isn't manly. Neither is talking to a .45.

So it is over for another year. Class won, as usual, but deviousness cannot be overcome without resorting to trickery, violence and large bodyguards.

So that's what I plan to do next year.

No more Mr. Nice Guy.

A Small Bite of the Big Apple

New York

You know those crosswalks in the middle of the block, the ones where drivers are supposed to — and usually do — stop and let pedestrians cross?

I'd like to see them try that in New York City.

The result would be pedestrians bouncing about the city like human pinballs.

This is not a city gushing with the milk of human kindness.

Don't let anyone kid you. New York is different. It is not just spectacularly huge; it is alien to everything most of us have seen, heard or done.

You can hear half a dozen languages while you wait for

breakfast in an ordinary midtown coffee shop.

You can walk out of Tiffany's on Fifth Avenue, among the most famous jewelry stores in the world on one of the ritziest streets in the world, and find men hawking hot designer clothes from the trunks of battered heaps parked bumper to bumper with gleaming limousines.

New York is bigger, brighter, noisier and flashier. It is a city of exquisite beauty, of stirring theater, of breathtaking architecture — a city where everything is for sale, and the sidewalks are the best show in town.

New York is a city of people running in a psychological maze, winding their confusing ways past uniformed butlers walking tiny little beribboned dogs just a handful of blocks from poverty so crushing that the buildings look as if they were bombed.

A first visit to New York begins with a careening, high-speed, throat-tightening taxi ride through some of the worst traffic in the nation, often develops into well-justified paranoia at the strangeness of the characters loose on the streets and ends with admiration for New Yorkers.

If you can survive living in New York — not set the world on fire and make the cover of People magazine, just go about the simple business of living — you can survive anywhere.

They plant bombs in New York. One killed a teenager at JFK airport the Saturday morning my friend and I arrived at LaGuardia. By Monday, they found four more bombs around the city, and there had been hundreds of bomb scares.

By Wednesday, it wasn't news anymore. The city had been captivated by a beauty queen caught padding her bra.

A gang of young toughs walked up to a middle-aged stranger in the subway not three blocks from our hotel and fired a bullet into his brain for no reason. A car racing down a Harlem street ran into four people in front of a candy store and killed them instantly. Neither event made the front page.

Three blocks away from that subway stop, a theater audience was brought to tears when an actress dramatically shook hands with an actor during a touching scene.

There is a shell around New Yorkers — a shell that at first meeting seems like rudeness, but it isn't. It is armor, a psychological defense to block out what is going on around them.

There is no private place in the city. It is jammed all the time, so the only way to have space is to create it inside, to find solitude in the mob by ignoring it.

The thousands of people walking the streets with headset radios — and you see them everywhere — are not following a fad. They are trying to survive by making their own sound track.

If you let yourself care about what is around you, if you open yourself completely to the asylum, you will go crazy. There is simply too much of it to let in, too many sensations screaming for your attention.

My friend summed it all up well. It is like living on the midway at the State Fair, he said.

It is fun. But sooner than you expected, you are ready to go home.

Sometimes Dreams Come True

Wilson

She was the prettiest girl in school — everybody said that. "Senior Superlatives" they called that section of the yearbook and there she was, voted Best Looking. It wasn't even a close race.

He was a poor kid from the side of town where there were more calluses than Cadillacs.

They had never been friends. There were too many miles between them, but with the luck of the alphabet, he had sat just behind her in high school.

She was more than just a pretty girl. She was everything he dreamed about — blond, smooth-skinned and a winning smile. She was Galatea to his Pygmalion.

He would think about her often as the years went on. When the guys would tell stories in those drafty barracks on the other side of the world, he would tell them of the prettiest girl he ever knew. They'd laugh at his enthusiasm; no one was that pretty. But she was, and he knew it.

He never touched her, never asked her for a date, never asked her to dance. He couldn't remember one conversation they ever had.

That wasn't the part she was to play in his life. She was not to be a real flesh-and-blood woman, she was to be only a dream, a shining moment of perfection.

They would go in different directions, their paths never to cross. But the dream never faded. Sometimes, walking down a city street or sitting at a traffic light, he would see a woman and think of her, wondering what had become of the prettiest girl in school.

She drifted back into his thoughts two months ago when he got a letter. The high school class was getting together, the letter said, for a 20th anniversary reunion.

She was the first person he thought of. What would she be like now? She would be 38, a dangerous time. She could be fat or wrinkled or graying. She could be hard now, embittered at life. She could be anything. But could she still be the prettiest girl in school?

He made plans to go to the reunion. There were friends he wanted to see, old times he wanted to relive. And he wanted very much to see her.

He got there early, dry-mouthed, nervous, wondering what it would be like. Going to a class reunion, he thought, is like looking in a mirror. You can pretend with other people, but not with class-mates. They show you how old you are.

She wasn't there when he arrived. He mingled for a while, laughing at the old yearbook pictures they wore as name tags, making jokes about who had hair and who didn't. And wasn't it amazing there were already two grandmothers and only one death after 20 years?

He saw her name tag on the table. She had registered to come but hadn't arrived. He joked about her to his friends of long ago. Many of them had felt the same way about the prettiest girl in school, but only he would admit it.

He was sitting, eating barbecue, when she stood in front of him.

Some people had come up to him that night and he'd had to sneak a peek at their name tags to remember them, but not her.

He knew her instantly; that face that had lived in his memory for 20 years was there again.

She was more beautiful than ever.

He felt great joy knowing that. His dreams had been real; she really was the prettiest girl in school. It would have been sad for that beauty to have faded.

He grinned, a 16-year-old grin, and didn't take another bite of food. He was mesmerized.

Later that night, a warm, sultry evening of loud laughter and "hey, do you remember," he walked up to where she was standing and asked her to dance.

The song was perfect, "Three Times a Lady," and as he held her in his arms she fit just the way he always knew she would.

She knew how he felt; he and others had told her, laughing about it. She looked up at him and smiled as they danced. It seemed to make her happy, too.

The others gave them room as they danced. He had never danced with more grace. It was so easy with her in his arms.

Some people took pictures of them as they danced; it became a time to remember for all of them.

The music ended all too soon and he walked her back to where her husband so patiently waited.

"Thank you, Priscilla," he said. "It was lovely."

He didn't stop smiling all the way home.

It Was Good
to Hear From You

This came in the mail over Christmas. But I lost the envelope, so I haven't the foggiest notion from whom or what the original source was. So, to the person who sent it, thanks.

It is called, "How to know you're getting old":

Everything hurts, and what doesn't hurt, doesn't work.

The gleam in your eyes is from the sun hitting your bifocals.

You feel like the morning after, and you didn't go anywhere the night before.

Your little black book contains only names ending in M.D.

You get winded playing chess.

Your children begin to look middle-aged.

You finally reach the top of the ladder and find it leaning against the wrong wall.

You join a health club and don't go.

You decide to procrastinate but then never get around to it.

Your mind makes contracts your body can't meet.

A dripping faucet causes an uncontrollable bladder urge.

You know all the answers, but no one ever asks you the questions.

You look forward to a dull evening.

Your favorite part of the newspaper is 25 Years Ago Today.

You turn out the light for economic rather than romantic reasons.

You sit in a rocking chair and can't get it going.

Your knees buckle and your belt won't.

You regret all those mistakes resisting temptation.

You're 17 around the neck, 42 around the waist and 96 around the golf course.

You stop looking forward to your next birthday.

Dialing long-distance wears you out.

You remember today that yesterday was your wedding anniversary.

You just can't stand people who are intolerant.

The best part of your day is over when the alarm clock goes off.

You begin burning the midnight oil at 9 p.m.

Your back goes out more than you do.

A fortune teller offers to read your face.

Your pacemaker makes the garage door go up when a pretty girl walks by.

You get your exercise acting as a pallbearer for your friends who do exercise.

You have too much room in the house and not enough in the medicine cabinet.

You sink your teeth into a steak, and they stay there.

● ● ●

These are making the rounds at Raleigh's Broughton High School. They are said to be reasons bad drivers give to insurance companies after their inevitable bang-ups:

"Coming home I drove into the wrong house and collided with a tree I don't have."

"The other car collided with mine without giving warning of its intentions."

"I collided with a stationary truck coming the other way."

"The truck backed through my windshield into my wife's face."

"The guy was all over the road and I had to swerve a number of times before I hit him."

"A pedestrian hit me and went under my car."

"In my attempt to kill a fly I drove into a telephone pole."

"I pulled away from the side of the road, glanced at my mother-in-law and headed over the embankment."

"I had been driving for 40 years when I fell asleep at the wheel and had an accident."

"To avoid hitting the bumper of the car in front of me, I hit the pedestrian."

"I was on my way to the doctor with rear-end trouble when my universal joint gave way, causing me to have an accident."

"My car was legally parked as it backed into the vehicle."

"I had been shopping for plants all day and was on my way home. As I reached the intersection, a hedge sprang up, obscuring my vision. I did not see the other car."

● ● ●

Melanie Heath is a teenager, but a special kind.

Most teenage girls, and I claim some authority in that area being the father of two of the breed, take themselves very seriously, especially in the presence of adults.

But not Melanie, a 13-year-old student at East Cary Junior High.

Melanie has put together a list of some clues to teenage behavior, and I've added a comment or so of my own.

According to Melanie, you know your daughter is a teenager when:

All telephone calls are for her (and she screams "I've got it!" every time it rings).

She has nothing new to wear to school, and you just spent $50 on clothes for her.

You drive up in the driveway, and her windows are open and the radio is blaring — and it is 35 degrees outside.

You find yourself becoming a taxi service.

Her room is a disaster, seven days a week.

You find her writing in her diary (and hiding it when you come in).

She is doing her homework at 10 p.m.

You find ice cream bowls, potato chip bags and candy wrappers under her bed.

She reads love stories instead of science fiction.

You check the pockets of her dirty jeans and find gossipy notes.

She is on the phone six hours a day (usually whispering about boys).

She starts watching soap operas.

You find that most of the clothes she wears are yours.

You find her spending more time on her hair (and trying every brand of shampoo sold).

You have to get her up 30 minutes sooner so she can put on makeup and curlers.

She stops sleeping with her stuffed cat (except when things go wrong).

She gets a fancy calendar (and fills it with cryptic notes).

Her jeans just have to be washed and dried tonight so she can wear them tomorrow.

She wears braces (and doesn't complain).

She does not wear socks with dresses.

She takes an hour in the shower.

She smells like a flower garden instead of an old tennis shoe.

She wants a one-piece bathing suit.

She is on a diet one day and off the next (one of mine drinks diet drinks with doughnuts).

She has three things in her life — partying, grades and boys (mostly boys).

She paints her toenails.

She stops watching "Captain Kangaroo" (and laughs at "Mister Rogers' Neighborhood").

She starts bringing boys over to meet you (and refuses to discuss them a week later).

She stops getting homesick.

And most of all, she finally figures out why God made parents.

● ● ●

A Greensboro friend sent this along the other day.

You know it's going to be a bad day when:

You wake up face down on the pavement.

You put your bra on backward and it fits better.

You call Suicide Prevention and they put you on hold.

You see a "60 Minutes" crew waiting in your office.

Your birthday cake collapses from the weight of the candles.

You want to put on the clothes you wore home from the party, and there aren't any.

You turn on the TV news and they're showing evacuation routes out of the city.

The woman you've been seeing on the side begins to look like your wife.

Your twin sister forgets your birthday.

You wake up to discover that the water bed broke and then you realize you don't have a water bed.

Your horn goes off accidentally and remains stuck as you follow a group of Hell's Angels off the interstate.

Your wife wakes up feeling amorous and you have a headache.

• • •

Alex MacFadyen, who gave the world the slogan, "If God is not a Tar Heel, why's the sky Carolina Blue," passed these along. They purport to be excerpts of correspondence received by social services departments across the country:

"Please send me my elopement as I have a 4-month-old baby, and he is my only support. I need all I can get every day to buy food and keep him close."

"Both sides of my parents is poor and I can expect nothing from them as my mother has been in bed one year with the same doctor and won't change."

"Please send me a letter and tell me if my husband has made application for a wife and baby."

"I can't get my pay. I got six children. Can you tell me why this is?"

"Sir, I am forwarding my marriage license and my two children. One is a mistake, as you can see."

"Please find out for certain if my husband is dead as the man I am living with can't eat or do anything until he knows for sure."

"I am annoyed to find that you branded my two children illiterate. Oh, the shame of it. It's a dirty lie, as I married their father a week before they were born."

"I have no children as my husband was a truck driver and worked day and night when he wasn't sleeping."

"You have changed my little boy into a little girl. Does that make any difference?"

"In accordance with your instructions, I have given birth to twins in the enclosed envelope."

"I am glad to say that my husband who has been reported missing is now dead."

"Unless I get my husband's money quickly, I will be forced to lead an immortal life."

"I want my money as quickly as I can get it. I've been in bed with the doctor for two weeks and he doesn't seem to be doing me much good. If things don't improve, I will have to send for another doctor."

"I am a poor widow and all I have is in the front."

"My husband had his project cut off two weeks ago and I haven't had any relief since."

●　●　●

Susan Giles of Roanoke Rapids sent this along from the April issue of Farm Wife:

"You know you're in a small town when:

"Third Street is at the edge of town.

"Every sport is played on dirt.

"The editor and publisher of the newspaper carries a camera at all times.

"You don't use your turn signal because everyone knows where you are going.

"You are born on June 13 and your family receives gifts from the local merchants because you are the first baby of the year.

"You speak to each dog you pass by name and he wags at you.

"You dial a wrong number and talk for 15 minutes anyway.

"You are run off the main street by a combine.

"You can't walk for exercise because every car that passes offers you a ride.

"You get married and the local paper devotes a quarter page to the story.

"You drive into the ditch five miles out of town and the word gets back to town before you do.

"The biggest business in town sells farm machinery.

"You write a check on the wrong bank and it covers it for you.

"The pickups on Main Street outnumber the cars 3 to 1.

"You miss a Sunday at church and receive a get-well card.

"Someone asks how you feel and then listens to what you say."

Footprints in Time

Davis

There comes a time in the human experience when trying hard isn't enough, when all your faith in self-reliance becomes meaningless, when no matter what you do the cards are stacked against you.

Life has never been easy for the fishermen and their families in this town that sits on a comma-shaped peninsula hanging down into Core Sound.

It is a place of hard work; the sea does not give up its bounty without a struggle. And when you live by the good graces of nature, you die when nature chooses.

They've been here a long time, these men and women who take their living from the sea. They have had gardens, grappled shellfish from the bottom, hauled their heavy nets from the gray water and killed wildfowl to vary their diet.

But in the winter of 1898, it all came to naught. The people of Davis almost died that winter. Were it not for a remarkable demonstration of faith, a desperate act by desperate men, Davis would have been nothing more than a memory.

The story is an old one, preserved by Mary and Grayden Paul, the wonderful storytellers of Carteret County:

Winter came early in 1898; at the time it was the coldest year ever recorded. There was a depression that had lasted for years, and people were going hungry. But as long as the sea was there, the people could survive.

Food ran short that winter, the wild birds went away, and it got colder and colder.

Ice began to form on the edges of Core Sound, slowly encircling the people of Davis in its chilling grip. Boats could not get out; they were trapped. Many people were sick that awful year, and some starved.

Finally, Core Sound was frozen solid all the way to the Outer Banks. Life was in peril.

There were several black families living near Davis who were led by Uncle Mose Davis. Uncle Mose, fearing for all the people, suggested that a community prayer meeting was in order.

Everyone well enough to leave his home met on the frozen banks of Oyster Creek. The men removed their hats, and all bowed their heads. Uncle Mose started to pray.

"Oh, Lord, we're gathered here to ask you to help us out of our troubles," Grayden Paul recorded, and his father and grandfather were there that day. "We've done everything we can for ourselves and unless you do something to help us, we are all gonna starve to death. Amen."

Suddenly, before another simple prayer could be lifted, someone looked toward Core Banks, a few miles across the frozen sound.

There was a slender column of smoke, reaching high into the winter sky, a common signal for help. There were people in trouble on the Banks.

Some said the men of Davis must go to help; others argued out that no boat could get through the ice and that only a fool would walk across and take a chance on falling through the ice to certain death.

Everyone looked at Uncle Mose. He said quietly: "Fellows, you ought to be ashamed of yourselves. We came here to ask God to help us, and we're not willing to help someone else."

So the desperate fishermen of Davis, spurred on by the gentle black man, took a 20-foot boat and tied three lines to the bow. Three men tied the lines around their waists and began slowly walking out onto the ice, pulling the skiff behind them.

The ice was thick enough, and they made it all the way to Core Banks.

When the men crossed the top of the sand dunes, they saw seamen gathered by a fire. Out on the shoals was their wrecked ship.

On that ship was a cargo of molasses and grain, a salvaged cargo that fed the people of Davis and saved their lives.

The people of Davis survived that dreadful time because of their willingness to risk their own already-threatened lives to save someone else. That, and faith and an old black man who prayed for all of them.

To Love a Memory

Whiteville

You just can't beat a good love story, and this is a goody.

It is the love story of Simms Memory and Memory Simms and how it came to be that Memory Simms became Memory Memory and how they lived happily ever after:

Thomas Memory was a successful Whiteville merchant in the years before the Civil War. Each year he traveled to New York on a buying trip, and on one of his trips he met Thomas Simms, a merchant from Atlanta.

The men became friends on the train heading north. There were no dining cars on the trains in those days, and Memory shared his larder of country ham with Simms. The men decided to combine their buying power and get lower prices, and for several years thereafter they made trips together.

On one trip, the men discovered that each was due to be a father when they got home. They decided that if one had a girl and the other a boy the children would marry each other when they grew up. Friends do that sort of thing, but no one really expects it to happen.

When Thomas Memory got home to Whiteville he found he had a son. He gleefully wrote to Thomas Simms: "I found in my home a wee boy when I came, and I have been pleased to give him your name. Simms Memory we call him, so do not forget, that while Memory lives I remember you yet.''

And, wouldn't you know it, when Simms got home to Atlanta he found he had a girl. He wrote to Memory: "I, too, found in my home a wee girl when I came, and how do you care for the little girl's name? Emily Memory is her name and I give her to you, for the bride of Simms Memory if Memory is true.''

So in North Carolina we have Simms Memory and in Georgia we have Memory Simms, promised by their fathers to each other.

Both children heard the story, and as each grew up they wondered what the other was like. But they didn't meet for a long time.

A warm exchange of letters began after the death of Thomas Simms, and in December 1877, Simms Memory got on a train and went to Atlanta to finally meet Memory Simms.

They tried to trick Simms Memory when he got to Atlanta. One by one, the Simms sisters, dressed in their prettiest frocks, came into the room where he waited. They wanted to see whether he could pick out Memory.

But as each girl came in and smiled at him, he said, "No, you are not Memory, you must be her sister.''

Finally, a little slip of a girl in a gingham dress came in a side door, and he spotted her watching him. He knew right off it was Memory.

He fell deeply in love during his week in Atlanta, and on the last day of his visit got up enough nerve to ask her to marry him.

She refused at first, telling him to go back to North Carolina and wait for six weeks to make sure he was marrying her for love and not to fulfill the silly promise their fathers had made.

Simms Memory tried to do that, but as soon as he got home he ordered a ring from Baltimore and wrote a letter to Memory. He spent the next week watching the mail from Baltimore and the mail from Atlanta until he ran the family crazy and his daddy told him to go back to Atlanta and get his precious Memory Simms.

He did just that, and on Jan. 29, 1878, in a church lit by candlelight, Simms Memory married Memory Simms.

They came back to Whiteville and lived together for 45 years. Memory, a talented musician, played the organ for the Baptist church, and Simms played the fiddle at her side.

Memory passed away in 1923. Simms lived to be 92 years old,

dying Jan. 29, 1948, the day that would have been their 70th anniversary.

Today their graves are side by side in Whiteville Memorial Cemetery.

Fifty Cents and a Dream

Durham

He was the son of a simple farmer, the eighth of 10 children. There would be no family inheritance to help the boy they called Wash.

So Wash did what he had to do. He knew farming but had no farm of his own. He became a sharecropper, working another's land for a share of the profit.

He married at 22. His wife, Mary, was not wealthy, but inherited land when her father died five years later.

Just when it seemed they had it made, just after they got her father's land, Mary died, leaving Wash alone to raise their two sons.

Wash was 27. He worked hard to make a go of it. He made a little money, and, within five years of Mary's death, he had 300 acres. He decided to get married again, this time to a lady named Artelia.

Those were good times. Soon there would be three more children to help on the farm. But it was not to last.

They had been married for six years when tragedy struck. First, the oldest son came down with typhoid fever. Artelia took it upon herself to nurse the young boy back to health, but the fever got her, too. Both his oldest son and his second wife died.

Once again Wash was without a wife. War came three years later, a war that Wash opposed. Not only did he oppose the war, but his sympathies were with the people his neighbors were fighting against.

Fate can be ironic sometimes, and it was at its ironic best when Wash, at 43, was drafted to go fight, not only in a war he opposed but on the side he opposed. The war also took one of his sons, the three other children being sent to a relative to be raised.

His military service was brief. He spent most of the time as a prisoner of war, suffering silently and wondering what had happened to the son who was drafted with him.

When the war ended, Wash was sent packing. He was nearly broke and had to walk 135 miles to his home near Durham. He arrived home with 50 cents in his pocket.

His farm, neglected for two years, was in shambles. He was 45, and he had buried two wives. It is hard to imagine anyone being further from the top than Wash.

But in 25 years Wash would be one of the most powerful men in America. He would be wealthy beyond anyone's dreams.

His full name was Washington Duke, as in Duke University, as in Duke Power Co., as in American Tobacco Co.

Just saying that doesn't really touch on just how big the Duke influence really was. American Tobacco Co. was made up of four other companies — the original W. Duke and Sons, Liggett and Myers, P. Lorillard and R.J. Reynolds. In modern terms, it would be as if one family controlled General Motors, Ford and Chrysler. At one time Buck Duke, Washington's son, controlled more than 80 percent of the smoking tobacco sold in the world.

And it all came from that first 50 cents that Wash Duke had in his pocket — after serving the losing cause of the Confederate states — when the Civil War ended.

The Duke fortune began on what is now called the Duke Homestead, 45 acres of land just outside Durham. It is now a state historic site and slowly is being put back in its original condition, when Washington and his children were working in outbuildings on the farm, perfecting the techniques of tobacco processing that would soon take them to the top.

Hangman in the Rain

Nashville

It rained hard that day. The sky was so dark the chickens went to roost.

It was March 15, 1900, the Ides of March, and the perfect setting for Nash County's last public hanging.

John Henry Taylor said the day before he died that his mother used to tell him he'd either die on the gallows or spend his life in the penitentiary. Mama knew her boy well.

Taylor was a small-time chicken thief and burglar. On the eve of his death, he said: "I have always been considered a mean boy. I was determined not to work for my living if I could help it.''

In November 1899, John Henry Taylor shot a man in Norfolk, Va., after an argument over a girl. It was his first killing.

A few days later, he robbed and killed a merchant seaman for $11, a silver watch and a hawk-bill knife, and dumped his body in the harbor.

He fled from Norfolk with a friend, Robert Fortune. In Weldon on Dec. 18, 1899, they spotted Lawrence Jackson leaving a small store. They followed him out of town, sneaked up behind him and shot him twice in the back. They got $4.85 and left Jackson to die.

Taylor and Fortune then traveled to Rocky Mount, where on Dec. 21 they spotted Robert Hester in a tobacco warehouse and, mistakenly thinking he was a rich farmer named Bob Ricks, plotted to kill him.

They waited by a bridge outside town. When Hester came by walking home, they stopped him and asked for change for a dollar.

When Hester opened his pocketbook, Fortune fired. Between them, Taylor and Fortune shot Hester four times — the last time after he threw them his money and pleaded: ''Have mercy on me. Don't shoot me anymore.''

Hester identified his assailants before he died. Taylor and Fortune also were identified by a 12-year-old boy who saw the shooting. They were arrested almost immediately.

Small groups of men began discussing the slaying in the Rocky Mount bars that afternoon, and a lynch mob soon was demanding that the two young men be handed over. But Sheriff Willis Warren had moved them to Raleigh for safekeeping.

Taylor and Fortune were found guilty and sentenced to be hanged.

The gallows arrived by train in Nashville a few days before the hanging. People gathered to watch the sheriff test the works. Everything was satisfactory.

The crowd started arriving at daylight March 15, 1900. A special train was chartered from Rocky Mount, and it was so full that flatcars with temporary bleachers were used to transport the morbidly curious.

When 1 p.m. — the appointed hour of death — rolled around, 35,000 people were in Nashville, the largest crowd to ever gather there.

People were packed around a 50-foot enclosure surrounding the gallows. When Taylor and Fortune were brought from their cell, 50 guards with shotguns protected them.

Fortune stood on the right, Taylor on the left. The crowd was silent. There was no sound but that of falling rain. Witnesses said the two men seemed composed.

Taylor and Fortune confessed on the gallows, and Taylor added: "Friends, I am now on the gallows to leave this world to go home to rest, to live with Jesus. You may hang me and stretch my neck, but you can't hurt my soul. Myself and Robert killed Mr. Hester, but I would not confess until God forced it out of me. I have no harm against anyone and want you all to meet me in heaven because I'm going to live with Jesus where I will never die but live always. Goodbye to everybody."

There was one shout from the crowd that ugly day. As Taylor ended his gallows confession, a man yelled out: "You ain't going to heaven; you're going to hell where you belong."

Sheriff Warren then placed a black hood over each man's head, tied it around the neck, stepped back, paused for a moment and pulled the lever.

Taylor took four minutes and 45 seconds to die. Fortune lasted for nine minutes.

The ropes were collected and cut into small pieces, which sold for 25 cents each.

Every scrap was bought.

Buster Brown and That Blasted Dog

Roxboro

"I'm Buster Brown, I live in a shoe. He's my dog Tige, he lives in there, too."

He was a yellow-haired lad with a Dutch boy suit and a lovable bulldog who gazed down at us from the walls of shoe stores, the advertising campaign of the Brown Shoe Co. of St. Louis. He was the perfect lad with his perfect pup, everything our mothers wanted us to be.

I hate to destroy your childhood memories, but Buster Brown loathed Tige. He often referred to him as "that blasted dog."

In fact, Buster Brown despised Tige so much that he quit

advertising shoes to run a service station.

Buster Brown was portrayed during the 1920s by Jack Barnett, one-half of the famous Barnett midgets from Roxboro. In their time they were one of the hottest acts in show business, starring with the Barnum and Bailey Circus and traveling the big-city vaudeville circuit. Herbert Barnett appeared in a George M. Cohan Broadway musical called "Little Nelly Kelly" in 1922.

Jack was born in 1891 and grew to 37 inches. Herbert, who often played female parts or appeared as Jack's son, was born in 1898 and grew to only 26 inches.

Together they toured the world. For 14 years they were with the circus, becoming one of the biggest draws under the big tent. Finally they were persuaded to leave the circus and for many years played the vaudeville houses.

They were written about everywhere they went. They were a personable pair — talented and friendly — and they knew how to get headlines. Had there been a People magazine, they would have been on the cover. Some of the tales about them were a press agent's dream.

In Milwaukee, Captain Jack, as he was called, was arrested by a traffic cop who saw a car go by with only two eyes peeking over the dash. The judge gave the small man a small fine, $1.

Another time they were in Chicago doing some Christmas shopping when, in the midst of a crowd, a woman grabbed Herbert's hand — thinking she had the hand of her son — and plunged into the mob of shoppers. It all ended after Herbert and Jack ran amok through scantily dressed women in the woman's clothing department, trying to find each other in a sea of knees.

They tell a story in Roxboro of the day that Herbert "robbed" the Thompson Insurance Agency. He marched in and stood before the high counter, which made him impossible to see by the clerk on the other side, and held a toy gun high above his head and demanded in a growl, "Give me your money." The clerk looked down and saw nothing but a gun waving at her and gave a scream, whereupon Herbert broke into gales of laughter and gave himself away.

The pair ended their act about 1920, and Jack signed on as Buster Brown, touring the country hustling shoes. He got so fed up with the dog playing Tige that he left in a huff and returned to Roxboro to run a service station.

Herbert, after a fling on Broadway, became the Meditation

Kid, crackerjack salesman and advertising symbol of the Meditation Cigar Co.

Jack married a 5-foot-8-inch showgirl and circus performer named Dorothy Warsfield and they had a normal-size son named Jack Jr.

Herbert never married, but he had a reputation as something of a ladies' man. With his big cigar, gold-headed cane, diamond ring and fancy suits, he was often surrounded by several comely lasses on his daily jaunts along the streets of Roxboro.

They did not live long. Herbert died in 1933 and Jack in 1936, both of heart attacks.

I keep thinking of an old cliche, one that goes: "When life hands you a lemon, make lemonade."

The Pirate Died Hard

It has been 261 years since he died, a death he well deserved, but to this day the legend lives on.

North Carolina is a state of legends — the Lowery gang down in Robeson County; Tom Dula, the Tom Dooley of folk-music fame; the lost colony of Roanoke Island. But when all is said and done, it is Blackbeard who still shivers our timbers.

Born Edward Teach in Bristol, England, he achieved fame as a privateer, in reality a hired gun for the queen. He robbed, or was supposed to rob, only Spanish ships.

Living up to writer Hunter Thompson's theory that when the going gets weird, the weird turn pro, Blackbeard, a name he gave himself, decided he'd rob whom he bloody well pleased. And he set out to do just that.

Part truth and part fiction, Blackbeard was the meanest of the lot, or so he liked people to believe. He was famous for tying fuses into his beard and lighting them just before a battle so the enemy would see this fearsome man, 6 feet 4 inches tall, seeming to burn like the devil himself.

Once he decided to raid the port city of Charleston, S.C. He sailed into the harbor, fired off a shot or two from the 40 cannons that graced the decks of the ship called Queen Anne's Revenge and then sent his emissary ashore.

The emissary merely informed the good people of Charleston that Blackbeard intended to attack their town. The townspeople filled chests with valuables and delivered them to Blackbeard and begged him to spare them. Such is the power of advertising.

Things got tough for piracy in North Carolina, always a haven for seamen up to no good, in 1717 and 1718. The shallow waters and hidden coves of the state had been so popular with pirates that it is said that 50 of them held a summit conference on Ocracoke Island in 1718. To this day, dope smugglers sail the same waters with their contraband.

But during those two years, the governors of South Carolina and Virginia had all they could take and declared war on the pirates — killing dozens of them. North Carolina didn't strike back against the pirates, legend has it, because the pirates protected North Carolina waters and, most of all, because they are said to have shared the booty with Gov. Charles Eden, who, in fact, did preside at Blackbeard's 13th wedding in Bath.

But on Nov. 22, 1718, Blackbeard's end came. Semi-retired from the high seas, he and his crew of just 18 were off Ocracoke when Royal Navy Lt. Robert Maynard, commanding the Adventure, fought the bloody pirate at the place they still call Teach's Hole.

Blackbeard fired first, raking the deck of the Adventure. He thought he'd killed almost all aboard and ordered his men over the side to attack the few survivors.

But Maynard was smart. His crew was hiding below decks, and when Blackbeard and his crew swarmed aboard the fighting began.

But as all good legends must, the whole battle came down to a confrontation between the king of the pirates and the young lieutenant.

It was Blackbeard's cutlass against Maynard's slim dress sword. But Maynard fired his pistol at Blackbeard, drawing first blood.

Staggered and bleeding, Blackbeard lived up to his reputation and swung a mighty blow at Maynard, breaking the sailor's slender sword at the hilt.

But then, from behind, a sailor delivered the killing blow, slashing his cutlass into Blackbeard's neck.

But the mighty pirate would not die. He tried to fight on until he drowned in his own blood, a fitting end for our greatest legend.

And they still haven't found one piece of his treasure, which is most likely still hidden 'neath the sands of North Carolina's famous coast.

Black Stallion in the Moonlight

Smithfield

He was black, coal black.

When the sun was shining, his coat gleamed with dark fire. His mane was long and full, his legs sturdy. When he ran, strength surged through those powerful muscles.

The earth would shake when those hooves pounded across the Johnston County farmland. Other horses that sensed him were afraid.

A plow mule would stop in its traces when the mighty black horse appeared.

Many feared the horse. No one would ever break that wild spirit.

The legend of Johnston County's wild stallion was told to me by another Johnston County legend, J.B. Coats. Coats is 85, and he remembers the years from 1907 to 1910 when the last of the wild horses was free. He saw the stallion and remembers.

The black stallion arrived in Smithfield the same way thousands of other horses and mules came, by rail from Tennessee.

"Back then they used to drive the horses down Main Street from the depot to one of the three livery stables in Smithfield," Coats said. "When farmers heard a shipment of horses was coming in, they used to come to town to watch them go down the street.

"And that black stallion was something special."

The horse was wild-eyed and powerful. He would fight when someone came to him with a harness or even a bridle. No man could ride him — no man could hold him.

But a man named Smith thought he'd try. He and his two sons took the stallion to their farm. They were tough farmers; they thought they could break the horse.

They penned him and hobbled him, but pens and hobbles could not hold the mighty stallion. He broke free.

For the next three years the stallion lived in the wild, roaming an area of several miles on the west side of Smithfield along Poplar Branch and later along Reedy Branch.

"It was his domain," Coats said. "And he roamed it at will."

There were those who wanted to capture the horse. Some said he was terrorizing their livestock. Others said they wanted to catch him simply because he had never been caught.

They would see the stallion on moonlit nights, stretching his long legs across the fields. They would see him on summer days as he appeared in the shadows by the deep woods.

The other horses and mules would sense him first — they could tell a wild thing was afoot; they were in traces and the stallion was wild. It frightened the plow horses, and they would rear and refuse to work. They didn't know about freedom, and the wild stallion didn't know about traces.

The men built fences to catch the horse. Among them were Coats' father, Joe Coats, and his older brothers. They built a fence like a funnel, down by the creek where the horse roamed. They baited it first with hay and then with a female pony, but the stallion was free because he was smart. And he stayed free.

Finally, the men decided the horse could no longer be free among them. So a pack of men and a pack of dogs went looking for the stallion.

They picked up his trail one afternoon, and the final chase began.

They chased the horse all afternoon — the dogs baying and yapping at those lightning hooves, the men following as best they could.

They chased him all night, by lantern light, through the thickets and brambles, through the barbed-wire fences that fell before the stallion. Along the way they began to see bits of hair, pieces of flesh, but the horse would not be caught.

They resumed the chase the next day when the sun came up. For 24 hours they chased him, seeing him now, losing him again.

Finally the mighty heart of the horse gave out. He was beaten. He sought refuge where he had never found it before, in a pen with other horses. He was wily.

When the men found him, he was near death. The brutal barbed wire had ripped his chest to ribbons. He was weak from loss of blood. They could see the bones of his legs where the shiny black hair had been ripped away.

And that night, the horse that no one would ever tame — and that no one could let be free — died.

I wonder how those men felt.

Taking Refuge From the World

Fort Fisher

He was called the Fort Fisher Hermit, and for 16 years he lived alone, out where the sand and the marsh and the wind answer to no one.

When you stand where the Hermit stood, you can better understand the wizened little man who sought refuge from an uncivilized world to live in an old blockhouse.

Before him stretched a flat salt marsh, a marsh teeming with the bounty of the sea. He once claimed to have eaten oysters every day for 16 years. Another time a visitor was shocked to see six green-head biting flies sitting on his back at the same time. The Hermit never noticed. He had become one with his world, a world of awesome beauty.

Robert Edward Harrill never fit too well in the world into which he was thrust at birth. He was a printer by trade, a Linotype operator at a Shelby newspaper for a time, a seller of jewelry other times.

He never talked about what drove him to leave his wife and children in Shelby and move to Fort Fisher. His son later said that his father was a harsh, angry man, but a brilliant one. He went to college, and some said he was a minister. One day back in 1955 Harrill gave it all up and became a full-time hermit.

"I didn't come here to be a hermit," he once said. "Other people made me a hermit. I just came here to write my book." The book, which he called *A Tyrant in Every Home*, was never published.

Harrill first moved into a tent near the Fort Fisher monument but later settled in a World War II blockhouse that squatted in the sand at the end of the Carolina Beach peninsula. There he lived alone, through hurricanes that drove him and his pack of mangy dogs to high ground, through blistering summers when the heat rose in shimmery waves over the baked sands, through cold, hard winters when the gales blew.

He lived with his few meager possessions hidden in the piles of debris that encircled his home. He ate what he could find — berries, shellfish scooped from the marsh. A tiny garden gave variety to his diet, and some of the thousands of visitors who would at the same time be his torment and his delight would leave money in his rusty old frying pan.

"He used to keep a quarter, a nickel, a dime and a penny in that pan, sitting out where people could see it and get the idea," said Harry Warren, a staff member at the Marine Resources Center at Fort Fisher. Warren has put together an exhibit of the Hermit's camp, stressing how one man lived in harmony with his often-hostile world.

The Hermit was a familiar figure on this peninsula. Dressed in nothing but a floppy straw hat and tattered shorts in the summer — and adding little more than an overcoat in the winter — he looked for all the world like a stooped Ernest Hemingway. Practically every writer who has made the pilgrimage to his bunker has made comparisons between the Hermit and Hemingway's *Old Man and the Sea.*

One day, when he was 79 years old, some boys went to call on the Hermit. They found him dead, lying by the front door of his littered blockhouse. He died, the coroner said, of natural causes.

It wasn't long before the scavengers came, the bloodsuckers looking for his fortune. They ripped apart his little world searching for it.

But they could have saved themselves the trouble. He would have given them his wealth for free. All they had to do was listen.

"He wasn't a bum," Warren said. "If you gave him money he'd tell you a story, give you a picture of himself or maybe a clam he had dug."

On his tombstone in Shelby are written the words, "He made us think."

Some say he was crazy; others say he was perhaps the most sane man they ever met.

How Hygiene Changed History

Swansboro

Hygiene has been the downfall of many a hardy college student.

I don't mean hygiene, as in washing your feet. I mean Hygiene, with a capital H, as in Hygiene I, a required course for many would-be college graduates.

It is a universally despised course, totally without redeeming social value. Anyone who takes it without protest is not to be trusted.

The only people who take it seriously are the people who teach it.

Hygiene once kept a brilliant newspaperman I know from graduating from the University of North Carolina at Chapel Hill; I had to appeal to God's representative in South Building to escape it when I was a student there. It almost did in Franklin D. Roosevelt when he was a student at Harvard.

Hygiene I did one good thing in its miserable life. It gave North Carolina one of its finest parks, Hammocks Beach State Park near Swansboro.

Return with us now to those thrilling days of yesteryear and Hygiene I, Harvard University style.

It was an early-morning class, and William Sharpe was used to seeing the student who sat on his left come in every day, answer the roll call and promptly crash on his desk.

Sharpe felt a little differently about the course than did his seatmate named Roosevelt. For Sharpe, attending Harvard was a crash course in trying to find enough money to eat, sleep and go to school.

For Roosevelt, it was something to do while he was waiting to be named President for Life.

Sharpe had gone to Harvard from the slums of Philadelphia on, of all things, a rowing scholarship. His father was a preacher who made $1,200 a year. His mother had borrowed $100 to get him to school.

He could row like crazy, and after his team won the Harlem Regatta in 1900 Sharpe was offered an athletic scholarship.

There was a problem. Sharpe was great at Philadelphia rowing, but he was stinko at Harvard rowing. After three weeks he was kicked off the team, and he lost the free meals that went with being an athlete.

So that first session in Hygiene was important to Sharpe. He was struggling to stay in school, and the last thing he needed was grade problems on top of the money woes, so he took a lot of notes that first year.

As a result, when fall grades were posted Sharpe had an A.

Shortly thereafter, Roosevelt, who spent most of his nights having one whale of a good time, came to Sharpe and asked whether he could borrow Sharpe's notes, according to Sharpe. Sharpe agreed, but Roosevelt couldn't read his handwriting.

So Sharpe agreed to become a Hygiene I tutor for FDR for $2.50 per hour. That was decent money in the first years of the new century.

Roosevelt showed up at the first tutoring session with two friends who also needed help with Hygiene I. When their first two-hour session was over, Sharpe had $15 in his pocket.

Word spread about Sharpe and his tutoring session. After all, you could sleep through class every morning and once a week show up for a two-hour session with a private tutor and pass the course. Not a bad deal.

By the spring exam, Sharpe had 35 students and was renting a room for his classes. By the finals that spring, he had 46 students. Of his group, only one failed and one got an A — Roosevelt. Sharpe made a B, and $2,000 in fees.

By the middle of the next fall, he was making $182.50 per hour. When he finished college and medical school, he had $50,000 in the bank from tutoring Hygiene I.

Sharpe went on to become a surgeon, and he used to spend time each year on an island retreat off the North Carolina coast, a retreat bought with his Hygiene money.

Sharpe, at the urging of his longtime guide and friend John Hurst, willed the island retreat to the North Carolina Teachers Association, a black teachers organization to which John Hurst's wife had belonged.

The association, in turn, gave the island to the state of North Carolina in 1961 for development as Hammocks Beach State Park.

But Hygiene is still a dumb course.

A Quare Bunch

Wilsonville

Country people always have been tolerant of their friends and neighbors, putting up with any sort of strange behavior as long as the strange ones were good neighbors.

But even the old-timers around Wilsonville in eastern Chatham County will tell you that the Jones family was "a quare bunch."

They don't say it to be critical; everyone who knew the Jones family thought the world of them. They were honest, hard-working people, friendly to neighbors, suspicious of strangers, but "a quare bunch."

It wasn't so much what they did as what they didn't do.

The story begins with Jim and Margaret Jones. No one knows where they came from, but they settled in a log house that Mister Jim built on some high ground near where B. Everett Jordan Lake is.

Their first child was named Jart, born in 1866. He was dear to his mother, for when he died at 19 in 1885, Margaret Jones "cursed the Lord and swore she'd never set foot on God's green earth again," recounts Vossie Horton, who still lives in the area.

And she didn't. Margaret Jones lived for 29 years after the death of her beloved Jart, and she never touched the earth again. She remained in the house most of that time, going to her log kitchen by way of a connecting breezeway. She was seen in the yard on occasion, but she would walk only on the exposed roots of the large trees around the house, never touching the dirt. And it was that way until 1914, when she died.

There were other children — a daughter Tillitha, and sons Dan, William, Simeon and James, who went by his middle name of Calvin. The children, in their own way, were just as unusual as their parents.

None of them ever married. They lived out their lives in the house their father fashioned from trees in the hardwood forest.

Every meal cooked in that house, in the 100 years from the time it was built until the last Jones child died in 1952, was cooked in an open fireplace. They never owned a stove.

They made their own cloth and clothes. There was never an electric light in the house. Not one of them rode on a train, although the tracks went by their house.

They did not go to church, although their land bordered the church grounds and all of the family are buried there. One time, however, Dan was spotted peeking in the church window.

Not one of them ever traveled more than 30 miles from their

house. Raleigh was as far as anyone ever went, then less than once a year.

They never saw a movie.

They never used a tractor, only mules.

There was no plumbing, or even a well; the water was brought from a spring.

They were suspicious of strangers. Legend has it that one time some con men slicked them out of a lot of money, telling them they were investing in Carolina Power & Light Co.

They kept all their money from then on, hiding it on the land. After the last Jones died (William), scavengers descended on the farm looking for the cache. Some will tell you a lot of money was found. But others say no, the money was taken away in a suitcase by a distant relative and deposited in a Raleigh bank just before William died.

The old log house, put together with pegs, is in vine-covered ruins now.

The front porch where they and their neighbors used to gather to play their fiddles and sing is covered, as is the corncrib where the community corn shuckings used to be held.

Simply, they were a people who chose not to participate in a changing world. Their father carved out a home in these hills and it was good enough for his children. Even when America was setting off atomic bombs, watching television and building cars, the Jones family kept what it had.

Few people, with all the luxuries in the world, can honestly make that claim.

She Sailed a Haunted Sea

Her name was Theodosia Burr Alston, the daughter of Aaron Burr and the wife of South Carolina Gov. James Alston.

On Dec. 31, 1812, she boarded the Patriot, a converted pirate ship, and set sail from Georgetown, S.C., for New York to visit her father. She was taking him a present, a painting of herself.

The weather was terrible in the Graveyard of the Atlantic that winter, and the United States was at war with England.

Sometime in January a British warship stopped the Patriot

off Cape Hatteras, but because of who Mrs. Alston was the ship was allowed to continue.

Theodosia Burr Alston, the crew and the Patriot were never seen again.

But like most legends from that lonely ocean, there is more to the story.

Some say the ship was boarded by pirates during a storm and that everyone was forced to walk the plank. A pirate later confessed on the gallows that he watched as the lovely face of Theodosia sank beneath the waves while the pirate band looted the ship.

But others say she lived. They say she came ashore in a small boat. Her experiences had driven the emotionally unstable woman stark-raving mad, they say, and she was taken in by a kindly fisherman's family.

She was clutching the painting when they pulled the crazed woman from the storm and the fisherman's family hung the picture on the wall of their little house. The woman was never able to give her name and when anyone spoke to her she would simply say, "I'm going to visit my father in New York."

Fifty-seven years later, the aging woman from the sea became ill, and a vacationing doctor was summoned to care for her. But because the family had no money to pay the doctor, they offered him anything they owned in payment.

He saw the painting on the wall and offered to take it.

The crazy old woman who had brought the portrait ashore heard the discussion and became enraged.

She leaped from her bed, grabbed the painting and shouted, one report has it: "It is mine, you shall not have it. I am on my way to visit my father in New York, and I am taking him this picture of his darling Theodosia!"

She ran from the little house and down to the ocean.

A terrible storm was lashing the beach but she stood for a moment on the shore and then calmly, with the painting clutched to her bosom, walked back into the sea from whence she had come so long before.

They searched for her throughout the night but they never found her body.

The next day the painting washed up on the beach.

So ends the legend.

The doctor, Dr. W.G. Poole, took the painting to Elizabeth City, where people began to say it looked like the mysterious Theodosia who had disappeared.

The painting stayed in the Poole family for years, and as late as 1967 it was hanging in a New York art gallery and was identified as being a portrait of the daughter of Aaron Burr. It was later sold to a member of the Burr family, and there the trail ends.

That Theodosia sailed on the Patriot and disappeared from history is factual. That the painting was with her when she sailed and was recovered years later from an Outer Banks house is factual.

Some say the painting washed ashore by itself and was found by a banker, who gave it to his sweetheart as a gift. She was supposedly the old woman who gave it to the doctor, and the part about a woman rushing into the sea is pure hogwash.

And some say Theodosia's body washed ashore in Virginia in 1813 and was buried.

No one will ever know for sure. Theodosia Burr Alston will sail forever on the haunted seas off North Carolina, her legend strong.